HOT TRASH

HOT TRASH

Cherie Bennett & Jeff Gottesfeld

BERKLEY JAM BOOKS, NEW YORK

THE BERKLEY PUBLISHING GROUP
Published by the Penguin Group
Penguin Group (USA) Inc.
375 Hudson Street, New York, New York 10014, USA
Penguin Group (Canada), 10 Alcorn Avenue, Toronto, Ontario M4V 3B2, Canada
(a division of Pearson Penguin Canada Inc.)
Penguin Books Ltd., 80 Strand, London WC2R 0RL, England
Penguin Group Ireland, 25 St. Stephen's Green, Dublin 2, Ireland (a division of Penguin Books Ltd.)
Penguin Group (Australia), 250 Camberwell Road, Camberwell, Victoria 3124, Australia
(a division of Pearson Australia Group Pty. Ltd.)
Penguin Books India Pvt. Ltd., 11 Community Centre, Panchsheel Park, New Delhi—110 017, India
Penguin Group (NZ), Cnr. Airborne and Rosedale Roads, Albany, Auckland 1310, New Zealand
(a division of Pearson New Zealand Ltd.)
Penguin Books (South Africa) (Pty.) Ltd., 24 Sturdee Avenue, Rosebank, Johannesburg 2196,
South Africa

Penguin Books Ltd., Registered Offices: 80 Strand, London WC2R 0RL, England

This is a work of fiction. Names, characters, places, and incidents either are the product of the authors'
imagination or are used fictitiously, and any resemblance to actual persons, living or dead, business
establishments, events, or locales is entirely coincidental.

HOT TRASH

A Berkley Book / published by arrangement with the authors

PRINTING HISTORY
Berkley edition / December 2004

ISBN: 0-425-20120-1

BERKLEY® JAM BOOKS
Berkley Jam Books are published by The Berkley Publishing Group,
a division of Penguin Group (USA) Inc.,
375 Hudson Street, New York, New York 10014.
BERKLEY is a registered trademark of Penguin Group (USA) Inc.
BERKLEY JAM and its logo are trademarks belonging to Penguin Group (USA) Inc.

PRINTED IN THE UNITED STATES OF AMERICA

10 9 8 7 6 5 4 3 2 1

Contents

TRASH

For Tammie Connors,
the coolest

ONE

"My father was a mass murderer."

Chelsea Jennings took a shaky breath and leaned forward into the microphone.

"Did I forget to mention that? Maybe you've heard of him. Charles Kettering? That's right, the guy who went into the Burger Barn Restaurant in Johnson City, Tennessee, oh, about seventeen years ago, and shot every single person inside on one sunny Monday afternoon.

"Then he drove home—I mean, no one in the restaurant was left standing to stop him—and I guess his plan was to murder Mom, too—even though she did have his favorite lunch all ready for him on the dining-room table. Probably he planned to kill me, too—but, hey, I was only ten months old, so I don't really know.

"Anyway, Mom ended up killing Dad instead—lucky for me, huh? And then, of course, Mom and me moved to Nashville, and changed our name, and then after that I really had a very normal life.

"Oh, and don't worry. I'm not much like him. I don't even have a bad temper—ha-ha.

"What else? Let's see. I'm valedictorian of my senior class. I'm a very hard worker. Oh, and I'm very interested in a future career in television. Which is why it means so much to me that you have hired me as a summer intern on your television show, *Trash*."

Chelsea put down her microphone—actually the hairbrush she had been *pretending* was a microphone—and stared at her reflection in the mirror over her dresser: shoulder-length golden-blond hair, large green eyes, all in all, a pretty, all-American-looking face gazing back at her. At the moment she was dressed in jeans, hiking boots, a man's white T-shirt with a beige suede vest over it, and a backward, gold-and-black Vanderbilt University baseball cap perched on her head.

Normal, she told herself. *I look totally normal. Like any other eighteen-year-old girl going off to New York City for her very first summer job as a TV intern.*

"It's a good thing being the only child of a psycho-killer doesn't show on your face," she told her reflection. "Of course, if you'd told them the truth, you'd probably be a guest on *Trash*, instead of an intern working for it."

No one knew the horrifying truth about her parents except her and her mother, and they never, ever talked about it. In fact, they both pretended that it had never really happened.

And most of the time, it doesn't seem as if it ever really did happen, Chelsea thought. *I can go days, weeks, sometimes even months, just living my life, hanging out with my friends, just normal me with my normal life.*

Except that my real name is Chelsea Kettering.

And up in the attic, hidden away, are the yellowed newspaper articles, the front-page headlines, about wealthy Johnson City attorney Charles Kettering, who just went bonkers one day and shot twenty-three people in a fast-food restaurant, and about his wife, Arlene, who stabbed her husband with a kitchen knife so he couldn't get to their innocent baby daughter.

And the front-page photos of me, the poor, innocent baby, wrapped in a white blanket with a duck on it, being carried out of the Ketterings' palatial home by some social worker.

Chelsea shook off her musings and picked up the glossy-covered folder that lay on her dresser, with the word TRASH on it in huge, raised neon letters. The folder had arrived in the mail a month earlier, and still Chelsea found it all somewhat hard to believe.

Chelsea's dream, ever since she could remember, was to one day become a producer of some important television news show like *60 Minutes*. She had no desire to be in front of the camera—in fact, the very thought made her cringe. Rather, she wanted to be the one who made it all happen, who pulled the strings, uncovered corruption, spoke for the powerless, and hopefully made the world a better place.

Corny, but true, Chelsea thought. *And TV—really good TV—can do all that.*

However, Chelsea knew that thousands—even tens of thousands—of high-school grads wanted careers in TV, too. And she knew that many of them began by getting internships in the industry the same summer they graduated from high school.

An internship would be the all-important foot in the door, crucial if one had any hope at all of succeeding.

That's when Chelsea had come up with her game plan: she would spend three months of the fall of her senior year applying for every single TV internship in the entire country available to graduating high-school seniors. And then she'd be able to pick and choose among all the ones that offered her an internship.

So, she spent all her money from her afterschool job at The Gap on postage and printing. She sent packets on herself everywhere, from prestigious shows like *60 Minutes* (her dream) to the lowest-rated local TV station in Nashville. When she had exhausted all possibilities, her records showed she had applied for three hundred and forty-eight internships.

She was turned down by three hundred and forty-seven.

It was the biggest ego-bruiser of her life to date.

Oh, she'd been a finalist as an intern at a local station in Nashville, but she hadn't even gotten that.

It turned out that being the best and the brightest at her high school simply put her up against the best and the brightest from thousands of different high schools across America. In other words, she was utterly ordinary. Didn't stand out.

Didn't get picked.

Except by *Trash*.

Trash, of all places.

Trash was the number-one-rated talk show on TV. Geared to a Gen-X and teen audience, it was the most audacious show that had ever been on the airwaves. Frankly, Chelsea thought it was a pretty awful show, but she applied for the internship simply because she was applying for every single TV internship that existed.

Never in a million years did I think I had a shot, Chelsea thought. *And I still have absolutely no idea why they picked me.*

After all, on paper I look so normal, and Trash *is anything but! So what if I graduated number one in my class, and so what if I was editor of the Hume-Fogg Honors High School newspaper,* The Foghorn? *Those credentials must be a big yawn, or else some other TV station or some other TV show would have offered me an internship.*

But no one did.

She figured maybe it was the first-person essay she had written for her *Trash* application that had done the trick.

The directions had instructed her to "be wild and fearless, just like *Trash*."

So Chelsea had written her essay as if she was a teen runaway and drug addict, a prostitute on the streets, doing whatever she had to do for a fix.

And it wasn't until the end of the essay that she had admitted that none of it was true, but she added that she believed a real journalist should be willing to go anywhere and do anything to get a true story.

Yeah, like I'd really go live on the street and sleep with strange men and become a drug addict for a story, Chelsea thought. *I am the most clean-living, virginal, normal (or so they think), boring eighteen-year-old left in Nashville, Tennessee. And why Trash picked me when everyplace else in the entire country turned me down, I cannot imagine.*

But they did. And it's a famous show. And I'll get to live in New York. And I'll actually be working in TV. Hey, it's a foot in the door. It's a start. Thousands of kids didn't get picked at all.

Chelsea ran her fingers over the raised letters on the cover of her folder from *Trash*, then opened it and read, yet again, the tantalizing letter that was enclosed.

Dear Chelsea,

Congratulations!

Out of over ten thousand applicants, you have been selected as one of the six summer interns for *Trash*, the most controversial and hippest teen TV talk show in America today.

***Rolling Stone* calls us hipper than MTV's *The Newlyweds*. *The New York Times* says we make Jerry Springer's show look like *Sesame Street*, and our ratings prove that we are a national phenomenon, expressing the daring cutting edge of American youth today.**

This summer, you will be a part of it.

Enclosed is all the information you will need regarding your housing in New York, job description, etc.

TRASH. EXCESS/ACCESS/SUCCESS.

Welcome aboard.

Barry Bassinger, Senior Producer

Chelsea flipped to the next page, which gave directions to the apartment on the Upper West Side of Manhattan that she would be sharing with the two other female *Trash* interns, only four blocks from the studios where *Trash* was aired daily in front of a live studio audience.

My own apartment, Chelsea rhapsodized. *And no mom there to have an anxiety attack if I'm five minutes late, or actually have a date with a guy she doesn't know, or—*

"Chelsea, honey?"

She quickly closed the folder and turned around. Her mother was standing in the doorway of her room, her face even more anxious looking than usual.

"Hi, Mom," Chelsea said, giving her mother a reassuring smile.

Her mother's eyes swept across Chelsea's packed suitcase and the small carry-on case with the rolled-up copy of *People* magazine sticking out. "So . . . all ready," her mother said, a slightly desperate edge to her voice.

"Please don't be upset, Mom—"

"I'm not," her mother assured even as she nervously patted her perfectly coiffed hair into place, which she always did when she was upset.

Chelsea tried to see her mother as a stranger might—the perfectly pressed navy pants and matching blazer, the understated strand of real pearls around her neck, the tasteful makeup on her attractive, unlined face.

Her mother always looked perfect. She taught music at an exclusive, private girls' school, she was on the board of a number of charities, and she sang in the church choir. In fact, everything on the outside was always perfect—clothes, hair, home, daughter.

To hide what's going on inside, Chelsea knew. *To hide our horrible secret.*

"So, I guess we'd better leave for the airport," Chelsea said, picking up her purse and slinging the strap over her shoulder.

"New York is so far away...." her mother began.

"It's going to be fine, Mom." She had been saying the exact same thing for a month, ever since she had received the letter in the mail telling her that she had actually, really and truly, been picked for the *Trash* summer intern program.

"Well, I'm going to worry about you in that city, all by yourself," her mother insisted, her brow furrowed.

"I'll be fine," Chelsea said again. She picked up her suitcase and headed for the stairs.

"I still don't understand why you couldn't have accepted an internship from a nice show," her mother said, trailing behind her.

"Mom, this is an incredible opportunity," Chelsea maintained. She hadn't admitted to her mother that every other internship in the entire country had turned her down.

She had been too embarrassed.

"It's just that I've heard that *Trash* is just so...so...unsavory," her mother said, fiddling with her pearls. "I have friends who watch it. Evidently they have on drug addicts! And gang members. And homosexuals—"

"We have all that right here in Nashville, Mom," Chelsea said patiently.

"Well, perhaps so, dear," her mother replied, "but we don't associate with people like that."

Chelsea kissed her mother's cheek and started down the stairs. "We have to go, Mom."

Her mother hurried down the stairs after her. "Just remember, Chelsea, dear, that you're a well-brought-up young lady, won't you?"

"I will, Mom." Chelsea put her stuff in the back of the car, then got behind the wheel. Her mother got in the passenger seat.

"Because if you lie down with dogs, you get fleas," her mother added, clicking her seat belt in.

"Right," Chelsea said. "Dogs. Fleas."

"And you'll call me every night," her mother went on.

"If I can," Chelsea said absently, backing the car out of the driveway.

Her mother sighed, long and loud. "Well, it's only a summer. In the fall you'll be right back here at home, safe and sound. You'll go to Vanderbilt with the right sorts of girls and boys, and you'll make lovely new friends. Won't that be nice?"

Chelsea didn't reply. Just the thought of living at home for college and going to Vanderbilt with "the right sorts of girls and boys" felt like a noose tightening around her neck.

But maybe this summer will change everything, Chelsea thought as she pulled the car onto I-440 and hit the gas pedal. *Who knows? Maybe some miracle will occur and I won't have to come back here and go to Vanderbilt at all....*

She felt hopeful. And scared. And daring. And on the edge of a million possibilities.

Ready for New York. Ready for anything.

So long as no one found out who she really was.

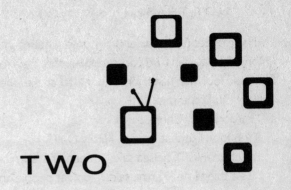

TWO

"I'm coming, I'm coming, keep your shirt on!" a nasal female voice with a definite New York accent called from inside the apartment.

From the other side of the door, Chelsea heard lock after lock turning, then a chain sliding, and finally the door opened as the head of a very pretty Asian girl, about Chelsea's age, peeked out.

She had gorgeous, long, straight black hair and wore lots of black eyeliner and very pale lipstick.

"Yeah?" the girl said in a guarded voice. "You're—?"

"Chelsea Jennings," Chelsea said, picking up her suitcase. "One of the *Trash* interns? Didn't the doorman downstairs just announce me?"

"Yeah, like that means anything," the girl said. Now she opened the door completely, and Chelsea got a look at the rest of her. She was tiny, not much more than five feet tall, Chelsea figured. She had on ice-blue silk pants with a drawstring waist that fell below her navel, and a matching, cropped, ice-blue silk camisole.

The girl stepped aside and gestured Chelsea into the living room. "Honestly, you can't be too careful in this city. I'm Karma Kushner." She held out her hand for Chelsea to shake, then pointed at her. "Hilary Duff," she said.

"Pardon me?" Chelsea said.

"You look like that actress, Hilary Duff."

"Well, thanks," Chelsea said. "I mean, that's a nice compliment—"

"It's a thing I do," Karma said. "I look at people and decide what famous person they look most like. It drives my mother crazy. She looks like Anjelica Huston. 'Karma,' she always says, 'stop with the famous people look-alike bit!'"

"Your name is Karma—"

"Yeah, I know, it's bizarre," Karma agreed. "I mean, look at me, I'm Asian—I guess you noticed that—"

"Right off," Chelsea admitted.

"Yeah, right," Karma agreed. "And I have this, like, huggie-veggie first name and this Jewish last name, right? And, okay, I'm perfectly aware that I've got a voice like Fran Drescher on *The Nanny*, and you're like, 'What's up with that?' Am I right?"

"Kind of," Chelsea admitted.

"Jewish former-hippie parents," Karma explained. "I'm adopted. They own a New Age health food and bookstore now, out on Long Island. They're still in mourning over the end of the Age of Aquarius. Meanwhile I own twenty-three cashmere sweaters. I mean, they're, like, dying that they raised this materialistic daughter. So, come on, I'll show you around."

She picked up Chelsea's suitcase—which was almost as big as she was—and carried it through the living room and down a long narrow hallway. Chelsea glanced into a bedroom and glimpsed a beautiful mahogany canopy bed, and a bathroom with a shower curtain covered with nude Roman statues.

They turned into the third door on the right. It was a small furnished bedroom. The bedspread was bright pink, the bed was brass, the carpet a worn Oriental centered on a polished hardwood floor, and the wallpaper featured giant pink cabbage roses.

"I moved in two days ago." Karma said. "I couldn't wait to get out of Long Island. And frankly I took the best bedroom, with the canopy bed. This is the second best, if you can stomach Pepto-Bismol pink, which frankly is not one of my better colors. The other bedroom is tiny, but it has a water bed, in case you're into sex on the high seas."

"This is fine," Chelsea assured her. She felt both dazzled and a little shocked.

No one I know would talk about sex on a water bed, Chelsea thought. *Mom would just die,* she added to herself, gleefully.

"So, listen," Karma said. "You wanna come out and gab? Because I've been dying for company. Or you need to put your stuff away?"

"I can do that later," Chelsea decided. "I didn't bring all that much, anyway."

"Smart," Karma said. "Because the shopping in New York is to die for. I know every great discount place for designer clothes. Come on, I'll make coffee."

Chelsea followed Karma out of the room and went into the living room while Karma went into the adjoining kitchen.

"I hope you like it really, really strong," Karma said, measuring out some coffee into the Mr. Coffee.

"Truthfully, I usually drink tea," Chelsea said.

"Oh, gag me," Karma snorted. "Reminds me too much of Mom and Dad. According to them, there's a tea for every occasion. Constipated? French vervain. Too aggressive? Camomile. Want to do past-life regression? There's a tea for it. Guaranteed."

Chelsea looked around the living room, trying to get acclimated. The furniture was old and substantial. She sat on a red velvet couch, shabby at the corners. A larger Oriental rug than the one in her bedroom covered most of the floor. The tables were dark brown and the lamps were old-fashioned and lace-covered.

Which made absolutely no sense when you looked at the artwork, which was modern, erotic, and, Chelsea thought, really, really bad.

"So, Chelsea, where are you from?" Karma asked as she got out two coffee cups. Clearly she had already learned where things were in the kitchen.

"Nashville, Tennessee," Chelsea replied. "You need help?"

"Nah," Karma said. "Yeah, you have a little accent. So, you ever been to New York before?"

"Never," Chelsea said. "I've always dreamed about it, though. And now I'm finally here...." She stared at the painting behind the couch. It featured a naked woman standing on her head, balancing pianos on her feet. "The artwork in here is very strange," she said.

"It sucks," Karma said cheerfully, bringing in the coffee. "Can you believe how weird this apartment is? Old-lady furniture, and then a water bed in one bedroom, and this dreck on the walls?"

"I guess *Trash* rented it for us furnished," Chelsea said, sipping her coffee. She practically gagged, it was so strong.

"Yeah," Karma agreed. "But what I want to know is, who the hell furnished it?" She sat in the red velvet chair across from Chelsea and took a long swallow of her coffee.

"I live on this stuff," she continued. "I have this night job I just started—bartending at this club in the East Village—it's called Jimi's—after Jimi Hendrix, ya know? The guy who owns the place's name is Arnold, which doesn't exactly ring a sexy bell, so I can see why he calls the place Jimi's." She took another sip of her coffee.

"Anyway," she continued, "I'm, like, doing a day job and a night job and I, like, live on caffeine. I should just do it intravenously!"

"Do you have to lie about your age to work there?" Chelsea asked. "Or are you older than eighteen—"

"Nah, I'm eighteen," Karma said. "I just graduated from South Long Island High School—that was three years of my life I'd sooner forget, thank you very much—but anyway, Jimi's is a teen club. No alcohol. They happen to be very hip at the moment. There's, like, this reverse thing happening with alcohol. It's really cool not to drink."

Chelsea nodded, as if all this information was normal to her. In actuality, her head was swimming and she felt overwhelmed. Clearly Karma loved to talk, though, so Chelsea didn't have to contribute too much for the time being.

"So, are you as psyched as I am about this *Trash* thing?" Karma asked. "I couldn't believe it when they picked me!"

"Me, neither," Chelsea agreed. "I mean, I feel like I'm so ordinary!"

"No one has ever described me as ordinary," Karma allowed, "but my grades in high school were so bad they barely let me graduate! I can't spell to save my life! God, I hope interns don't have to spell."

"You just use spell-check on the computer," Chelsea explained.

"Oh, yeah?" Karma said. "Great! Hey, you aren't one of those super-brains, are you?"

"Well, no—"

"Like one of those girls who got, like, fifteen hundred on her SATs—"

"No . . ." Chelsea said carefully.

Karma eyed her. "You got higher. I can tell."

"Well . . ."

"You did," Karma accused. "What did you get?"

"Fifteen-sixty," Chelsea admitted meekly. "But I'm just one of those people who test well, and—"

"I'm dying here!" Karma whined. "Oh, my gawd, you are, like, *brilliant!*"

"Oh, I don't think I'm brilliant, I just—"

The buzzer next to the front door went off, loud and insistent.

"Our third roomie!" Karma cried, jumping up from her chair. "If she's another brain I'm killing myself." She pressed a black button on the wall and spoke into a small speaker. "Yeah?"

Static and noise came out of the speaker, followed by a garbled name neither girl could understand.

"Try again, Antoine," Karma called into the speaker.

More static and noise from the speaker.

"Yeah, sure, Antoine, have a nice day," Karma said into the speaker. "It could be a friggin' ax murderer and Antoine would send 'em up."

"He's the guy downstairs—?"

"Doorman," Karma said. "He stays up all night playing the trotters, he told me. Gonna hit it big and leave this job in the dust."

"Trotters?" Chelsea echoed.

"Yonkers Raceway? The horses? You got a lot to learn...."

"And he actually told you that?" Chelsea asked.

"What can I say?" Karma shrugged. "People confide in me. Antoine suffers from serious sleep deprivation. And the intercom system is totally broken. Welcome to New York."

"Maybe we should report it to the manager of the building," Chelsea suggested. "And he'll see that it's fixed."

"Yeah, and maybe I'll find a Todd Oldham original at Target, but I doubt it," Karma said, draining her coffee.

Chelsea blushed and studied the bad art on the wall again, while Karma took the coffee cups into the small kitchen. "Hey, do you cook?"

"Not much," Chelsea admitted.

"Me, neither," Karma said. "Let's hope our third roomie is the Galloping Gourmet, or we'll be living at the Greek diner on the corner."

The doorbell rang, and Karma went through her who-is-it routine at the door again. Of course the response was unintelligible, but Karma unlocked the locks, undid the chain, and opened the door anyway.

"So, what we wanna know is, can you cook?" she asked the girl.

Chelsea couldn't see her, since Karma was standing in front of the door.

"I can boil water," came a throaty reply, "but I only do it under duress."

"We're screwed," Karma said cheerfully, ushering the new girl into the apartment. "I'm Karma Kushner, by the way." She turned to look at Chelsea, pointing at the new girl. "Angelina Jolie," she pronounced, "but younger."

The new girl walked in and looked around, and Chelsea studied her. She had short, shaggy brown hair that fell sexily over her forehead, into her large, almond-shaped blue eyes. She wore a pair of teeny tiny cutoffs and a sleeveless black T-shirt, and black boots that laced almost up to her knees. Chelsea could see the outline of a tattoo on her shoulder, though she couldn't make out what it was. The girl was utterly confident, curvy, sexy, and cool.

And totally intimidating.

All she carried was a shabby backpack, which she dropped in the center of the living-room floor.

"Wow, weird," the girl said, looking around at the conservative furniture and the bad erotic art.

Something about her is familiar, Chelsea mused, *something about her voice....*

"What's with the tacky art?" the girl asked in her throaty, sexy voice, making a face at the upside-down nude.

"We wondered, too," Chelsea said.

And then, for the first time, the new girl looked at Chelsea. Really looked at her. She blinked slowly. "No," she said. "It can't be."

"Pardon me?" Chelsea asked, taken aback.

The new girl stared at her for another beat, and then she laughed.

"She's laughing," Karma commented as she shut the door. "I didn't hear a joke, but the girl clearly finds something hilarious."

"It's a pretty good joke, too," the girl said, her hands shoved into the tight pockets of her cutoffs. She looked right at Chelsea. "You don't recognize me?"

Chelsea studied her. "I'm sorry. I mean, if we've met before, I guess I don't remember. Your voice sounds familiar, but—"

"It should," the girl said. She took a step toward Chelsea. "You're Chelsea."

Chelsea's heart thudded in her chest. *Oh, God, please don't let this be my worst nightmare come true,* she thought. *Please don't let this be someone who knows the truth about me. No. I'm being paranoid. No one knows. It can't be—*

"Chelsea," the girl said, taking her hands out of her pockets. "It's Alyssa."

Now it was Chelsea's turn to stare. Alyssa *Bishop*? Alyssa Bishop had been Chelsea's best friend all through grade school and junior high, but then she and her family had moved to Denver, and after about six months of letter writing, they had lost touch with each other.

But this couldn't be Alyssa. Alyssa was overweight, with an overbite that made her top teeth stick out. She was shy and quiet, and an excellent student.

But even if some kids thought Alyssa was kind of geeky, Chelsea knew how smart and funny and irreverent Alyssa really was, how she was the most fun person in the world to be with, how she could make anything exciting. She wasn't the lump her parents or the other kids thought she was at all. In fact, behind her thick glasses were the sparkling, mischievous blue eyes of—

Chelsea stared into the new girl's eyes.

Blue. So blue. Just like Alyssa's. And the voice, the funny, froggy, sexy voice that didn't seem to go with the plump, funny-looking little girl at all...

"Alyssa Bishop?" Chelsea whispered.

"It's really me," the girl said. "Only everyone calls me Lisha now."

"But...you changed," Chelsea managed.

Lisha laughed. "You didn't."

And the next thing they knew, they were hugging and laughing and crying, all at the same time.

"I love happy endings," Karma said, "but I feel like I missed the first reel of the movie here."

Chelsea broke away from Lisha, a huge grin on her face. "We were best friends when we were kids," Chelsea explained. "But Alyssa moved to Denver—"

"And I changed, thank God," Lisha added. "I used to be fat—"

"You?" Karma asked incredulously. "I would kill to have a body like yours. I have to practically buy my clothes in the children's department."

"Believe me, I was a lump," Lisha said. "And I had this overbite, and glasses...."

"But you were always wonderful," Chelsea said. "I missed you so much when you moved away.... God, I just can't believe this!"

"Me, either," Lisha said. She shook her head in wonder. "This is really out there. What are the odds that the two of us would both get picked to be interns at *Trash?*"

"Slim to none," Chelsea said. She felt as if her mouth would break from smiling so hard. "I want to hear about everything that's happened to you!"

"Oh, this means I need to make more coffee," Karma announced. "Hey, I hope you like water beds," she added to Lisha as she hurried into the kitchen.

"Depends on who's in it with me," Lisha said. She sat on the couch. So did Chelsea. "So, tell me—"

There was a knock on the door.

"Who's that?" Karma asked. "The doorman didn't buzz us."

Chelsea and Lisha just shrugged.

Another knock.

"We could buzz down to Antoine," Karma suggested. "Not that he'd be conscious enough to offer an opinion."

"Let's just open the door," Lisha said, getting up from the couch.

"Oh, sure," Karma said sarcastically, hurrying across the room. "And if any of us could cook we could invite Freddy Kreuger out there to dinner. He'd supply the fresh meat."

She stood on tiptoe so she could see through the peephole in the door. "Who is it?" she yelled.

"Ick!" came a male voice.

"Okay, there's a guy standing at our door yelling 'ick.' I can't see a thing through the stupid peephole. What do we do?"

Lisha strode over to the door. "Who?" she called.

"Nick!" the voice yelled.

Karma shrugged. "So kill me. It sounded like 'ick' to me."

Lisha looked through the peephole. "There's more than one guy out there," she said. "In fact, it looks like three," she reported. "I'm opening the door."

"Are you on drugs?" Karma screeched. "This is New York! You can't just—"

The door was open. Chelsea and Karma both peered around Lisha to see who was there.

It was, as reported, three guys.

Three *cute* guys.

Three *incredibly* cute guys.

"Hi," the one standing in the front with the Brad Pitt blue eyes and dirty-blond ponytail said. "I'm Nick Shaw. This is Alan Van Kleef and Sky Addison," he added, cocking his head toward the two guys with him.

One had dark hair and a sensitive, finely chiseled face, and the other had short brown hair and the lean, muscular body of a serious athlete.

"We're the other three *Trash* interns," Nick explained. He gave a dazzling smile.

"And we live right across the hall."

THREE

"So, you got it?" the assistant producer, Cindy Sumtimes, asked Chelsea, her voice harried. She looked down at the three wristwatches on her left wrist, saw the time, and swore under her breath.

"Yes," Chelsea said tentatively, "I think so. I mean—"

"You can't *think so*," Cindy said, as if Chelsea was the slowest, most annoying kid on the block, "you have to *know so*."

She checked her watches again, then ran her hand nervously over her entirely shaved scalp. Her eyebrows were shaved off, too, and new eyebrows drawn on. But Cindy Sumtimes was so beautiful that she actually managed to look good anyway.

"Listen . . . Chutney, was it?"

"Chelsea," Chelsea said politely.

"Yeah," Cindy said distractedly. She pulled up a folding chair and slid onto it backward, her legs splayed. "Because if you screw this up, Jazz'll eat me alive. All you have to do is—"

Riiiiiing. Riiiiiiiing.

It was a tiny mobile phone that Cindy wore tucked into the over-sized pocket of her hot-pink leather overalls.

"Sumtimes," Cindy barked her last name into the phone. "Yeah... uh-huh..."

As Cindy began pacing the office with the phone, Chelsea's mind wandered.

It was her first day of work at *Trash*—actually, Chelsea's first hour on the job. She'd hardly been able to get to sleep the night before, she had been so revved up—a combination of excited and exhilarated—and also very, very nervous.

Imagine me, Chelsea Jennings, working in television, she thought to herself, for maybe the hundredth time. *So what if it's Trash—it's national TV! I'll make great connections that can launch my career. I'll meet famous people. I'll learn all about how television really works.*

I'll work with incredibly cute guy interns.

And they're so nice, Chelsea thought, smiling dreamily. *Really, really nice guys.*

When they had arrived in New York, neither she, Karma, nor Lisha had known that the guy interns for *Trash* were going to be housed right across the hall from them. The night before, they had all ordered in Chinese food—so much better than any Chelsea had ever tasted in Nashville—and it had been delivered by a young Asian guy on a bicycle!

Chelsea had eaten squid for the first time—actually, Nick had bet her that she wouldn't eat it and then he had actually fed her a pink, dangly, icky-looking piece, dropping it into her mouth from between two chopsticks, and then—

"Yo, Chutney?" Cindy said, standing over her. "Can we focus here?"

"Sorry," Chelsea replied, embarrassed, turning her attention back to the task that the producer had outlined for her. She didn't want to tell Cindy yet again what her name really was.

"So let me repeat it for you," Cindy said slowly, tapping her fingers on the desk. "This is the expert file. Jazz wants each expert's name, address, phone, and specialty on a separate *Trash* index card."

"The cards go in the box," Chelsea recited, pointing to an enormous case on the floor by her side, filled with four-by-six-inch index cards, in colors ranging from pale yellow to deep purple, all with the distinctive *Trash* logo printed on the back.

"That's right," Cindy said, nervously checking her watches again. "Keep it alphabetical, and make each expert's specialty a separate color. You've got ten thousand cards and a hundred fifty colors, so you should be all set."

"And I take the information off the computer," Chelsea said, indicating the screen in front of her.

"You got it," Cindy said. "Okay, I gotta run, Jazz'll kill me if I'm late. Okay, if you need me, it's extension three-four-one, Sumtimes."

"Thanks, Cindy," Chelsea said politely.

But Cindy was already gone, on a dead run to somewhere or other, leaving behind only the scent of some great perfume.

Chelsea looked at the huge pile of cards on the floor and sighed. *Well, okay, so it's a weenie job,* she thought. *But, after all, I have to expect that some of the stuff I do is going to be boring. I mean, I'm only an intern.*

For now.

But someday... someday I'll be a big producer, she dreamed, *on some fantastic show like 60 Minutes. I'll uncover corruption and travel all over the world, I'll make a fortune, I'll win the Pulitzer Prize for journalism, and they'll do a profile on me for People magazine...*

... And some young, hungry reporter will dig for the dirt about me, and she'll find out who I really am.

Oh, God...

Chelsea dropped her head into her hands. *You have to stop this,* she told herself. *You've never in your whole life spent time obsessing about what happened with your parents. You've always ignored it and pretended it never happened, and now is not the time to change things!*

Chelsea got up and looked around the office. The gold nameplate on the large Lucite desk read BARRY BASSINGER, SENIOR PRODUCER. The large office featured all modern, beige suede furniture that sat on beige carpeting so thick that Chelsea's steps felt springy when she walked. A huge window gave a view of the street scene below.

Chelsea walked over to the wall closest to the window, where a series of photos hung.

I guess that's Barry, Chelsea thought, since the same small, dark-haired, good-looking guy, about thirty-five, Chelsea guessed, was featured in each photo.

In one photo he had his arm around Madonna. In another he was on a boat with a bikini-clad Tyra Banks in his lap. And in another Sandra Bullock was kissing his cheek.

"Where's Barry?"

Chelsea swung around guiltily. A tall, handsome Hispanic guy with gorgeous hair that hung halfway down his back stood in the doorway.

"I—I don't know," Chelsea stammered, her face red. She felt as if she had been caught looking through drawers or something.

"I got papers for him," the guy said impatiently, waving a bunch of papers in his hand.

"I guess you can put them on his desk," Chelsea said with a shrug.

"You his new secretary?" the guy asked, flipping his gorgeous hair over his shoulders.

"Oh, no, I'm—"

"Didn't think so," the guy said, crossing to the Lucite desk and dropping the papers. "You're not the type." He strode back to the door and slammed it on his way out.

"I feel like Alice in Wonderland," Chelsea murmured out loud. "People just keep coming and going. . . ."

She looked down at the outfit she'd so carefully chosen for the first day of work, and wondered what the guy had meant by "you're not the type."

Chelsea had spent an hour that morning trying to figure out the best thing to wear, and had tried on practically everything in her meager wardrobe. She hadn't lied when she'd told Karma that she hadn't brought much, but it wasn't because she planned to shop in New York. It was because she didn't own much. Her mother didn't make very much money teaching at a private school, and Chelsea had earned money for her clothes at her after-school job at The Gap at the Bellevue Mall.

The Gap discount was a huge help. Just about all of her clothes were from that store. Today she had on a pair of black cotton trousers and a white muslin collarless shirt. Her hair was tied back with a black ribbon, and she wore flat, men's-looking oxford shoes on her feet.

Businesslike, but cute, she had thought to herself that morning, adding some mascara to her blond eyelashes.

She had felt confident about her choice, until Karma and Lisha walked out of their bedrooms that morning.

Lisha had on a pair of baggy, faded jeans that rode low on her hip-bones. With this she wore the top of a Cub Scout uniform, tied under her bust. The merit badge on her shoulder was for wildlife.

Karma had on a red felt poodle skirt, circa 1950s, only whereas poodle skirts usually came down to the calves, Karma's was mid-thigh. With it she wore a tiny, sleeveless white cashmere vest and very high heels.

"Wow, you guys look nice," Chelsea had managed.

"You, too," they had both told her.

But now she knew they were just being nice. Because everyone at *Trash* seemed to have this wild sense of fashion. No one looked like anyone else.

And clearly no one else here but me shops at The Gap.

I guess I'm the token boring-looking person, Chelsea thought with a sigh, fiddling with a button on her white blouse.

The buzzer on the Lucite desk went off, startling her. She hurried over to the desk and picked up the phone, as Cindy Sumtimes had instructed her to do.

"Barry Bassinger's office," Chelsea said into the phone, her voice sounding thin and nervous in her own ears. "Chelsea Jennings speaking."

"How many?" the voice on the phone barked.

"Excuse me?" Chelsea said, bewildered.

"I said how many," the voice repeated irritably, and now Chelsea recognized it as Cindy Sumtimes. "How many cards have you done by now?"

"Uh, well, uh . . ." Chelsea stammered, embarrassed that she'd been daydreaming for the past ten minutes. "Not too many yet . . ."

"Look, Chutney, get to it!" Cindy yelled, then she hung up.

Chelsea hung up the receiver and turned to the task she'd been assigned.

I mean, the whole assignment is so pointless, she thought. *It's so much easier to access this information on computer, and if Jazz wants a printout, it can just be printed out and put on cards.*

I said that to Cindy, Chelsea remembered. *And Cindy looked at me like I was crazy. And then she said, "If Jazz had said that she wanted this stuff handwritten on file cards while you're standing on your head, you'd be upside down right about now. Understood?"*

She stared at the list on the computer.

There were hundreds of topics, ranging from Animals (teens who have killed or mutilated) to Yacking (teens who can't stop). And everything in between. Most of which seemed to deal with either sex, drugs, alcohol, or crime.

Chelsea sighed one more time and, beginning with Animals, dutifully began transposing the data onto file cards. It was excruciatingly boring work, but she vowed that these were going to be the very best file cards that Jazz had ever had put into her hands.

She worked for two hours straight before she stopped to stand up and stretch her legs. Idly, she walked over to the window and looked out. The offices and studio of *Trash* were located in a building overlooking the Hudson River, and because it was such a warm June day, there were many pleasure boats on the river.

Last night Sky said that his uncle captains a fishing boat, Chelsea recalled. She could just picture Sky's open and friendly face, his large brown eyes and strong jawline.

He's so nice and sweet, Chelsea thought. *He's even in the Big Brother program in Brooklyn, and he showed us pictures of his family. He's interested in the tech stuff, like camera work, and I guess it didn't hurt that his dad is really big in the TV tech union when he applied to be an intern here.*

And he's so cute. Karma says he's teenage Keanu Reeves. He's so nice, so easy to talk to, I feel like he could have been one of my buds from high school, and—

"Hey!"

Chelsea turned around.

As if she had willed it, Sky Addison had stuck his head in the door. "How ya doing?"

"Hi!" Chelsea said, happy to see a friendly face. She walked over to him. "How did you know I was in here?"

"Karma told me," Sky reported. "I ran into her in the Xerox room. She already seems to know where everything and everyone is. So, how's it going?"

"Well, to tell you the truth, it's basically boring," Chelsea admitted. "I'm writing things on file cards. What have they got you doing?"

"Well, first I Xeroxed papers for the audio engineer—I have no idea what they were—and now I'm on my way to the control room, to learn how the cameras work."

"Lucky you," Chelsea said enviously.

"Well, keep your chin up," Sky said. "Don't let 'em drown you in file cards!" He flashed his great grin again and left.

He's definitely the friendliest of the three guy interns, Chelsea thought as she forwarded the computer to more experts' names.

Now Alan Van Kleef—Johnny Depp, according to Karma—is the most sensitive, Chelsea mused, picking up a tangerine-colored index card. *He wants to be a writer. Last night he told us that his dad was really disappointed in him because he didn't want to work in the family business. And I bet there are a lot of sons out there who would want to work in the family business, if their dad owned a National Football League team like Alan's dad does! But Alan thought that working on Trash would give him good material for a book.*

Chelsea looked up at the computer screen. She was up to the Cs—Cannibals (teens who claim to have eaten human flesh). She shuddered at the thought.

That has to be made up, she decided. *Half the stuff in here has to be made up.* She reached for another index card, and her mind wandered off again.

To Nick. Nick Shaw.

Her heart jumped, just thinking his name in her mind.

He's Brad Pitt. Definitely Brad Pitt.

Chelsea had been so attracted to him the night before that it was hard for her even to be around him. She had felt breathless and tongue-tied, stupid and flushed.

I hope no one noticed, she thought. *God, that would be so totally humiliating.*

And what is his deal, anyway? Chelsea thought, the sky-blue index card in front of her blurring. *He's a total slacker, as far as I can tell. Last night he was wearing jeans and a huge flannel shirt, and today he's wearing exactly the same thing.*

Chelsea smiled and closed her eyes, images of Nick dancing in her mind. *I like the fact that a guy that fine isn't into his looks,* she thought. *It's like he's not even aware of how impossibly hot he is. Even though he is so hot that...*

She opened her eyes. *No. I am not the kind of girl who falls for some guy just because he's hot.*

"But it's more than that," she murmured out loud, as if she were having an argument with herself. *When I talked—Lisha and Karma, too, for that matter—Nick really listened,* she recalled. *So many great-looking guys just pretend to listen to girls, some fake the Mr. Sensitive thing, meanwhile all they're really thinking about is getting your clothes off....*

Not Nick. I can tell.

Or maybe it's Belch, she thought, smiling at the memory of Nick's mongrel dog, whom he had brought over later in the evening the night before. *Belch is the cutest, coolest dog I ever met in my life.*

And he can belch on command. Nick said "belch," and he—

The phone rang again. Chelsea answered right away.

It was Cindy. "How many?" she barked into the phone. "How many cards?"

Chelsea took a quick look at the table in front of her. She'd organized the piles of file cards into piles of ten, and there were thirteen piles on Barry's desk, along with three cards directly in front of her, in the category of Cross-Dressers (Teen).

"I've done one hundred and thirty-three," Chelsea said hesitantly.

Silence on the phone.

"Is that okay?" Chelsea asked anxiously.

"Yeah, not bad," Cindy allowed. "So, take a coffee break. The staff lounge is the third door on the left when you turn right out of Barry's office. I'll stop by and check your work while you're there."

Once again, Cindy hung up the phone without saying good-bye.

"Coffee break, right," Chelsea mumbled as she made her way down the hallway to the *Trash* employees' lounge.

The room was a disaster. Half-consumed foam cups of coffee sat on a scarred wooden table. Some stale-looking jelly doughnuts spilled out of a box on the counter. Someone had left a half-eaten bagel on the lumpy orange tweed couch. Above that a bulletin board overflowed with haphazardly placed notices, notes, and photos.

"It's a total dump," Karma said as Chelsea took in the disaster of the room.

Karma was sitting on the couch, holding a photocopied article from some newspaper in her hands. She had kicked off her high heels and her feet were up on a small gold vinyl footrest with the stuffing coming out of it. "Why didn't you stop me from wearing these shoes this morning?" Karma whined. "My feet are killing me."

"So don't wear them tomorrow," Chelsea said, pouring herself a cup of the thick-looking coffee.

"It's the worst," Karma said, indicating the coffee. "Swill. I gotta bring in better stuff."

"So, what have you been doing?" Chelsea asked. She took a sip of the coffee. Karma was right. It was vile.

"Oh, you know, glamorous stuff," Karma said in her nasal whine. "I filed papers. I answered a phone." She thrust the photocopied page she had been reading at Chelsea. "You gotta read this."

It was an article photocopied from that morning's New York *Daily News.*

TRASH'S JAZZ STEWART SET FOR
BARBARA WALTERS TELEVISION SPECIAL

Jazz Stewart, the white-hot, white-blond, nineteen-year-old host of the TV-talk-show phenomenon *Trash,* has been invited by television interviewer Barbara Walters to join her in a half-hour-long, one-on-one special, to be broadcast over the Labor Day weekend.

Stewart's story, and her rise from being a sexy dancer on an afternoon music-video channel's teen dance show to being the cover story of last week's *People* magazine, is well-known.

"We want to go beyond the brains and the great legs," one of Walters's producers said, "and we want to make this daughter of rock-and-roll groupie Pamela Brewer real to our viewers. No one can do it like Barbara can."

Stewart, who claims to be the illegitimate daughter of Rod Stewart, has had her show for only nine months, but, in syndication, it has penetrated every major television market in the

> USA, and has achieved higher ratings in a shorter time than any
> other talk show in history.

Accompanying the article was a quarter-page photo of Jazz, taken on the beach at Saint-Tropez, France, last month.

In it, Jazz was wearing nothing but the world's tiniest bikini bottom and a sultry sneer, her arms crossed across her breasts.

"She's a sluttier-looking Mischa Barton," Karma decreed, looking at the photo over Chelsea's shoulder. "Gawd, I would kill to have Jazz's body."

"Why bother?" Lisha said, striding in the open door to the lounge. Evidently she had overheard Karma's comment. "I mean, you, too, could buy those body parts at your friendly neighborhood plastic surgeon's."

"What, you're telling me she had a boob job?" Karma asked, squinting at the photo.

"I heard she had an *everything* job," Lisha said, pouring herself some coffee. "So, how's life in the fast lane, you guys?"

"We did secretarial stuff," Chelsea said, still studying Jazz's photo. "Do you really think she's had plastic surgery? I mean, she's only nineteen!"

"Who'd you hear this dish from?" Karma demanded.

"What difference does it make?" Lisha asked. "Jazz did what she needed to do. And now she's hot."

"And we work for her," Karma added, "which makes us very, very warm."

"Right," Lisha agreed, making a face at the vile coffee. "Which is why when Jazz tells us to jump, we will say 'how high?' "

The phone on the table next to Chelsea rang loudly.

Is there anyplace in this office that is less than ten feet from a phone? Chelsea thought, automatically reaching to pick it up.

"Uh, employees' lounge, Chelsea Jennings speaking," she said, hoping she was answering the phone the right way.

"Why didn't you tell me your name was Chelsea?" Cindy barked into the phone. "I've been walking around calling you Chutney all morning!"

"Well, I—"

"Glad to see you found the lounge. Listen, is Karma and what's-her-name—the other intern—"

"Lisha," Chelsea said.

"Right," Cindy agreed. "They both in there?"

"Yes," Chelsea replied.

"Well, cool," Cindy said. "I've got a little surprise for you guys. Why don't you come down to the set? Barry wants you guys to see an actual taping in progress. Usually we air live, with a six-second delay, but Jazz wants some shows in the can for when she goes on vacation."

Cindy hung up. No good-bye, but Chelsea was used to it by now.

"We've been summoned," Chelsea said, getting up from the couch.

"All of us?" Lisha asked.

Chelsea nodded. "We're supposed to go to the set. I think we're about to find out exactly why *Trash* is the trashiest hit of all time!"

FOUR

"Ladies, ladies, ladies!" a short, slight guy in faded jeans and a Good Charlotte T-shirt called out as Chelsea, Lisha, and Karma entered through the side door of Studio C.

Studio C hadn't been easy to find. And once they had found it, they had to give their names to a monitor, who stood just outside the door. A sign over the door read LIVE, but as the girls entered, it was not lit up.

"I'm Barry Bassinger, senior producer," the guy said, a warm smile on his face. "You met Sumtimes this morning, right?"

Next to him, in the rear of the room, Cindy Sumtimes waggled her fingers at the girls, her eyes on the technicians moving cameras around the stage area.

Chelsea took it all in, wide-eyed. She recognized the *Trash* set from what she'd seen on TV, although she was surprised to find that it was much smaller than it looked on the tube.

But there was the infamous *Trash* logo painted on the nude, faux-marble statue of David. There was the comfortable overstuffed furniture, the wooden coffee table, the inflatable man now lolling on the couch with a top hat hanging over his crotch, the inflatable woman hanging upside down from a curtain.

And every show, the inflatable people hang somewhere else, Chelsea recalled, thrilled in spite of her general dislike for the show. It was all just so . . . so magical and seductive.

And there, on the coffee table, is the bowl of M&M's that Jazz always eats. I've seen it all so many times on TV, but now I'm really, truly here. I actually work here!

"Hey, Sumtimes!" a woman wearing white go-go boots and a lime-green micro-mini called as she ran over to them. "We got a problem with today's shrink."

"What, a hair problem?" Cindy asked.

"Well, her hair looks like dog meat," the other woman said. "But also she's wearing houndstooth, which, as you know, will go all blurry on camera. Plus she claims she's allergic to all cosmetics, so she won't let José touch her face with a makeup brush."

"Geez, just what I need, a neurotic shrink," Cindy said with disgust, getting up from her chair. "Lemme see her."

They hurried off together.

"So, who's who?" Barry asked.

They quickly introduced themselves.

"Great, great," Barry said. "So, you're about to see your first *Trash* show. Remember our motto: Excess, Access, Success!"

"Okay, Mack, let 'em in!" a guy with earphones on called from the stage.

At that moment, as if they were in a marathon and someone had just shot off the starter pistol, throngs of people swarmed into the studio. The quickest—or rudest—elbowed their way to the front and claimed seats.

"Brenda! Over here!" a skinny, sallow-faced teenage girl in a sweatshirt featuring a puffy pink kitten called to the back of the room.

"Excuse me," said the Hispanic guy that Chelsea had seen earlier, coming over to the girl. "The front seats are reserved. You need to sit back there."

"I don't see no sign that says that!" the girl exclaimed huffily.

"And yet it's true," he said.

He looked the audience over, moving people around, some to the front and some to the back.

"Why is he doing that?" Chelsea asked.

"I know," Lisha said, watching the audience reseating continue. "He's moving the hip, good-looking people to the front, because they'll be on camera more, right?"

Barry grinned at her. "Smart girl," he approved. "So, this is how it works. Roxanne or Demetrius—he's the dude over there who looks like a Spanish superhero—the one with the hair—and Roxanne you'll see later on—one of them will warm up the audience. Then Jazz will come out—the audience always goes wild, of course—and we go live, and we're happening!"

Chelsea looked over the buzzing audience. They were all young, she realized, and there was a reason for that. No one over the age of thirty was allowed in the studio audience. ID was checked at the door.

"What's the subject of today's show?" Karma asked.

"Transvestite Teen Girls versus Real Teen Girls—who's sexier?" Barry recited.

"You mean guys who dress up like girls versus real girls?" Chelsea asked, wanting to make sure she knew what he meant.

"You got it," Barry said. "Sumtimes took them shopping yesterday. We dropped a bundle at Victoria's Secret. One guy had to have two corsets sewn together to get something that would fit him."

"Gee . . ." Chelsea said, at a loss for words.

Barry smiled at her. "Where you from?"

"Nashville," Chelsea admitted. She felt utterly provincial, standing there in her little Gap outfit.

"Oh yeah, right," Barry said. "I remember that from your application. Let's see. You want a career in TV, something serious," he continued. "You probably read classics for fun. Am I right?"

Chelsea blushed at being so transparent.

"Hey, it's cool," Barry said easily. "Just remember that more people's lives are affected by pop culture than have ever read *Ethan Frome*."

"Good," Karma said, "because I was forced to read that book my junior year and I, like, totally hated it."

Barry laughed. He turned to Lisha. "How about you? You an intellectual, too?"

Lisha shrugged and eyed him coolly.

How does she get away with that? Chelsea wondered. *It's like nothing in the whole world intimidates her. How did she change so much between junior high and now?*

"Okay, we're set down here," Demetrius said into his headphones. "Who's doing the warm-up, me or Roxanne?"

Chelsea could hear because there was a set of headphones on the chair where Cindy Sumtimes had been sitting.

"Roxi," the guy in the booth said. "She's on her way."

At that moment the curtain at the side of the stage parted, and an incredible-looking girl walked out onto the set. She was very tall and thin, with sexy red hair that fell over one eye, and cheekbones so high you could serve dinner off of them. She wore a perfect white designer suit with a very, very short skirt. Underneath the jacket she wore nothing but her perfect, creamy skin.

No one in the audience knew who she was, but she was clearly *someone,* and their excited conversations dropped off expectantly.

"Hello," the girl said coolly. "I'm Roxanne Renault."

"Uh-uh," Karma whispered to Chelsea. "She's Gwyneth Paltrow with red hair."

"Welcome to *Trash,*" Roxanne continued. "As you know, the audience is a major part of our show. You'll be on live, which means that all of America is about to see you and hear you."

The audience tittered their excitement to each other.

"Ask lots of questions," Roxanne continued. "Don't be afraid to be outrageous. After all, that's what we're known for. There's nothing you can't do or say on *Trash*."

"Don't mention that to the censors," Barry whispered to the girls.

"How does that work?" Chelsea whispered back as Roxanne continued her spiel down front.

"We're on a six-second delay," Barry explained. "They try to bleep out anything that doesn't live up to FCC standards. They fail a lot."

"So, now," Roxanne continued, "to get you into the *Trash* frame of mind, we're going to make two of you into superstars." Her eyes scanned the audience. Hands flew into the air, even though, as far as Chelsea knew, they had no idea in the world what they might be volunteering for.

"You," Roxanne said, pointing to the girl in the puffy-print sweatshirt who now sat near the back of the studio, "and you." She pointed to a very overweight girl in bulging stretch leopard-print pants.

The two girls eagerly came down on to the stage.

"Would you like to win some money?" Roxanne asked them in her purring voice.

"Sure!" Puffy Print exclaimed.

"Uh-huh," the other girl agreed eagerly. She waved to someone in the back of the room.

"Okay," Roxanne said.

Demetrius and Alan Van Kleef pushed a large box on wheels—about eight feet by eight feet—out on to the stage. It appeared to be filled with mud.

"There are ten twenty-dollar bills hidden in that box of mud," Roxanne said. All you two ladies have to do is to jump in and mudwrestle for one minute. Whoever is left standing gets all the money."

Puff Print jumped up and down with excitement. The other girl looked reluctant.

"Oh, come on," Roxanne coaxed her. "This is *Trash*. You have to get into the spirit of the show, right?"

"I guess," the heavy young woman agreed.

"Cool," Roxanne said, smiling. "Oh, and one other thing. We have outfits for you to wear while you're wrestling—we wouldn't want you to get your nice clothes all messed up. Just step backstage and an assistant will give them to you."

Dutifully, the two girls walked offstage.

"They're really going to mud-wrestle for money?" Chelsea asked dubiously.

"Yeah," Barry confirmed. "This is one of our tamer warm-ups."

Roxanne talked to the audience for two more minutes, and then the two teen girls came back out onto the stage.

They were both wearing pig outfits.

"Okay, you two little oinkers!" Roxanne said gaily. "Go for it!"

This is just so humiliating, Chelsea thought. *I feel so embarrassed for those girls.*

But evidently the girls didn't share Chelsea's sensibilities. They eagerly got into the box of mud and went at each other. Over a sound system came a singsong version of "The Farmer in the Dell."

The audience cracked up, and the girls in the mud box got more and more into it, falling, sliding, hurling mud at each other.

After a minute of this "hilarity," a gong went off.

"Time for the audience to vote," Roxanne said. She held her hand over the skinny girl, and there was polite applause. Then she held her hand over the fat girl, who egged the audience on for more accolades, and the audience went wild.

"You win!" Roxanne said as the two girls climbed out of the mud box. "Did you have fun?"

"Oh, yeah!" the skinny girl said enthusiastically, wiping some mud out of her eye. "I coulda whipped her butt if we'd gone longer."

"Well, go backstage and someone cute with bulging muscles will hose you down," Roxanne promised. She turned to the heavy girl. "You get all the money," she told her.

"Great!" the girl said happily, wiping some mud off her eye.

"Of course, you have to dive back in the mud pit and dig for it," Roxanne added.

The audience hooted at this turn of events, and the heavy girl's face fell.

"Hey, just kidding!" Roxanne said gaily. She turned to the audience. "How about a nice hand for a good sport?"

The audience applauded dutifully and the girl walked offstage, waving to the studio audience as they left.

"And now," Roxanne said, her voice reverential, "the person you've all been waiting for. Please welcome . . . Jazz!"

The audience came roaring to its feet, screaming and cheering with excitement.

Nothing happened.

The stage was empty.

And then, over the roar of the audience, came the sound of a motor. A Harley motor, revving.

Jazz roared onto the stage, on a huge chopper. She was dressed all in black leather, from head to foot. She parked the bike in the center of the set and pulled off her helmet. Her gorgeous, trademark white-blond hair came flying around her incredible face.

"Don't you hate it when people tell you what to do?" she asked the audience without preamble.

"Yeahhhhh!" the young audience cheered.

"And don't you hate it when people tell you what you should be?" Jazz went on.

"Yeahhhh!" the audience cheered, even louder.

"I can't hear you," Jazz said, giving the audience a look that told them they had disappointed her.

"Yeahhhhh!" they screamed as one.

"Again," Jazz commanded.

"Yeahhhhhh!" they screamed again.

"Live from New York," a deep male voice said over a sound system, "it's *Trash!*"

The applause sign lit up and the audience went wild, yelling and screaming, jumping out of their seats. As they did this Jazz slowly and wordlessly began to strip out of her black leather, as hot rock and roll blared over the sound system.

This, of course, only egged the audience on even more.

Finally Jazz had stripped down to a tiny black leather bikini.

"What's sexy?" she asked, staring into the camera. "Who knows? My guests today do. Some are real girls. And some are guys who dress like real girls. And they're all hot. But who's hotter? And who cares what people like your third-grade teacher think?"

Here Jazz turned around so that her back was to the audience. Then she undid the top of her leather bikini and pulled it off. She turned her head and spoke over her shoulder.

"The ultimate showdown, real teen girls and transvestite teens. Betcha Mom and Pop don't know what little Bobby wears when he's all alone, know what I mean?"

Jazz smiled a sardonic little smile at the camera. "After all," she concluded, "it's all just *Trash*. Isn't it?"

The show went to a commercial, and Jazz walked off the set, never allowing the audience to see her from the front.

"Pretty amazing, huh?" Barry said, his voice full of admiration.

Many words came to Chelsea's lips, but *amazing* wasn't one of them.

Unbelievable.

Tacky.

Humiliating.

These were but a few of the words that came to Chelsea's lips.

But the valedictorian of Hume-Fogg Honors High School was smart enough to keep her mouth shut.

Because this was *Trash*.

And now she was a part of it.

"Look, how much can we bitch?" Karma asked, carrying her bowl of ice cream into their living room. "I mean, we knew what *Trash* was when we entered the contest to be interns, right?"

It was that evening, and after eating at the Greek diner on the corner, the three girls had come home to find a note on their door from Nick, Sky, and Alan, telling them they'd stop over about nine-thirty.

The girls had changed into shorts, and they had just scooped up three heaping bowls of Ben & Jerry's ice cream they'd bought on the way home.

"Did you apply for a lot of different internships?" Chelsea asked with feigned casualness.

"Just at *Trash* and *The Wall Street Journal*," Karma said, dipping her spoon into her ice cream. "But *Trash* seemed like more fun."

Meaning she got them both, Chelsea realized. *She wasn't rejected three hundred and forty-seven times.*

"*Trash* is the only one I applied for," Lisha said. "A free ticket to New York City, a TV gig, an apartment—I can dig it."

"But doesn't *Trash* seem...I don't know...even trashier than you thought it would be?" Chelsea asked, spooning some ice cream into her mouth. She thought about her mother's comment about lying down with dogs and getting up with fleas.

It's a good thing she's never watched Trash, Chelsea thought, *or she would drag me home so fast I wouldn't know what hit me.*

"The way I look at it," Lisha said, "is that it's a means to an end. We've all got summer jobs in TV, right?"

"Right," Karma agreed. "So who cares if it's the sleaziest TV ever broadcast in the history of TV? The whole world is sleazy today."

"I guess," Chelsea said reluctantly. She shuddered as she recalled a scene from the show that day: a seventeen-year-old girl in a pushing fight with a tall, thin, desperate-looking transvestite guy who was wearing the same outfit the girl was wearing. "It's just so...so sad. And sordid."

"People like sordid," Lisha said. "They like to see weird, dysfunctional people on TV. It makes them feel so superior." She spooned some ice cream into her mouth. "Remember my mom, Chels?"

"Sure," Chelsea said. "She was so sweet. She used to bake the best chocolate-chip cookies...."

"She still does," Lisha said. "And she still teaches Sunday school. But she's addicted to talk shows, the trashier the better."

"Your *mother*?" Chelsea asked in shock.

"Wake up and smell the cappuccino," Karma advised. "These shows are wildly popular. And *Trash* is the most popular of all."

"I guess...." Chelsea said with a sigh.

"People love the titillation," Karma continued. "And then, Jazz has this way of turning the worst of pop culture on its head, you know what I mean? And she's got that in-your-face I-don't-give-a-damn-what-you-think thing, which they love on the college campuses. Face it, it's brilliant."

"But—"

"And just because you work there, it doesn't mean *you're* trash," Lisha added. "Like I said, it's just a gig."

"Yeah..." Chelsea agreed reluctantly.

"Hey, you want to be this TV producer, right?" Lisha asked. "How do you think Geraldo started?"

"And he's a lawyer, too," Karma put in, licking some ice cream off her spoon.

"Y'all are right, I guess," Chelsea said.

"Someday when Barbara Walters is interviewing you, you'll be able to say how you started out as an intern on the sleaziest show in the history of TV. It'll make a great story."

Chelsea smiled at Lisha. "When we were kids you wanted to be a rock star," she recalled.

"Too bad there aren't any rock-and-roll internships available," Lisha said. She made a face. "God, I was such a joke. Pudgy, bucktoothed little me, a rock star."

"You were cute," Chelsea said loyally. "I mean, you're cuter now . . . how did you do it, anyway?"

"What?" Lisha asked.

"Make yourself over," Chelsea replied.

Lisha shrugged—something she seemed to do whenever she didn't want to answer a question.

"Well, now you're a total babe," Karma said. "So maybe you could tell me how to put on ten pounds of curves—and three inches in height while you're at it."

"You're tiny and darling," Chelsea told her.

"I am so sick of being tiny and darling," Karma whined. "I want to be tall and intimidating, like Roxanne. What's her deal, anyway?"

"I don't know," Lisha said. "I saw her in the hall after the show, and she asked me who I was. Then she just walked away."

"Very bizarre," Karma said. "I get a major bad vibe from her."

"My guess is she's a Jazz wannabe," Lisha said, getting up to put her ice-cream bowl in the sink.

Karma checked her watch. "Oh, wow, I gotta go. My shift starts in an hour."

Chelsea had completely forgotten about Karma's night job as a bartender at Jimi's. "Aren't you beat?" she asked as Karma raced around gathering up her stuff.

"What can I tell you, I have the energy of an elephant," Karma said. "Remember to triple-lock the door after I leave."

As Karma opened the door Nick, Alan, and Sky practically fell into the apartment.

"What did you do," Sky asked, "just divine that we were out here?"

"I'm on my way to my other job," Karma explained. "And don't bring Belch in unless you gave him a bath since yesterday. I found dog hair on everything."

"She doesn't mean it," Nick told Belch as the three guys and the dog came into the apartment.

"Anybody want ice cream?" Chelsea offered.

"I'm stuffed," Alan said, sitting in the comfortable chair. "We just ate at the Mexican restaurant on Broadway. It was great."

"They wouldn't let Belch in," Nick said, roughhousing with the dog.

"'Cuz—I don't know if this concept has escaped your notice—he's a dog," Lisha pointed out.

"Shhh," Nick said. "Belch doesn't know that."

"I'm beat, man," Sky said, sitting on the rug, right next to Lisha. He lifted a lock of her hair and let it drop. "How about you?"

"I didn't do anything any more strenuous than file papers," Lisha said.

"I answered some guy's phone all day," Alan said. "It never rang. I don't know who he is or what he does."

"What did you do?" Chelsea asked Nick, trying to sound casual. Just being near him made her feel quivery.

Nick lay down on the rug and Belch climbed on his stomach. "Not much," he said.

"Like what?" Chelsea asked.

"I didn't get there until after lunch," Nick said.

"And no one even noticed?" Lisha asked him.

He put his hand in Belch's mouth, and the dog play-bit at him. "Jazz told me I didn't have to come in until one."

"*Jazz?*" Lisha repeated. "What, you mean you *know* her?"

"Yeah," Nick said, pushing some hair off his face. "I met her in a club downtown about a month ago. That's how I got this gig."

"I guess that means the contest was fixed," Sky said wryly. "It's an American scandal."

"So, you mean Jazz Stewart, like, walked up to you in a club and said, 'Do you want to be an intern on my show?' " Lisha asked dubiously.

Belch licked Nick's face, and Nick laughed. "Kinda," he replied. "I mean, we talked, and then we went out for coffee, and then she asked me."

"You're kidding, right?" Lisha asked.

"Hey, look at the guy," Alan said in his gentle voice. "I've only known him for two days and I already know that gorgeous women, total strangers, will stop him on the street to give him their phone number."

"It doesn't mean anything," Nick mumbled.

"So, since we're all earning squat, I guess it's my man Nick here who could put in a good word for us about a raise," Sky teased.

"He's probably earning more than we are," Lisha said. She looked over at Nick. "Are you?"

"Hey, chill with that," Nick said, sounding embarrassed. "It's no big thing."

Nick put his hand out and reached for Chelsea, barely making contact with her knee. "You aren't gonna tease me about this, too, are you?"

"Maybe," she said, trying to sound as cool as Lisha always sounded. *What I really want to do is to fling my body on top of you and kiss you wildly,* Chelsea thought. *And then I want to—*

"I guess Nick could ask Jazz if he's making more money than we are," Sky said, folding his arms behind his neck.

"Really soon," Alan added, nodding.

"Why, you have her home phone number?" Lisha asked.

"Better," Sky said with a grin. "There was a message on the answering machine when we got in. Jazz is picking Nick up tonight in her limo at eleven o'clock."

Sky leaned into Lisha and nudged her playfully in the shoulder. "But I don't think it's raises that they're gonna talk about, do you?"

There was more teasing banter, but Chelsea didn't hear it. She was too depressed.

Great, she thought. *Just great. I get a crush on a guy, and it turns out he's dating Jazz Stewart, the girl* People *magazine calls the sexiest girl in the world.*

Just great.

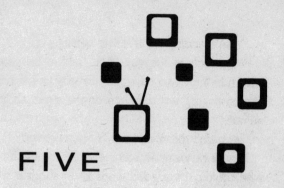

FIVE

Oh, no!

Chelsea looked down at the sidewalk, hoping against hope that what she'd just stepped in had been an ice-cream sandwich someone had dropped on the sidewalk by accident, or maybe even a Chinese egg roll that had fallen off some delivery guy's bicycle.

No such luck.

"Yuck," she muttered. "Yuck, yuck, yuck."

Quickly, she pulled on the leashes of the two dogs she was walking, yanking them toward the street, and began scraping her right shoe furiously against the well-worn concrete curb.

Oh yes, she thought to herself, lifting up her foot awkwardly to see if it was now clean. *This is why I left Tennessee. The television business is just soooo glamorous.*

It was a week later, and in that brief span of time Chelsea's mood had gone from euphoria over working in the TV industry, to guilt about the kind of show she was working on, to utter depression at the banal reality of her job.

She spent her days answering phones, filing papers, and doing endless errands for various executives and, most often, for Jazz.

Not that Jazz even knew who she was. Oh, no. It was always Cindy Sumtimes who told Chelsea what Jazz wanted her to do.

Like walking Jazz's two dalmatians, Luke and Ian, which was exactly what she was doing at the moment. Supposedly the dogs were named after two guys from a hit TV show, both of whom Jazz had dated and ditched.

"Come on," Chelsea said impatiently, pulling the two dogs along on their polka-dot leashes. It was only ten o'clock in the morning, and already the air was so hot and humid that her cotton floral dress was sticking to her back.

She'd arrived at the *Trash* studio that morning at nine o'clock, and Cindy Sumtimes had immediately handed her Jazz's dogs, secured by two matching black-and-white polka-dot leashes, and a black-and-white polka-dot cellular phone.

"Don't come back for an hour," Cindy had barked.

"You told me that the last two times I did this job," Chelsea pointed out.

"Yeah, yeah," Cindy said, reaching for a cigarette from the pack in her pocket. "You want Jazz's parasol? It's pretty hot outside."

Chelsea had graciously declined the polka-dot parasol.

I wonder if Jazz wears a polka-dot jumpsuit when she walks these monsters, Chelsea had thought nastily, the dogs pulling on their chains. *Or maybe teeny, tiny polka-dot panties, which she flashes to every cute guy that drives by.*

Luke, the larger of the two dogs, snarled at Chelsea as they turned the corner. "Shut up," she snarled back.

She was in a terrible mood, and Luke and Ian were the very first dogs she had ever met that she could not stand.

"Well, hi, fancy meeting you here," Karma said, coming from the opposite direction on the street. "I see you got the exciting assignment this morning."

Luke snarled again and lifted his leg against a fire hydrant.

"I hate these dogs," Chelsea confessed. "What are you doing out in the real world?"

"Just came from Zabar's," Karma explained. "Had to buy Barry Bassinger his Jamaican coffee beans. You know he doesn't touch the swill we drink in the lounge."

Ian lifted his leg and added his urine to Luke's, barely missing a passerby, who swore as she hurried past.

"I ran into Lisha on Eighty-ninth Street," Karma continued. "She had to pick up Jazz's dry cleaning. Do you think the guys get assigned as much crap work as we do?"

"Alan is doing something or other boring with credit-card receipts," Chelsea reported. "Sky gets to follow a camera guy around all day—lucky him. And Nick never seems to be around at all."

"Oh, he's probably around—around Jazz," Karma said knowingly. She adjusted the suspenders that held up her red raw-silk baggy pants, under which she wore a cropped, sleeveless, purple-and-red-striped shirt.

"It's so gross," Chelsea said crossly. "It's like he's her boy-toy."

"Nice toy if you can get it," Karma said with a grin.

Chelsea made a face at her. "Very funny. You'd just think that Nick would have more self-respect than that, wouldn't you?"

Karma nudged her elbow into Chelsea's side. "You only say that because you're crazed for him."

"I am not!" Chelsea denied vehemently.

"You lie like a rug," Karma said good-naturedly.

"I'm not interested in him," Chelsea insisted, her face turning red.

"You are a terrible liar," Karma said with a grin. "You turn this really bright red color. It's just hilarious!"

Chelsea blushed even harder. "I am not into Nick," she said again.

"Anyway, according to Alan, not only is he spending time with Jazz, but he's had two other girls over this week."

"Gawd, I miss everything by working nights," Karma whined.

"And besides," Chelsea continued, "it just so happens that I like Alan. Really."

"Alan is a doll," Karma agreed. "But Nick turns your bones to jelly."

Luke snarled at Chelsea, and then Ian barked at her.

"I gotta walk these monsters," Chelsea said as the dogs began to pull her away. "I'll see you later."

"Have a blast," Karma called as she headed back toward the *Trash* offices.

Chelsea walked across to West End, where Ian and Luke stopped and sniffed every hydrant, picking their two favorites to stop and deposit their doggie doo. Chelsea dutifully picked it up in the black-and-white plastic bag that Cindy had given her, which she deposited in the nearest street-corner garbage can.

"Hey, pretty mama." A toothless guy on the corner leered at her. Chelsea had already learned to ignore this sort of behavior. She pulled the dogs away from another hydrant, and the black-and-white cellular phone in her pocket rang.

"Chelsea Jennings, intern," she answered.

"How many?" Cindy's voice demanded.

"I'm sorry," Chelsea said, feeling a little weird to be holding a work-related conversation right in the middle of the street, and completely baffled by what Cindy was asking about. "I don't understand."

"Then let me spell it out," Cindy said, exasperated. "How many times did each of Jazz's dogs poop?"

"You're kidding," Chelsea replied, the words popping out of her mouth before she could think about them.

"About Jazz's dogs' poop I don't kid," Cindy replied. "Now, Jazz is sitting right across the table from me, and she really wants to know. She's concerned that Luke and Ian need to go to the vet because of some digestive thing. So you'd better answer me in like two seconds flat. Got it?"

Chelsea nodded, even though Cindy couldn't see her. "Uh, right," she said. "They both went twice, I think."

"You think, or you know?"

"I know," Chelsea answered firmly.

"Gotcha," Cindy said. "Call me when you get back."

My life is so glamorous, Chelsea thought as she tried to lead the dogs back toward the office. They were not interested.

"Come on," Chelsea said impatiently, tugging on their leashes.

Luke trotted over to her.

"Good dog," she told him, reaching down to pat him on the head.

Whereupon he lifted his leg and peed on her favorite shoes as if they were the nearest fire hydrant.

"Hey, girlie! That dog just—" the toothless guy began, pointing at her shoes.

All Chelsea could do was to turn around and head miserably back for the *Trash* offices, her feet squishing every revolting step of the way.

Chelsea was in the world's most terrible mood. Stopping at a cheap shoe store to replace her ruined shoes had done nothing to improve her mood.

"Hi," Nick said, walking into the employee lounge.

It was two hours later, and Chelsea was on her lunch break. None of her friends had been free, so she had bought a tunafish sandwich at the deli across the street and glumly brought it back to eat in the lounge.

"Hi," Chelsea said, taking a sip of her Coke. "You on lunch?"

"Kinda," Nick said. "I mean, I just got here." He put some coins in the Coke machine and pushed a button.

"Must be nice," Chelsea said, an edge to her voice.

Nick shrugged and popped open his Coke.

"I mean, you never have to do the demeaning things the rest of us do, do you?" she continued. "You never walk dogs, or pick up dry cleaning, or call restaurants you'll never see the inside of to make reservations for other people."

Nick sat next to her on the couch and took a slug of his Coke. "That's what they've got you doing?"

"I haven't used my brain since I got here," Chelsea fumed. "But then again, neither have you."

Nick shook some hair off his face. "You ticked off at me or something?"

"Oh, no," Chelsea said sarcastically, "why would I be ticked off just because you basically slept your way into your job?"

"Who says so?" he asked.

"It's obvious." Chelsea got up and threw the paper from her sandwich into the overflowing trash barrel, then turned to Nick again. "I hope you're not going to tell me you got hired because you wrote a great essay or something like that."

"You think I can't write a great essay?" he asked mildly.

"I don't really care," Chelsea said coolly. "I mean, I don't even know if you graduated from high school."

"Is that important?" Nick asked.

"In your case, evidently not," Chelsea said.

Nick stood up. "Hey, did I do something to you or something? I mean, did you have a dream where I was real wicked to you, and now you're taking it out on me?"

"I don't dream about you!" Chelsea insisted. She could feel her face growing red, since that was a big, fat lie. In fact, she spent most of her nights dreaming about him.

And a lot of her days, too.

"I had a dream about you," Nick said, his voice low. He walked over to Chelsea and stood close enough so that she could hear him breathing.

"You did not," she managed, unable to look him in the eye.

"I did," he said softly. "And you were a lot nicer in the dream."

He picked his Coke up from the table and walked to the door, then turned back to her. "Oh yeah, one other thing. I graduated from high school. A year early. And then I got a scholarship to Brown." He put his hands in the pockets of his faded jeans. "Later," he added, and walked out the door.

Chelsea sat down on the couch and put her face in her hands. "You are a total idiot!" she yelled out loud. "What did you just do? You wrecked everything!"

Nick stuck his head back into the lounge. "No, you didn't," he said.

Oh my God, he heard me, Chelsea realized, her face burning with embarrassment and humiliation. *Please just let the floor open up and let me fall through it, right now....*

Nick flashed his incredible smile at her. "Don't worry about it. I've been thinking about you, too."

And then he was gone.

"Hi, Cindy?" Chelsea said into the phone in the lounge. "This is Chelsea. I just finished lunch. What did you want me to do?"

"It's not Cindy," the girl replied.

"I'm sorry," Chelsea said quickly. "Did I dial the wrong extension? I was trying to reach—"

"It's Julia," the voice said.

It sure sounded like Cindy.

"Uh...Julia?" Chelsea asked carefully.

"I was Cindy last week. This week I prefer Julia," Cindy-Julia said. "Anyway, everyone just calls me Sumtimes. Like sometimes I'm one name and sometimes I'm another. Get it?"

"Right, got it." Chelsea was trying hard not to laugh, since she had a feeling that Cindy-Julia did not find this amusing.

"Okay," Sumtimes said. "Go to Room 401, fourth floor, left out of the elevator. You'll find some of the other interns there, and they'll bring you up to speed. Good luck. You'll need it."

Click.

Chelsea took the stairs rather than wait for the endless elevator, then she made her way through the small warren of offices to Room 401, dodging producers and other staff people who always seemed to be on the run. She pushed open the door to the room.

As Sumtimes had said, there were Alan, Karma, and Lisha, each of them sitting at a separate desk in front of a computer, typing away, with a set of headphones perched on their heads.

They all looked up when Chelsea walked in.

"Hi," Lisha said, slipping off her earphones. "Welcome to insanity."

"What are you doing?" Chelsea asked.

"Listen to this," Alan said, pushing a couple of buttons on the panel in front of his desk. "You're not going to believe it."

The sound of Jazz Stewart's famous voice issued from one of the speakers in the room.

"Hey, this is Jazz," Jazz's voice said coolly. "Thanks for calling 1-900-I'M TRASH! That's right, it's your chance to be with me, Jazz, live on TV, coast-to-coast, and now in Holland and Argentina, too! Just tell me why you should be on my show, and what your TRASHy show idea is. Leave your name and address and phone number, too! This call costs you just a buck ninety-nine a minute. Oh yeah, if you're under eighteen, get the parentals' permission—big duh. Go for it at the beep!"

Alan pushed another button to cut off the recording and shook his head ruefully. "Can you deal? They actually pay for the privilege of leaving Jazz a message."

"It's kind of fiscally brilliant," Karma commented, "when you think about it. A thousand calls a day, more or less, at two bucks, and that's if they talk fast. I bet they make a million a year."

"And I'll bet it's people who can least afford it who make calls to her," Alan said sadly. "It doesn't seem right."

"No one's making these people call," Lisha said with a shrug.

Chelsea edged over to the empty desk and chair next to Alan and sat down. Obviously, it was meant for her, as there was a blank computer screen and keyboard and a set of headphones. And obviously, her friends were transcribing the calls, presumably so that the producers could see if any of them were worth using as a show idea.

"So, what kind of stuff do people suggest?" Chelsea asked.

Alan grinned. "Listen and weep," he said. He pushed another couple of buttons on his panel. Instantly, a girlish voice with a flat Midwest accent filled the room.

"Oh, yeah, hi, Jazz, um...my name is Margie Blackwell, and I think you should do a show on sexy mothers and their sexy teen daughters. And it should be, like, a competition, you know? Where the mothers and daughters go out and try to pick up guys, and whoever picks up the cutest guy wins? And, like, you, Jazz, would be the judge. My mother and I volunteer because we do this together all the time here in—"

Alan snapped off the sound and looked at Chelsea, whose jaw was hanging slack with shock.

"You're kidding me," she said.

"No kidding," Lisha commented. "It must be a trend out there in the heartland, 'cause I had some girl in Nevada suggest the same thing on my tape."

Chelsea tried to picture her own mother in a sexy outfit. The idea was so ludicrous that she almost laughed out loud.

"We better get cracking," Karma said. "If Sumtimes catches us talking, she'll probably grow hair."

Chelsea put her headset on. She turned on the computer, which automatically booted to a screen entitled 1-900 SHOW IDEAS, with the day's date on it. Chelsea pushed a switch on the control panel that read PLAY, and the voice of a teen guy filled her headphones.

"Hi, Jazz!" the voice said. "I'm calling from Bend, Oregon. Wow, I can't believe I'm talking to you. Wow, this is so awesome. So, listen, I totally love you. I mean for real. Like, I would marry you, no lie. Call me sometime, but not too late because my parents are like prison guards. Here's my number and you can call collect if you have to...."

Chelsea shook her head in disbelief.

He called to propose marriage to Jazz, and paid two dollars for the privilege? Who would do anything that stupid? she thought.

Do I enter it as a show idea? Probably not. I guess I'll just type his name and number and type Marriage Proposal *next to it.*

For the next half hour Chelsea listened to, and carefully transcribed, many show ideas.

There were the two teen girls in New Hampshire who wanted to have a beer-guzzling contest on the air.

There was the guy in Arkansas who claimed to have slept with four of his high-school teachers. And he was still in high school.

There was a girl in Florida who claimed that she knew at least four other girls who, like her, were really space aliens.

Yeah, right. Chelsea chuckled to herself as she dutifully typed in the call.

And then, there was a call that stopped her heart.

"Yeah," a gravelly young male voice said, as if he'd been chain-smoking for years. "My name is Wade Cooley. My dad's in prison doing time for murder, and my mom's in prison doing time for murder. What a family, huh? It would be bitchin' if you did a show on teens whose parents are murderers, you know? Like, you'd never believe how normal I look. Hey, you guys pay for hotels and stuff, right? So, here's my phone number...."

Chelsea snapped off the tape player. Her hands were trembling and she felt sick to her stomach.

Because from a sicko *Trash* point of view, Chelsea knew this was a terrific show idea, exactly the kind of thing that Jazz loved to do.

I could ignore the tape, Chelsea thought, her hands growing clammy, her heart pounding in her chest. *No one will ever know that this guy called in.*

But what if Sumtimes comes and checks my work? What if she listens to the tape and finds that I skipped a message? What if, what if, what if...

No way out.

Slowly, shakily, she started to type in the information from the tape.

She felt a tap on her shoulder, and jumped guiltily into the air.

"What's your problem?" Roxanne Renault asked, staring down at her.

Chelsea took off her headphones. "You startled me."

"Like a rabbit?" Roxanne asked, looking her over. "Yeah, you kind of have rabbit coloring."

Chelsea's friends kept typing, watching her out of the corners of their eyes.

"Did you want something?" Chelsea asked, trying to sound polite.

Roxanne shook her gorgeous red hair out of her eyes. "You're Chutney, right?" she asked.

"Chelsea. And you're Roxi—"

"Roxanne," the tall girl corrected her. "Only my friends call me Roxi."

Chelsea was taken aback by the girl's utter nastiness. She really didn't know what to say.

"So, how's it going?" Roxanne asked, though she sounded utterly bored.

"Fine," Chelsea said. "We're all...you know...um, transcribing the phone calls to the nine-hundred number." She hated the way she sounded—tentative and stupid.

"Anything hot?" Roxanne asked.

"Uh..." Chelsea's heart hammered in her chest.

"It wasn't such a tough question," Roxanne said.

"Well, no, I don't think so," Chelsea lied. Sweat began to trickle down the center of her back.

"It doesn't sound as if you'd know something hot if it jumped up and bit you," Roxanne said with disgust. "When you're done, print it all out and bring it to my office.

"If there's anything hot on there," she finished smugly, "I'll find it."

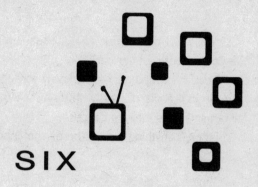

SIX

"So," Barry said to Chelsea as the waiter brought over their drinks—
Glenlivet single-malt Scotch on the rocks for him, cranberry juice for
her. "Here's to a great summer for the one and only Chelsea Jennings!"

He picked up his glass and held it above the bar, for a toast.
Chelsea took her cranberry-juice glass self-consciously and clinked it
lightly against Barry's.

"Here's to a great summer," she echoed, hoping that her voice
didn't betray her nervousness.

She looked around the bar of the Empire Hotel, right across from
Lincoln Center. Everywhere she looked, beautiful, sophisticated-
looking people were drinking, laughing, talking about their sophisticated lives, she supposed.

"I'm glad you decided to have a drink with me," Barry said with a
smile. "When I saw you in the employee lounge this afternoon, you

were kinda long in the tooth, as we say. You looked like you needed a friend."

Chelsea stared into her cranberry juice. "I guess...I was kind of having a bad day," she admitted.

"Feeling better now?"

"Much," Chelsea said, and she found, to her surprise, that she actually was.

I mean, so what if Luke ruined my favorite shoes, and so what if I spent my day doing stupid errands and typing out crazy ideas from the 900 line. And so what if Roxanne seems to hate my guts for absolutely no reason, and I made a total jerk out of myself in front of Nick.

Here I am, out for drinks with Barry Bassinger, senior producer. He's nice and friendly and he seems to be on my side.

"It was nice of you to invite me," she added.

"Hey, I know how tough it can be," Barry said, swiveling around on the bar stool to face her. "A new town, new job, new faces—I've been there."

He took a sip of his drink and Chelsea studied him. Though small, he was good-looking, and he dressed like a teenager. Today he was wearing jeans, sneakers, and an old Ozzy Osbourne T-shirt, underneath a great-looking black sport jacket with padded shoulders and a slim, European cut.

And everyone seemed to know him, from the coatcheck girl to the bartender. In fact, they were practically fawning over him.

I guess it helps to be a senior producer on the hottest TV show on the air, Chelsea thought as a beautiful woman stopped to chat with Barry.

"Sorry," he said, after the woman left. "Didn't mean to ignore you."

He's so kind, Chelsea realized, her heart warming. *I guess there really is one nice person who works at Trash—besides the interns.*

He took a sip of his drink and studied her. "So, what do you think of *Trash* so far?"

"It's really great!" Chelsea replied brightly.

He raised his eyebrows at her, an amused look on his face.

"I mean, I'm so lucky to be an intern. . . ." Her words sounded lame and hollow even to her own ears.

"A real dream come true, huh?" Barry said, his face still amused.

"Right!" Chelsea agreed, her voice too bright.

Barry took a sip of his Scotch. "You know, Chelsea," he said, leaning toward her confidentially, "I was the one who really pushed to get you on the show."

Chelsea was surprised. "You did?"

"I did," he said cheerfully. "Roxi was completely against you—don't ever tell her I told you so. I mean, I'm speaking in total confidence here, and—"

Another gorgeous woman stopped to talk with him.

Chelsea rubbed her finger nervously along the rim of her glass. Roxi. Roxanne Renault. Just the sound of her name filled Chelsea with dread. Tomorrow Roxanne would be reading through the show ideas Chelsea had transcribed.

Which means tomorrow she could decide that teen children of murderers is a great topic for a show, she thought, her stomach turning over. *Which means—*

"Sorry," Barry said, turning back to her. "Where was I? Oh, yeah. A group of us went through the finalists. We had it narrowed down to eight, and we were only going to take six. We had to drop one girl and one guy. . . ."

Chelsea nodded again.

"So Karma and Lisha were in. I mean, Karma is so cool she could be a *Trash* covergirl, right? What with her making all that money in the stock market—"

"She what?" Chelsea interrupted.

"She didn't tell you about that?" Barry asked. "The girl is brilliant. She's been dabbling in the stock market for two years. She's made thousands. Her record is better than some of the top analysts—it just slayed us! And she said on her application that her goal was to be a millionaire by the time she's thirty, and to own a TV station before she's forty. Cool, huh?"

"Wow." Chelsea marveled. "I thought she was just into designer fashions...."

"It doesn't hurt that she's Asian and gorgeous, either," Barry admitted. "And Lisha...well, after spending a year bumming around Europe—"

"Lisha spent a year in Europe?" Chelsea echoed.

"You didn't know?" Barry asked. "What, don't you guys talk to each other?"

"We do," Chelsea said. "At least, I thought we did."

"Well, anyway, she's utterly cool, smart, confident, hot looking—and ask her about Europe," he added. "So it came down to you and a girl from Alaska who's a dog sledder."

Chelsea felt overwhelmed, and suddenly very depressed. She looked down at her little dress and the cheap shoes she'd run out to buy to replace her wrecked ones.

I'm ordinary, she thought. *I'm utterly ordinary. And the only thing that makes me anything but ordinary is a big, horrible, shameful secret that I can never, ever share with anyone....*

"Hey, I didn't tell you all this to bum you out!" Barry reached out to chuck her lightly under the chin. "I wanted you to know how special I thought you are—how special I still think you are!"

Chelsea tried to smile. "The truth of the matter is...well, ever since I got the letter telling me that I got this internship, I've been trying to figure out why I was picked," she confessed. "There are a million girls out there like me—"

"Exactly!" Barry exclaimed.

"Pardon me?" she asked, confused.

"Roxi said you were boring and preppie. She passed your photo around with your two front teeth blacked out with a Magic Marker—I guess she did that herself—and the word *hick* written in real big letters."

Chelsea felt as if someone had punched her in the stomach. "But...but that's so mean—"

"I said, 'Rox, there are a million girls out there like Chelsea—smart, cute, all-American-type girls in the hinterlands. What we need around here is that real Middle America thing. It'll be refreshing—someone who isn't jaded and experienced!'"

"I guess that means my essay didn't fool you," Chelsea said.

"You mean where you pretended to be a runaway hooker living on the street?" Barry laughed. "No runaway hooker has the vocabulary you used. It was priceless!"

Chelsea's face burned with embarrassment. "Meaning that you were all laughing at me."

"Hey, don't feel bad," Barry said, reaching out to touch her arm. "We picked you as an intern, didn't we?"

"You did," she agreed.

"Right," he said cheerfully. "As far as I'm concerned, at *Trash*, you are a breath of fresh air. I pushed for you big-time, and here you are."

"I guess you have more power than Roxanne," Chelsea said.

"She started last summer as an intern," Barry confided. "She thinks she's hot stuff because she hangs out with Jazz. I mean, give me a break. She's, like, nineteen years old and she grew up in Seattle! What's so exciting about that? I'd better have more power than her, huh?"

"She hates me," Chelsea admitted. "Now I know why."

"Oh, don't mind Roxi," Barry said. "She comes on like she's so tough—she'll chill out after a while."

"Well, it's really nice of you to tell me all this," Chelsea said.

Barry smiled at her. "Like I said, Chelsea, I'm on your side. What can I tell you? I have a weakness for cute, smart, preppie girls."

Chelsea tried to smile back, but her mouth felt funny.

Is he flirting with me? she wondered nervously. *Nah, he couldn't be. He has to be at least thirty-five years old! And Trash is filled with gorgeous women. No, he's just being nice.*

"The way I figure it," Barry went on, "so much of our audience is in places like Nashville, and Little Rock, and Oklahoma City, that we need interns and fresh blood from places like that. Do you know there hasn't been a single week since we went on the air when our Nielsens haven't gone up in Coeur d'Alene, Idaho?"

"No, I didn't know that," Chelsea said honestly, remembering dimly from someplace that the Nielsens were the important television ratings, and that talk shows like *Trash* lived and died on their results.

"Everyone says we have to concentrate on sweeps," Barry continued, taking a big slug of his Scotch. "But I think that if we don't do the week-to-week thing well, we're in big trouble. What do you think?"

What do I think? Chelsea thought. *I barely know what he's talking about.*

"I, uh, agree with you, Barry," she stammered.

"I guessed you would." He smiled broadly. "So, tell me what you think."

"About what?" Chelsea asked, picking up a shelled almond from a bowl on the bar and nibbling it nervously.

"About *Trash*, of course," Barry said. "You must be thinking about the show. Hell, I think about it all the time. Give me the interns' perspective. Hell, tell me your best show idea. Here's your chance. Better yet, why don't you give it to me over dinner? They make a great steak here."

"Oh, that's really nice of you." Chelsea glanced quickly at her watch. She had been stuck transcribing tapes until seven, and it was already eight-thirty. "But I'm meeting my friends down at Jimi's at nine-thirty. That's where—"

"Karma's night gig," Barry put in. "I know. It was on her application. Okay, so you're booked." He sounded slightly annoyed and reached for a handful of almonds. "Anyway, that's cool." He looked deeply into Chelsea's eyes. "I want you to know you can talk to me, Chelsea. Really talk to me."

"Thanks."

He chewed the almonds contemplatively. "I bet you're getting sick of the scut work they've got you doing, am I right?"

"Kind of," Chelsea admitted.

"Of course you are," Barry said. "I know how smart you are. And I'll bet you have all kinds of creative ideas, and there you are, you're walking Jazz's monsters—"

Chelsea laughed. "You call them that, too?"

"I hate 'em," Barry said with a laugh. He leaned toward her. "So, Chelsea, listen. I'm not like that. I value your brains. You got a show idea? I want to hear it."

Chelsea's heart nearly skipped a beat. Was the senior producer of *Trash*, the person on whom Jazz leaned more than anyone else, actually asking her for her ideas for a perfect *Trash* show?

What an opportunity, she thought.

Don't blow this, Chelsea.

"You want to hear my best show idea," she said, buying some time.

"That's what I said," Barry said, looking soulfully into her eyes.

Chelsea did have a show idea. And she was convinced that it was a good one. She'd just been waiting for the right chance to tell someone about it, but she was also convinced that no one would listen to her because she was just an intern.

"Here's my idea," she said, choosing her words carefully. "I think that *Trash* should introduce a bunch of teens from all over America to each other by computer, on the Internet, and then bring them on the show and see if they really like each other. If they do, great. If they don't, it's TRASH!"

There. She'd done it. She had agonized over this idea many nights in the dark, before she'd gone to sleep, and had finally decided that it conformed both with her personal value system and with the kind of shows that Jazz tended to do.

It's actually moral, Chelsea thought, *something I could feel proud of. It doesn't exploit anyone. And if it works, it would show everyone that Trash doesn't have to be so sleazy to be successful. . . .*

She waited, holding her breath. Barry stared intently into her eyes.

"Brilliant," he finally said. "It's so . . . brilliant."

"It is?" Chelsea asked, shocked.

"Totally," he affirmed. "I knew I was right when I picked you, Chelsea. You've got a creative mind—"

"My honors English teacher told me the same thing!" she said with excitement.

"Chelsea Jennings, you are definitely going places," Barry predicted with a smile. He picked up his drink and drained it.

"I can get your idea on the air," he said. "Listen, what say we go over to my apartment? I know you can't drink here because they've got that stupid underage law, but I've got plenty of Glenlivet at my place. We can talk about your idea and whatnot."

"B-but I have to meet my friends downtown," Chelsea stammered.

"Oh, yeah, right," Barry said. He put his hand on her arm and rubbed softly. "But this could be much more important. *Much*," he added significantly.

"Oh, gosh, I couldn't stand them up," Chelsea heard herself say.

I sound like a ten-year-old, she thought. *A really stupid ten-year-old. And I'll bet he was only pretending to like my idea so I'd go back to his apartment with him. And now that I turned him down he's going to be really mean—*

"Hey, no prob," Barry said, dropping some money on the bar. He stood up. "So, did I cheer you up just a little?"

Chelsea stood up, too, and happiness flooded through her. So he wasn't a jerk! He really was a good guy! Impetuously she leaned over and planted a kiss on his cheek. "You cheered me up a lot," she said. "Thank you."

"Don't mention it," Barry said easily. "I'll be thinking a lot about your great show idea. Let me help you get a cab downtown, okay?"

Barry gave her a quick hug before he put her into the taxi, which he insisted on paying for, and Chelsea sat back as the driver zoomed wildly in and out of Manhattan traffic.

Well, well, well, she thought. *So Barry Bassinger really is a good guy after all. He likes my idea. And he likes me.*

And he has a lot more power than Roxanne.

"ID," a three-hundred-pound bouncer in a black leather jacket said, holding his hand out.

"I thought you didn't have to be twenty-one here—"

"You gotta be *under* twenty-six," the bouncer explained, still holding his hand out.

"Oh, that's right, I forgot." Chelsea scrambled in her purse for her driver's license and flashed it at the bouncer.

"Tennessee?" he said. "Is that in America?"

"Very funny," Chelsea said. "You should do stand-up."

"I do," the guy said seriously. "Check me out at the Comedy Factory on Monday nights." He put out a huge, meaty hand. "Five-dollar cover, sweetheart."

Chelsea pulled the one and only five-dollar bill she had out of her wallet and handed it to him. He waved her in.

Outside, Jimi's looked like any gray stone building in New York's so-hip East Village. In fact, there was only the tiniest sign on a blacked-out window that read JIMI'S.

Inside, it was insane.

Loud rock music pulsed off the walls. A large dance floor was lit here and there by colored lights, and on a raised stage area fake snow was falling on the dancers. Against one wall was a bar, but it was too far away and too dimly lit for Chelsea to see if her friends were there.

She looked up. A balcony ran all the way around the room. She could dimly make out a pool table, and a huge robot-looking mechanical creature wearing a T-shirt that read JIMI.

As the music changed, so did the light, and on the raised area where it had been snowing before, it now rained. Real rain, from some system in the ceiling. The water fell on the dancers, and then disappeared down tiny, recessed drains in the floor.

"Chelsea!" Alan yelled over the pounding music.

"Oh, hi!" she yelled back. "Wow, this place is wild!"

"No kidding! Come on."

Alan took her hand and led her through the maze of bodies until they reached the bar in the corner.

"You found us!" Karma said happily from behind the bar. She was wearing a black T-shirt that said JIMI'S in bright pink letters. "Want the house special?"

"What is it?" Chelsea asked.

Karma didn't reply; she just poured something orange into a tall glass.

Chelsea took a sip. It was cold and fruity. "This is great!"

"Twelve different fruit extracts," Karma said. "And ginseng, which is supposed to rev up your energy or something like that. My parents live on the stuff."

"Where's everyone?" Chelsea asked, sipping her drink.

"Sky and Lisha are out there dancing somewhere," Alan said.

"Where's Nick?" Chelsea asked, trying to sound casual. It was difficult. Very difficult.

"Nick hasn't shown up yet," Alan said.

"Probably tooling around Manhattan in Jazz's white SUV with the polka-dot doors," Karma said. She hurried off to wait on some people farther down the bar.

The music changed to a ballad by Bon Jovi. Alan smiled at Chelsea. "Dance?"

"Sure," she said.

They walked over to the dance floor—fortunately, it had stopped raining—and Alan took her into his arms. He felt good—warm, comfortable.

"You smell nice," he said, sniffing her hair.

"I doubt it," Chelsea said with a laugh. "I'm still wearing what I wore to work. I never made it home to shower and change."

"You look perfect to me," Alan said softly. " 'Shall I compare thee to a summer's day'?" he quoted lightly.

"Shakespeare, right?" Chelsea asked.

"Big Bill himself," Alan confirmed. "Can you imagine one guy writing all that great stuff? It blows me away."

"Maybe you'll write something that great one day," Chelsea said.

Alan laughed. "I doubt it. Sometimes I feel paralyzed just trying to write a short story. I keep hearing my dad's voice in my head, telling me I'm this big, worthless disappointment. Why don't I go out and do something *manly* instead of sitting in my room trying to write?"

"That's so cruel," Chelsea said. "And unfair."

"My dad lives and breathes football," Alan said. "But I never understood the thrill of big guys banging into each other in the mud. What can I say? I'm his only son and a major disappointment."

"Well, that's his loss." Chelsea leaned her head on Alan's shoulder and closed her eyes, swaying to the music.

"Hey, did I mention what a totally great girl I think you are?" he whispered into her hair.

"No," she whispered back. She felt warm and safe and happy. Barry Bassinger liked her show idea. Alan liked her. And she liked Alan.

And he's so much nicer than Nick, she thought. *He's kinder. And more sensitive. And I don't feel like a stuttering idiot around him.*

Slowly Chelsea turned her mouth to Alan's, and she kissed him softly, just at the corner where his lips met his cheek.

"Chelsea," he whispered. His arms tightened around her and he kissed her fully, his body pressed against hers. She kissed him back, wrapping her arms around his neck.

"Yo, the music stopped, you two," Sky said as he walked by, hand in hand with Lisha.

Chelsea opened her eyes. The music really had stopped.

"Hey, I kiss her, I hear music," Alan said lightly, draping his arm around Chelsea's shoulder.

"Having fun?" Lisha asked Chelsea as the music started up again. Kurt Cobain's voice wailed through the sound system.

"It's great here," Chelsea said. Her stomach growled. "Hey, have you guys eaten dinner?"

"No," Lisha said. "I'm starving. Do they serve food here?"

"Karma says it sucks," Sky said. "There's a Thai place down the street we could check out."

"Thai food?" Chelsea asked.

"You've never had it?" Alan said.

She shook her head no. "Believe me, Nashville is a fried-chicken-and-ribs kind of town."

"Well, allow me to broaden your culinary horizons," Alan said.

They went back over to the bar to tell Karma where they were going, then the four of them headed out the door. Alan had his arm draped around Chelsea's shoulders, and Sky was telling a joke that a cameraman at *Trash* had told him that afternoon.

Chelsea looked up, feeling happier than she had felt since she arrived in New York.

There was a white SUV parking at the curb. With the famous dalmatian polka dots on the doors.

And there was Nick, getting out of the SUV.

And Jazz, jumping into his arms.

SEVEN

"Wonderful girl that I am, I have brought you slackers breakfast," Karma said as she sailed into the apartment the next morning.

It was Saturday, and Chelsea and Lisha were sitting around in T-shirts and cutoffs, drinking coffee and trying to wake up.

After running into Nick and Jazz the night before, Chelsea vowed to herself that she was going to stop wasting her time dreaming about Nick Shaw.

I mean, what more proof do you need? she asked herself. *There was Jazz herself, in Nick's arms.*

At least Nick looked embarrassed, she recalled, taking another sip of her coffee. *And when Alan invited him and Jazz to come to dinner with us, he looked like he wanted to say yes.*

Of course, Jazz wouldn't be caught dead with us. And she just laughed and said they were heading to some chic restaurant down the block. So maybe it was just my imagination that Nick wanted to be with us....

Wanted to be with me.

Yeah, right. What a joke.

After eating at the Thai restaurant—Chelsea was crazy about the coconut soup and the curried chicken—they had gone back to Jimi's, where the four of them had danced until two in the morning.

Alan had kissed her many more times, Chelsea recalled. And it was . . . nice. Not thrilling. Not earth-shattering. But really nice.

Nick's kisses wouldn't be nice, Chelsea thought. *They would sear my lips. They would make me melt. . . .*

"I hope you brought something with lots of sugar," Lisha said in her throaty voice. "I need the rush to wake up."

"Oh, forget sugar, darling," Karma said, setting her bag of groceries on the kitchen table. "We are talking bagels, lox, and cream cheese, better known as Jewish soul food."

"What's lox?" Chelsea asked, padding over to peer into the large brown bag from Zabar's.

Karma stared at her. "Surely you jest." She pulled a copy of *Barron's* out of the bag and set it on the counter.

"I've had bagels," Chelsea said defensively.

"Well, my dear, you have not lived until you've had a really fresh New York bagel with cream cheese and lox, also known as smoked salmon."

"Smoked, as in . . . raw?" Chelsea asked tentatively.

"It's great," Lisha said, reaching for a packet of oily-looking white paper. "I had it at my ex-boyfriend's house." She unwrapped the paper. Pale, orange-y, fishy-looking things lay there.

"That's it?" Chelsea asked, peering at it dubiously.

"Trust me," Karma said. She took out a poppy-seed bagel, sliced it, and spread it thickly with cream cheese. Then she took some paper-thin slices of the orange fish and put them on top. Then she handed it to Chelsea. "Bite."

Chelsea took the bagel and took a tentative bite. She let the taste swarm around her tongue for a moment. "It's . . . good!" she said with surprise. She took another big bite. "It's fantastic!"

Karma laughed. "She's hooked now. Watch out, world!" She and Lisha quickly made their own bagels, which they carried into the living room, along with fresh cups of hot, strong coffee.

"I love this!" Chelsea said, licking some cream cheese off her finger.

"Good, then we can still be friends," Karma said sweetly. "So, did you guys have fun last night?"

"The Thai food was great," Chelsea said, taking a sip of coffee.

"I wasn't referring to the food," Karma said slyly. "I saw you and Alan sucking serious face on the dance floor."

"He's sweet," Chelsea said.

"I hate sweet," Lisha said blithely.

"What's wrong with sweet?" Chelsea asked.

Lisha sighed. "I don't know. Sweet is just so . . . so *good*. I like bad boys. Well, I used to, anyway."

"My shrink told me that is a very dangerous romantic outlook," Karma said. "Here's his theory. If a girl doesn't like herself, then she thinks she isn't worth anything. Hence, any guy who would like her and treat her well isn't worth anything, either. But if a guy treats her like crap, he's sexy and wonderful." She took a bite of her bagel.

"You're in therapy?" Chelsea asked.

"Not anymore," Karma said. "My parents made me go my junior year of high school. They thought I was antisocial because I stayed in my room reading *BusinessWeek*."

Chelsea remembered what Barry had told her the evening before. "Hey, Barry told me you play the stock market."

"Oh, yeah," Karma said, "here and there."

"I don't even understand how the stock market works," Lisha admitted.

"Me, neither," Chelsea said. She looked over at Karma. "Barry said you're really good, that you've made a lot of money at it."

"And since when did you and the senior producer get so chummy?" Karma asked.

Chelsea smiled. "He took me out for a drink after work yesterday."

"Get out of here!" Karma cried.

"How soon was it before he tried to put his hand down your dress?" Lisha asked dryly.

"It wasn't like that," Chelsea insisted. "He was just really nice to me."

"Please," Lisha said. "He wants to get in your pants."

"We're just friends," Chelsea said. "He told me a lot of stuff—like why Roxanne hates my guts, for example." She quickly told them what Barry had told her about Roxanne's opposition to Chelsea during the intern selections.

"So, it's just a stupid power struggle?" Karma asked. "And she hates you for that, even though you didn't have anything to do with it?"

"I guess so," Chelsea said.

"She was such a bitch to you yesterday in the computer room," Lisha said. "I wanted to throw my headphones at her."

"I know," Chelsea agreed. "And listen to this! She's only nineteen, and she started at *Trash* as an intern!"

"So, who'd she do to get promoted from intern to ... whatever it is her job title is—I can't figure it out," Karma said, polishing off her bagel.

"Who'd she 'do'?" Chelsea echoed. "What does that mean?"

"It means who'd she have sex with," Lisha translated.

"Oh," Chelsea said, chagrined. "I don't know. Maybe she's just smart and good at her job."

"She's the Wicked Witch of the West, even if she does look like a younger Gwyneth Paltrow with better hair," Karma said. "Have you noticed that I come up to, like, her kneecaps?"

Lisha's eyes narrowed. "She's power hungry, if you ask me."

"But what a wardrobe," Karma said with a sigh. "I could kill for that little number she had on yesterday. Of course, the right sleeve alone would've covered my entire body...."

"She's perfect looking." Chelsea sighed, too. "And she knows it."

"Not perfect," Karma said. She rose to get another bagel. "I have found her fatal flaw."

"What?" Lisha asked.

"The dawgs," Karma said, reaching into the bagel bag.

"The what?" Chelsea asked.

"Dawgs—feet," Karma translated. "The girl has feet the size of an ocean liner. She must go a size twelve at least."

"Bigfoot!" Lisha cried with delight. "Now the story can be told— we have found Bigfoot, and she's at *Trash!*"

The girls cracked up.

"Hey, I think there's a *Trash* episode in it!" Chelsea said. "Teens Who Have Been Stomped by Bigfoot!"

"You could go on the air and tell your sad and tawdry tale," Karma snorted gleefully.

"My guess is that Bigfoot is doing Barry Bassinger," Lisha said, sipping her coffee. "That's how she got her big promotion."

"Oh, no, I don't think so." Chelsea was quick to disagree, loyal to her new friend and mentor, Barry.

"You're being naive," Lisha said. "Barry's the guy with the most power at *Trash.*"

"But he's not like that, I mean it," Chelsea insisted.

There was a knock on their door. Karma opened it.

"Notice how she doesn't think it's a mass murderer anymore," Lisha told Chelsea with a laugh.

A mass murderer, Chelsea thought. *Like my father. And Roxanne is going to love the show idea, Teen Kids of Murderers. And everyone is going to find out.*

"Hi," Sky said, leaning on the door frame. "Can a neighbor borrow some coffee?"

"Don't you guys ever shop?" Karma asked as she went into the kitchen for some coffee beans.

"Hi." Sky looked over at Lisha. "How you doing?"

"Fine," Lisha said coolly.

"It's really nice out," he told her. "Want to go to Central Park with me later? We could go for a run, go to the zoo—"

"I don't think so," Lisha said. "Thanks anyway."

"Oh, okay," Sky said. Karma handed him the coffee beans. "Well, see you guys later. Hang loose."

Karma shut the door. "Oo, you just broke his heart," she chided Lisha.

"I thought you liked him," Chelsea added.

"I do like him," Lisha said. "I like him the same way you like Alan."

"I'd go to the park with Alan," Chelsea said. "I like Alan a lot."

"What happened to you and Nick?" Karma asked from the kitchen.

"There is no me and Nick," Chelsea said. "That is totally obvious. I'm with Alan. He's with Jazz. End of story."

"Oh yeah, right," Karma snorted, clearly not believing Chelsea.

"I'm serious," Chelsea insisted. "I'm not like you guys. I don't let myself get carried away by a purely physical attraction. I mean, a relationship has to be based on more than that...."

"Well, I don't want any kind of a relationship," Lisha said lightly, getting up from the floor. She put her coffee cup in the sink. "Frankly, I've had it with guys. They're highly overrated."

"Did you get burned or something?" Karma asked, coming back into the living room with her second bagel.

"I just know what can happen when you get in too deep," Lisha said.

"In Europe," Chelsea blurted out.

Lisha and Karma stared at her.

"Something happened to you in Europe—"

"How do you know about that?" Lisha asked sharply.

"I don't," Chelsea confessed. "But Barry said I should ask you about Europe—"

"And Barry should keep his mouth shut." Lisha's voice was tight.

"When were you there, you lucky dog, you?" Karma asked.

"Last year," Lisha said. She sounded closed off and suddenly cold.

"So you were, like, an exchange student?" Karma asked, taking a huge bite of her bagel.

"Something like that," Lisha said. "Hey, how is it that you can eat like that and stay so tiny?" she asked Karma, clearly anxious to change the subject.

Karma went into a long story about her unbelievably fast metabolism. Chelsea thought about what Lisha had just said.

I feel like I don't even know her anymore, Chelsea realized. *It's as if she has these huge secrets and she doesn't really want to let us in. And Karma has made all this money in the stock market, but she acts like she's an airhead. So I guess she has some kind of a secret, too.*

And I have the hugest secret of all, she realized. *And whatever it is that Karma and Lisha are trying to hide, I bet anything that my secret is a hundred times more shocking than theirs.*

"You sure you don't want to come to Jimi's with me?" Karma asked as she buttoned her clear plastic raincoat over her all-black outfit.

A streak of lightning was followed by a deep roll of thunder and wind lashed against their windows. The beautiful day had turned into a stormy night.

"Nah," Chelsea said. "It's so horrible outside. I'm just going to curl up with a book. I don't think I've read anything decent since I got to New York."

"No one reads in New York," Karma teased. "They just read the coverage."

Chelsea laughed. She knew that Karma meant the short descriptions the underlings wrote about possible "properties"—meaning novels, plays, or screenplays—for their bosses, who were too busy to read anything. In fact, Sumtimes had asked Alan to write "coverage" for a new horror novel that supposedly had inspired a teen reader to murder his best friend.

"See how much you've learned here in Sin City?" Karma quipped, reaching into the front closet for an umbrella. She turned back to Chelsea. "You really don't mind staying home alone on a Saturday night?"

Chelsea shook her head no. Lisha had gone to the movies with Sky—though she insisted to him that they were just "friends"—Alan had gone to visit a relative of his who lived in New Jersey, and as per usual, no one knew Nick's whereabouts.

"Don't open the door to anyone," Karma cautioned her. "You know you can't trust Antoine to screen guests."

"Thanks, Mom," Chelsea said with a laugh.

Karma waved and walked out.

She's so nice, Chelsea thought, locking the door behind Karma. *I totally lucked out, ending up roommates with her and Lisha. I haven't really had a best friend since Lisha moved away,* she realized as she padded back into her bedroom to get the book she wanted to read. *I mean, I had tons of friends, but no one to really confide in.*

Not that I could confide my deepest secret to Lisha or Karma, anyway, she told herself. She sat down on her bed, lost in thought.

What would happen, I wonder, if I told them the truth? If I could just talk to them, just confide in them . . .

Never. They'd be horrified, she decided. *They'd watch me every moment, afraid I was going to gun them down in their sleep. They'd want me to move out, but they'd be too afraid to say anything.*

Chelsea shook off those horrible thoughts and grabbed her book. "Just don't think about it," she told herself. "You're not going to say anything, so you don't have to worry about it."

She lay down on her bed and opened her book, *The Chosen,* by Chaim Potok, which Karma said was her favorite novel of all time.

Chelsea was startled by a knock on the front door. She looked at the clock on her dresser. She had been reading for two hours straight without even realizing it.

She walked into the living room and peered through the peephole in the front door. "Who is it?" she called. She could just make out a blurry male figure.

"Ick."

This had become a joke between them all. She opened the door. There was Nick, looking impossibly perfect in worn jeans, a T-shirt, and a flannel shirt. And he didn't even have Belch with him.

"Where's man's best friend?" Chelsea asked.

"He's getting his beauty sleep," Nick said. "Do I get invited in?"

Chelsea shrugged—she hoped she looked as cool and sophisticated as Lisha did when she shrugged—as if she didn't much care what Nick did one way or the other.

"No one's home?" Nick asked, plopping onto the couch.

"Just me," Chelsea said. She sat in the chair near him, but not too near. "So, you're not out with Jazz tonight, huh?"

"I'm here," Nick said, as if that explained everything.

"What, she didn't summon you?" Chelsea sneered.

"I think you have the wrong idea," Nick said. He jumped up from the couch. "Got beverage?" He already had the refrigerator door open.

"Help yourself," Chelsea said dryly.

"Want anything?" Nick asked.

"No."

He came back into the living room with a Coke. "So, how you doing?"

"I *was* doing fine," Chelsea said pointedly. "I *was* reading."

"So I'm disturbing you, in other words," Nick said.

"You're a very perceptive guy," Chelsea replied.

He shook some hair off his face. "I seem to bring out the worst in you, Chelsea. How come?"

She shrugged again.

"I mean, everyone is always saying how nice you are, sweet, good-natured—"

"But you don't think so," Chelsea said.

"Well, you always seem ticked off at me."

"That would presume I care enough about you to *be* ticked off."

"Don't you?" he asked softly.

She couldn't look at him. She got up and went to the CD player, and put on a Joss Stone CD.

"Hey," he said, his voice low.

He was standing right behind her. She could feel his breath on her neck. She didn't turn around.

"Look, Chelsea, I knew you were home alone. That's why I stopped over. I wanted to talk to you."

Still, she didn't turn around.

"You're right," he went on. "I got the gig at *Trash* because Jazz liked me. And yeah, I've been dating her. I thought it would be a kick. I mean, she's beautiful and famous. But I don't care about her. I never, ever cared about her."

Chelsea looked down. She could see her hands trembling. "So why are you dating her, then?" she asked. "Isn't that kind of hypocritical?"

"Yes," Nick said. He reached for her shoulders and gently turned her around. "That's why I'm gonna stop seeing her."

She looked into his blue eyes, eyes as blue as the ocean, eyes she could fall into, fall in love with. . . .

"She'll fire you," Chelsea whispered. "Won't she?"

"I don't know," Nick admitted. "But it's not like I've been doing any work around there, anyway. Jazz just thinks it's a gas to be dating a carpenter—"

"I thought you went to Brown," Chelsea said.

"I did," Nick said. "But I dropped out. I just couldn't figure out what the hell I was doing there, you know? I mean, what does it all mean, anyway? My dad's a carpenter, and his dad was a carpenter, and they wanted me to go to college so badly."

"And then you dropped out," Chelsea said.

Nick's eyes searched hers. "You can't live anyone's dream but your own. Don't you know that?"

"I . . . I . . ." She felt as if she couldn't get her breath, couldn't speak.

"Chelsea."

The way he said her name made her knees turn to Jell-O.

He reached for her, slowly pulling her close, until she could feel his heart beating against hers. Then he kissed her hair, her cheek, her neck, until she thought she'd just die if he didn't put his lips on hers, and then finally he did . . .

. . . And the room flew away, there was only the sizzling heat of Nick, Nick's arms, Nick's lips, and her own voice, softly calling his name.

EIGHT

Roxanne "Bigfoot" Renault—Chelsea couldn't look at her or think of her anymore without snickering inside at their nickname for her—looked up from the pile of papers in front of her, and then down her nose at Karma, Lisha, Alan, and Chelsea, who all sat across the conference-room table from her.

Evidently, Bigfoot had taken the transcripts of their tapes from the 900 number home with her over the weekend. When they had all arrived at work that morning, there was a note from Roxanne telling them to write up any of the ideas from their tapes that would make a good show for *Trash*. These ideas were to be dropped off in Bigfoot's office within the hour.

Chelsea had agonized over her transcripts.

I'm not about to point out that Teen Offspring of Murderers is a great Trash *idea,* she thought. *She's going to have to come up with that one herself.*

Only please, God, let her miss it.

All Chelsea had written up was an idea from a girl in Michigan, whose entire body was tattooed, and who thought Jazz should be tattooed on the air.

Now it was eleven-thirty, and they were all in Roxanne's office, their transcripts and the ideas they had picked in a big pile on Bigfoot's desk.

"Your ideas all suck, Karma," Bigfoot said to Karma, who Chelsea could see was not in the least bit cowed. "You can go."

Then she looked at Lisha.

"These suck, too, so get out of here," she said to Lisha, in the same cold tone of voice.

"And you, too, Alan," she added, not even looking up at Alan to acknowledge his presence.

Silently, Karma, Lisha, and Alan got up out of their chairs, pushed them under the clear glass table, and left the room. Karma rolled her eyes at Roxanne's feet, clad today in gigunda brown suede heels, which matched her perfectly cut brown silk suit, and walked out.

Bigfoot stretched her long legs, enclosed in sheer hose, ending in those astonishingly large feet, under the table. She shuffled a few papers on the desk as Chelsea waited and watched, growing more anxious by the second.

Roxanne picked up the idea Chelsea had written up. "A girl who's tattooed?" she asked, her tone withering. "That's your idea of a hip show for *Trash?*"

"Well, maybe we could work with it," Chelsea said tentatively.

"It's stupid. It's lame. It sucks," Roxanne said.

"Gee, I guess that means you don't like it." Chelsea was unable to keep the sarcasm out of her voice.

"Have you got a problem?" Bigfoot snapped at her.

"No," Chelsea said with a sigh.

"There were two usable ideas on your tape," Roxanne said, "not that you picked up on that. Although I can't think of any reason that should surprise me, can you?" Bigfoot stared at her.

"I'm assuming that was a rhetorical question," Chelsea said, trying to keep her voice neutral, lest she antagonize Roxanne even more.

"Oh yes." Roxanne sneered. "I forgot, you went to an honors high school. That's why you know big words like *rhetorical.*"

Chelsea fumed, but kept silent.

"Anyway," Roxanne went on, "there are two good ones here. Barry told me to tell you that he wants you to work on the marriage one as a long-term show concept, though I can't imagine why he'd think you'd be the right intern for it."

"The marriage one?" Chelsea asked. She had no idea what Roxanne was talking about.

"We're gonna bring a whole bunch of different guys who want Jazz to marry them on the show, and let them play the Dating Game. The last one standing gets to do a quick change, then we'll do a civil ceremony right then and there. And then Jazz will divorce him. So call that guy in Bend, Oregon, and tell him he's about to be famous."

"B-but that wasn't a show idea!" Chelsea protested. "That guy was for real."

"You've got to learn you can find trash for *Trash* anywhere," Roxanne pontificated, as if she were repeating an axiom she'd used a hundred times before. "Anyway, those are Barry's orders, not mine. I would have given it to Kushner."

Roxanne shuffled some papers on her desk, read something, then looked back at Chelsea. "Then there's this other one," she said slowly. "A good one. A really good one."

No, no, no, Chelsea screamed inside her head. *Please, don't let it be what I think it is—*

"This children-of-murderers thing," Roxanne went on. "Now, this has really good possibilities."

I knew it. I knew it.

"You totally missed it." Bigfoot was again sneering. "I guess you were too busy getting all rah-rah over girls with tattoos."

Chelsea kept silent.

"Of course, it has no possibilities at all, as is," Roxanne continued. "Maybe for *Jerry Springer,* but not for *Trash.* You know why?"

"It's been done before?" Chelsea ventured hopefully.

"Wrong," Roxanne said. "Because it's too tame for *Trash.* But I have figured out how to make this the *Trash* hit of all time. Want to know how?"

Chelsea got a sickening feeling in her stomach again.

"How?" she squeaked out.

"We make it into a show about the teen kids of *mass murderers.*" Roxanne was leaning forward in her chair, visibly gloating. "Now, am I brilliant, or am I brilliant?"

This cannot be happening, Chelsea thought. *This is my worst nightmare come true. There's got to be something I can do, some way out of this....*

"I mean, think about it," Roxanne went on, her eyes shining, "did Charles Manson have kids? Or what about that guy who shot all those people from the bell tower at the University in Texas years ago? It's so hot, it's sizzling!"

"Uh-huh," Chelsea managed. She felt her stomach turning over.

"I'm going to run with this one all by myself," Roxanne decided. She stood up, clearly meaning that Chelsea should stand up, too, which she did.

"I'm going to find the offspring of the worst mass murderers of all time," Bigfoot promised. "And believe me, I am the girl to do it."

"Chelsea," Barry said happily, giving her a warm embrace, "it's great to see you again."

"It's good to see you, too, Barry," Chelsea said sincerely as she stood up from her bar stool to embrace Barry back.

Barry and Chelsea were once again in the bar of the Empire Hotel. He had stopped by her tiny cubicle in the early afternoon to see how she was doing.

Chelsea had been sitting there, her head in her hands, agonizing over Roxanne's show about the kids of mass murderers.

All day long she hadn't been able to think about anything else. Not even thoughts of Nick could penetrate her wall of fear and anxiety.

"Hey, killer, you okay?" Barry had asked her.

Killer. Funny joke. If he only knew.

"Oh, yeah, just thinking," she had said lamely.

At which point he had invited her out for a drink after work, to talk about her "terrific show idea."

Anything to get my mind off Bigfoot, Chelsea had thought, and gratefully accepted.

"Cranberry juice, right?" Barry said now. "I took the liberty." A glass of cranberry juice sat on the bar in front of Chelsea.

"Thanks," she said, and took a sip of the cool, tart liquid.

"So, lucky girl," Barry said, a big grin on his face, "I've got great news for you, and I do mean great."

"About my show idea?" Chelsea asked, getting excited in spite of herself.

"I got to pitch it to Jazz this morning." Barry leaned forward conspiratorially. "And she loved it! I mean, she *loved* it!"

"Really?" Chelsea asked, thrilled. "That's . . . that's fantastic!"

"And"—he took a momentous pause—"she wants you to run the damn thing!"

"Me?" Chelsea squeaked. "She wants me—?"

"Well"—Barry chuckled—"I sort of gently nudged her in that direction. I merely suggested that the person who came up with the idea should be the person who puts it into motion."

"I can't believe it!" Chelsea cried. "That was so nice of you, really!"

"Hey, I'm a good guy," Barry said. "And like I told you, I have a weakness for cute, preppie girls with just the tiniest trace of a Southern accent." He traced the line of her hand from her thumb to her wrist.

"Well, I really appreciate it," Chelsea said, casually moving her hand away from him. "I won't let you down."

"Good." Barry grinned. "Because the show's airing on Friday."

Friday? Chelsea thought, astonished. *But that's just four days away from today! How can I possibly get this together by Friday? I've never even worked on any part of a real* Trash *show before. All I know how to do is walk Jazz's monsters and transcribe tapes.*

"Do you really . . . I mean, how am I supposed to . . . I mean . . . Friday is really soon," Chelsea stammered.

Barry laughed deeply, and took his sport jacket off, so that now all he wore with his jeans was a T-shirt featuring John Mellencamp playing at Farm Aid.

"Hey, not to worry," Barry told her. "You won't be working alone. I'm gonna put Karma and Lisha on it with you, and Sumtimes—she does the work of any three people. I'll be in charge, and I promise not to let you get in over your pretty head, okay?"

Chelsea gulped. "Okay," she said shakily, thinking already of the millions of things that would have to be done in order to get her show together in four days.

"I can see I freaked you out with this," Barry said, patting her thigh. "We don't always work this fast. But Jazz hated the show that was set for Friday, so we canned it. You got a lucky break."

He took a sip of his Scotch. "Jazz said to make this a number-one priority. That means open the checkbook wide. Do you know how many people would kill to be guests on *Trash,* get flown first-class to New York, and be put up in The Plaza Hotel?"

"Lots, I suppose," Chelsea said.

Barry chuckled. "Babe, I've seen people quit their jobs for less." Just then he glimpsed someone he knew walk in the door of the bar and gave a quick wave. Then he reached in his pocket, took out an envelope, and handed it to Chelsea.

"This'll give you a head start," he said.

Chelsea tore the letter open and scanned it quickly. It was a memo to Barry, from Sumtimes, detailing some research she'd done about an online dating service called Young Love Online. Evidently, the producer had already talked with the service, and the company was ready to cut a deal with *Trash*.

"This is fantastic," Chelsea said, quickly reading the memo. Sumtimes had just saved her hours and hours of hard work.

"I've got some other ideas," Barry said, picking up his drink and draining it. "I'd like to invite you over to my place now—we can continue over there. I've got a cold bottle of Aligote in the fridge. French, it's the best."

"Gee, I can't," Chelsea said. "I mean, I'd like to, but I promised Karma and Lisha we'd see the new Woody Allen movie tonight."

"I just handed you a gig that half the staff would kill for," Barry said sharply.

"I know, and I'm really grateful—"

"You don't act really grateful," Barry told her.

"Well, I want to . . . log on to Young Love Online myself tonight," she said quickly. "I mean, I don't have much time to get this show together. . . ." she improvised.

"A go-getter, huh?" Barry laughed. He threw his hands up in the air. "Okay, I can't argue with that. But I've got a computer at my place. We can log on together. For research." He leaned forward and lifted a lock of Chelsea's hair. "I truly am partial to blondes," he said, his voice low.

"Gosh, look at the time!" Chelsea said, jumping up from the bar stool. "I promised my friends. But I'm sure we'll be working together a lot in the next few days."

Barry grinned. He didn't seem too upset, she realized with relief. "Okay, Chelsea," he said, wagging a finger at her. "We've got plenty of time, right?"

"Right," Chelsea agreed, but she wasn't exactly sure to what she was agreeing.

And she wasn't so sure that she wanted to find out.

"So, what are you up to, this fine-but-ridiculously-hot New York night?" Alan asked Chelsea as he stood grinning in her doorway.

She hadn't been expecting anyone. She'd bowed out of going to the movie with her friends so that she could come home and log on to Young Love Online. Karma and Lisha had come home from the movie, which they said was great, and then they'd decided they were still hungry, so they had gone out to the diner on the corner. They promised to bring Chelsea back a burger.

"Not much," Chelsea said, opening the door for him. She kissed him on the cheek. He turned to give her a real kiss, but she eased herself away.

I've really got to talk to him, she thought to herself. *He's too terrific a guy for me to lead on. After all, Nick is breaking up with Jazz, so I've got to just tell Alan the truth.*

But how?

"So, how was your weekend?" Chelsea asked, sitting on the couch. Alan sat down next to her. "I mean, I know I saw you at work this morning, but we didn't get to talk or anything."

"Well, let's see," Alan said, "my cousin in Tenafly is very rich and very boring. She's a senior in high school and the extent of her conversation is guys, fashion, and movie stars."

"That bad, huh?" Chelsea sympathized.

He put his arm around her. "And what's up with you—besides getting reamed out by Bigfoot this morning, that is."

Chelsea laughed. "Who told you her name?"

"Karma," Alan said. "In the lounge. I almost split a gut laughing."

"God, Bigfoot hates me." Chelsea sighed. "She's so vicious."

Alan noticed her laptop computer, which was still on, sitting on the table. "You working?"

"I logged on to Young Love Online," she explained. Then she quickly told him about her show idea, and how it had to be together for Friday.

"Wow, good for you," he said. "So how does this Young Love Online thing work?"

For the next fifteen minutes or so Chelsea gave Alan the guided tour of Young Love Online, a computer chat service, which, unlike some of the other commercial services, was wholly dedicated to introducing teens to one another. And the best part of it all, it was absolutely free. That was because one quarter of every computer screen was dedicated to an advertisement, which changed every five minutes or so. In fact, at that very moment there was an advertisement for *Trash* on the screen.

"So," Chelsea said as she showed Alan around the service, "this is the wave of the future in how teens are going to meet."

Alan lifted a lock of her hair and tickled her face with it. "I think I prefer the old-fashioned way." He smiled, his voice soft and seductive. "Like how I met Chelsea Jennings."

Chelsea leaned forward abruptly and snapped the computer off.

I really need to talk to him, she thought. *He's such a great guy, I have to tell him the truth, and there's no time like now to do it. About Nick. And me. And us.*

"Alan, I . . . need to talk to you," she blurted out.

"Uh-oh," Alan said. "Bad sign."

"I . . . oh, shoot, I don't know how to do this," Chelsea groaned.

"Uh-oh, again," Alan said. "Okay, hit me with it. I promise I won't cry."

"About me and you," Chelsea added.

"And no one else?" Alan added. "Don't you want to talk to me about you and me and Nick?"

"Did he talk to you?" Chelsea asked hopefully.

Alan smiled, though his eyes were sad. "C'mon, Chels," he said. "I see how you get when you're around him. It's like your IQ drops thirty points. Which still leaves you smarter than the vast majority of the world, I might add."

Chelsea sighed. "You're way too nice for me."

"Well, that kind of comment is always the kiss of death," Alan said lightly.

"I guess I didn't realize that I'm that easy to read."

"You're not," Alan said. "I'm just a good reader. So, you and Nick—"

"I like you," Chelsea blurted out. "I mean, I think you're the greatest, nicest, most terrific—"

"But Nick gives you sparks, huh?" Alan asked.

Chelsea nodded, her head low.

"You give me sparks," Alan admitted. "Geez, aren't we a cliché here. Hey, maybe I could write about our little triangle. What do you think?"

"I don't want to do anything to hurt you," Chelsea said earnestly. "I would never—"

"Chelsea," he said softly, "you can't make a person feel sparks. Can you?"

"No," she admitted, her voice just as soft as Alan's. "I guess you can't."

He hesitated a moment. "I just hope . . . I hope he doesn't hurt you."

"He's breaking up with Jazz," Chelsea said quickly.

"How about the others?" Alan asked.

"I . . . guess I don't know . . . I mean, I'm sure he's breaking up with them, too," Chelsea said, flustered.

"I don't know if Nick is into a one-girl, one-guy kind of thing," Alan said. "I mean, I like the guy. He's my roommate. He's my friend. But . . . I don't know. . . ."

"Don't worry about me," Chelsea said, kissing his cheek.

"Okay." Alan sighed. "You've got to follow your heart, wherever it takes you. Right?"

"Right," Chelsea agreed.

"But we're still friends?" he asked, his gorgeous brown eyes glistening slightly.

"Always," Chelsea said fervently. "Always."

"Then I consider myself a lucky guy," Alan concluded, his voice betraying his Texas roots a little.

He's from the South, like me, Chelsea realized. *I never even thought about it before.*

"I'm lucky, too," she said. "To have a friend as terrific as you."

Alan hugged her, and it was the warmest, best hug she'd ever gotten from a guy friend in her entire life.

She thought about what he'd just said about Nick, but she quickly put any doubts about him out of her mind.

She and Nick belonged together.

Alan was right. She really did have to follow her heart.

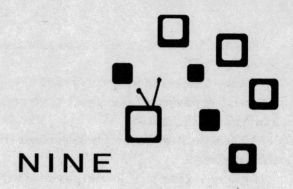

NINE

Karma barged into Sumtimes's office—this week she was Laura Sumtimes—and triumphantly dropped a six-inch-tall stack of files, newspaper clippings, computer printouts, and magazines on the desk. Chelsea was sitting in Sumtimes's chair, her feet up on the desk, rubbing her eyes with exhaustion.

"Read 'em and weep," Karma said gleefully. "I'm telling you, I have this mass-murderer research thing down cold. If I were Sumtimes, I would be offering me a major raise. So, read!"

Chelsea looked up at her blearily. Karma had on a silver stretch tube dress, silver lipstick, and white go-go boots. Chelsea had on her oldest jeans and a Vanderbilt sweatshirt—she felt lucky to have managed to put on clothes at all.

She was both utterly exhausted and incredibly nervous and excited, from lack of sleep, too much work, and too much caffeine, not to mention the reality that it was fifteen minutes to show time for Young Love Online.

And now Karma wants me to read about mass murderers and their kids, she thought. *Little does she know how close that subject is to my heart.*

"You want me to read this stuff *now?*" Chelsea asked. "I have worked like a dog for five days to get my first show idea on the air, which is going to happen in"—she checked her watch—"fourteen minutes, and you want me to read your research files *now?*" She jumped up from her chair. "I ought to be down there—"

"Relax," Karma said to her, plopping down onto one of the red wet-look vinyl chairs. "I heard Sumtimes get the call from the car phone—your star guest is, like, twenty blocks away in the limo."

"But what if they hit traffic? I'm finished."

"They hit traffic, Sela Flynn will fly to the studio," Karma said. "That's how badly the girl is dying for her fifteen minutes of fame."

"It's not funny," Chelsea retorted. "I've got to have that girl here—"

"Tell you what," Karma said. "I'll stay here until she gets here. If she doesn't show up, I'll go on as her."

"You're a peach," Chelsea said with a smile.

A big laugh came from the television monitor in the corner of Sumtimes's office. All the producers had closed-circuit TV monitors in their offices, directly connected to the *Trash* studio on the ground level. Right now, in the studio, Demetrius, the gorgeous Hispanic guy with the beautiful, long hair whom Chelsea had run into her very first day at *Trash,* was warming up the audience. He picked a girl out of the crowd, stripped off his shirt, and was dancing down and dirty with her to some loud rock music while the audience hooted and whistled their approval.

"That guy is seriously hot," Karma said, watching Demetrius dance on the monitor. "I could be falling in love. Or at least in lust. Gawd, with my luck he'll turn out to be gay. No guy that good-looking is ever straight."

As Karma watched the monitor Chelsea put her head down on

the desk again. She thought back on the previous five days—the five hardest days she had ever worked in her entire life.

In the office at seven in the morning, she recalled, *and home after ten o'clock every night. I've been so busy, I haven't even had a chance to see Nick. I made more phone calls than I ever thought possible, ate more delivery Chinese food and pizza than I ever wanted to, and spent more time typing notes into the computer than I ever did on any paper I wrote in high school.*

And the meetings! With Sumtimes, with Barry, with the others...but never with Jazz.

And now, here it is. Thirteen minutes to air time. And my star guest is stuck in traffic.

The show, though, was set. Chelsea—with the cooperation of Young Love Online—had managed to put together five pairs of teen guys and girls from across the United States, Canada, and England, who had been corresponding with one another and "chatting" live on Young Love Online for weeks or even months.

In most cases, they'd even exchanged photos already, although in two cases *Trash* had to intervene and set up the photo swap. Barry had handled that part of the process.

He's been so great, Chelsea thought. *The only reason I got this break was because of him.*

Barry had made certain that all the show guests were flown to New York first-class and put up in separate hotels, where they were allowed unlimited room service.

And now here they were, thirteen minutes from going on the air. The guests were in separate offices at *Trash,* with the exception of Sela Flynn, from Gallup, New Mexico, who was scheduled to meet Nigel Wynn, from York, England. They'd been writing and "chatting" for several weeks, and according to Chelsea's preshow interviews, she thought they were the couple most likely to really hit it off big in person.

"That guy Demetrius is poetry in motion," Karma said, her eyes still glued to the monitor. "Do you think I should ask him out or what?"

The phone on Sumtimes's desk buzzed. Chelsea picked it up.

"Chelsea Jennings, intern," she croaked. Her voice was weary.

"We're sending Sela Flynn up to you now," the receptionist said. "Barry says to bring her down to makeup at four-twenty P.M., and she's going on the air at four-forty P.M. Got it?"

"Got it," Chelsea said, though it seemed a very short time for Sela to spend in the makeup room.

"Thank God," she told Karma, "Sela's here."

"Told ya," Karma said. On the monitor, Demetrius had finished dancing, and now two guys from the audience were volunteering to dress as hula dancers and dance for Bigfoot.

Karma tapped her perfectly manicured finger on her stack of research. "So, where was I? Oh, yeah, check this out. I've outdone myself this time." She put her hands out in front of her, palms up, on either side of the stack of papers she'd just brought in.

Mass-murderer files.

Word of the upcoming but as yet unscheduled show on the teen children of mass murderers had spread like wildfire around the *Trash* offices. This was another one of Jazz's pet projects, and it seemed as if everyone was working on it, under Bigfoot's direction.

Everyone but Chelsea, that is. So far, anyway.

"The guy that killed and ate all those people in Chicago," Karma said triumphantly, holding up a computer printout. "He had three kids. Two of them are teens. One of them said yes already."

"That's ... great," Chelsea managed.

"Then," Karma said, pawing through her papers, "we've got a whole fifteen minutes in the works on teen kids of postal workers who've gone berserk." She held up a big magazine article. "See?"

Chelsea got a sick feeling in her stomach. "Uh-huh."

"And Bigfoot's working on the whopper herself," Karma said

confidentially. "About sixteen years ago there was this really rich lawyer in some hick Tennessee town—I forget where—who totally flipped out one day and shot up everyone in a Burger Barn."

Chelsea felt nauseated.

"But that's not the kicker," Karma continued. "He went home to off his wife and his kid, and his wife stabbed him in the throat with a butcher knife. Can you deal?"

I am going to throw up. Right here, right in Sumtimes's office....

"His kid, was like, only a few months old, so she'd be a teenager now," Karma continued, "and Roxanne is trying to—" She stopped talking and peered at Chelsea. "You okay? You're getting kind of green. Chels?"

There was a rap at the door. One of the *Trash* security guys stuck his head in. "Chelsea Jennings?" he asked. "I've got Sela Flynn waiting at the elevator. I'll go get her."

"Are you okay?" Karma asked again. She felt Chelsea's forehead. "You're all clammy! You have the flu?"

"I'm fine," Chelsea lied. "I'm just tired."

"Well, get some rest tonight, sweetie," Karma instructed her. "I'll make you a big pot of homemade chicken soup. It cures anything, and it's the one and only thing I know how to cook."

Chelsea managed a sick smile.

The guard opened the door. Chelsea stood up.

"That's my cue to exit stage right," Karma commented. "Break a leg today."

"Thanks," Chelsea said as Karma and Sela passed each other in the doorway.

"Hi," Sela said shyly as Chelsea got up to greet her.

"Hi," Chelsea said. "I'm really glad to see you!"

Sela smiled at her, and Chelsea tried not to look shocked.

This is one of the most unattractive girls I've ever seen in my life, she thought. *I hoped that it was just that her photo wasn't very good, but she's worse looking in person than she was in the photograph. She's got to be eighty pounds overweight. And look at that bad skin! And the receding chin. And the size of the nose! And that terrible lank, greasy hair...*

"So, welcome to *Trash,*" Chelsea said brightly. "I'm Chelsea Jennings, and I'll be your host until we get you on the air. Is there anything I can get you? Coffee? Tea? Bottled water?"

"How about a Coke?" Sela asked nervously.

"Diet?" Chelsea asked automatically.

"Regular," Sela answered, "if you've got it."

"Coming right up," Chelsea promised. She went to the little refrigerator next to the TV monitor, picked out a bottle of regular Coke, and handed it to Sela.

The girl opened it and drained half of it in one fell swoop.

"Thirsty," she confessed. "I am so nervous."

Chelsea knew her job was to put Sela at ease. "There's nothing to worry about, I promise you."

"I hope he likes me," Sela confessed. "I mean, everything went so well online, but..."

"I know, this is a little nerve-racking," Chelsea sympathized.

"I just hope he likes me when he sees me," Sela said, twisting a lock of her dank hair between her fingers.

"He's going to love you," Chelsea promised. "You guys swapped pictures, right?"

"*Trash* did it for us," Sela said, her eyes shining. "He is so cute. Did you see his picture?"

Chelsea nodded. She'd seen pictures of both of them before. Nigel Wynn was as handsome as Sela was unattractive.

"And our last names rhyme!" Sela went on. "That's destiny, don't you think?"

"Absolutely," Chelsea agreed, smiling at the girl.

"I believe in destiny," Sela said seriously. "So does Nigel. He told me that online. We've talked over the computer for hours and hours."

Chelsea nodded her encouragement.

"I can really talk to him, you know?" Sela said earnestly. "I mean, we talk about everything. We both love to read Keats and P. B. Shelley poems out loud. We both love politics, and we were both born in September. We both love hot chocolate. He plays soccer—well, he calls it football—and I'm a big football fan. I mean, it's destiny. Isn't it?"

"I guess it is," Chelsea said, a small smile curling at the edges of her mouth. She was beginning to like Sela. There was just something so open and innocent about her, it was, well, refreshing.

"Have you met Nigel?" Sela asked eagerly.

"No," Chelsea answered. "But I've seen his picture."

"And he's seen mine." Sela shook her head in wonder. "Don't you think it's wonderful that he loves the real me? I mean . . . well, I know what guys like. Girls who look like models. And I don't look like a model."

"All guys aren't like that," Chelsea said. "Nigel isn't!"

"I guess not," Sela said with wonder. "How lucky can Sela Flynn get, huh?"

Chelsea smiled at the girl again. *And that's why I saved this story for last,* she thought to herself. *Because it is the most wonderful of all. Most guys wouldn't look at Sela twice, except to make some joke at her expense. But Nigel fell in love with the real Sela. The audience is going to love this.*

"Oh look!" Sela said, pointing to Sumtimes's TV monitor. "It's the show! It's Jazz! Ohmigod, I *love* Jazz!"

Trash was live on the air. Chelsea turned up the volume so that Sela and she could hear Jazz's show intro—Jazz delivered it as she stood, apparently naked, inside a huge Apple-style computer, which covered her body from just above her breasts to just below her crotch.

"Cyber-sex?" Jazz asked. "Cyber-love? Teens falling in love with teens by computer. Is it possible? You're going to see for yourself, as we bring together five teen couples who've never met each other in the flesh, but who've been talking by computer forever. With the help of Young Love Online, you're going to see how love can blossom—or not—in cyberspace!"

The audience applauded loudly, and across the bottom of the screen, a feed from a live "chat" conversation currently under way on Young Love Online scrolled, along with the information number for Young Love Online.

That was my idea, Chelsea thought proudly. *This way, the viewing audience can actually see how the service works.*

After the commercial, Sela watched, transfixed, as Jazz introduced two different couples who'd met in cyberspace. First, she brought out one of the partners, blindfolded that partner, and then brought out the other one. Once the second teen was on the set, she pulled the blindfold off the first teen, who was now seeing the person they'd been writing to for the first time in the flesh.

The meetings were sweet and romantic. Both couples gave each other long, soulful kisses, egged on by the studio audience. Then Jazz waded into the audience to field questions for the couples.

"That's going to be me," Sela said happily. "That's me and Nigel in a little while. This is the greatest day of my life!"

Chelsea looked at her watch. It was four-fifteen P.M., just about time to take Sela down to makeup.

"Okay, Sela," she said. "Are you ready to be a star?"

Sela's grin was so bright that it seemed to light up the room another notch.

"You betcha," Sela replied eagerly. "Do I get my makeup done and everything?"

"By a professional makeup artist," Chelsea promised. "Sela Flynn is about to become a star."

"All right!" Jazz cried. "Let's bring out, all the way from York, England, Nigel Wynn!"

The *Trash* audience applauded, and the applause turned to cheers, whoops, and wolf whistles when Nigel actually appeared on the set and walked slowly across it to where Jazz was standing.

Nigel was drop-dead gorgeous. Over six feet tall, lean and muscular, with brown hair and green eyes, a cleft in his chin, and a boyish, dimpled smile. He was dressed simply, in black jeans, a black jacket, and a white T-shirt.

Taller, better looking Tom Cruise, Chelsea thought, automatically reverting to Karma's habit of comparing everyone with famous people.

"Oh, gosh," Sela breathed, grabbing Chelsea's hand. They were standing in the wings, watching the set. Nigel had been brought on from the other side of the stage. "He's so hot." She turned nervously to Chelsea. "He really likes me?"

"He likes you," Chelsea assured her, giving her hand a little squeeze.

Jazz went over to Nigel and gave him a big hug, which he returned with enthusiasm. Then they both sat on the couch. Next to them were the inflatable man and the inflatable woman, upside down.

"Maybe I oughta trade in my current model for this guy," Jazz quipped, and the audience cheered.

"So, what's a great-looking guy like you doing flirting in cyberspace?" Jazz asked him.

Nigel shrugged. "You can meet some great people," he said, in his soft British accent. "Like Sela."

"You really like her, huh?" Jazz asked eagerly.

"She's fabulous," Nigel said. "Sometimes I feel as if I dreamed her up, she's so terrific."

The audience awwwwwed its approval, and Jazz smiled.

"You're a sensitive guy, right, Nigel?"

"I like to think so."

"I mean, you're not into surface things, right? You look at a girl's soul, right?" Jazz asked earnestly.

"Absolutely," Nigel said firmly. "That's what's so great about meeting online. You get to really know the person before looks even enter into the picture!"

Jazz nodded in agreement. "So, you ready to meet Sela?" Jazz asked.

"Absolutely," Nigel said, standing up.

"Oh God, oh God, this is it—" Sela yelped.

"Cool," Jazz said in her laconic style. She took the big red blindfold out of her back pocket and tied it around Nigel's eyes. Then she took Nigel by the elbow and guided him to the middle of the set, putting him in front of the other "cyber couples" who'd been united for the first time on the *Trash* set.

"Let's bring out"—Jazz was reading from one of the *Trash* file cards she always seemed to be holding—"from the happenin' burg of Gallup, New Mexico, Miss Sela Flynn!"

A recording of the old Chuck Berry rock standard "I'm So Glad I'm Livin' in the USA" started playing, and Chelsea gave Sela a gentle tap on the arm.

"Get out there!" she commanded gently.

"Wish me luck!" Sela murmured. Then she took a deep breath and ran onto the set, prompting a huge reaction from the live audience. There was a mixture of cheering, whooping, and catcalls.

Jazz greeted Sela warmly as the music stopped. She waited for the crowd to hush, as it did, following the signs that read QUIET, PLEASE that were flashing all over the set.

"So, Sela Flynn," Jazz asked Sela, casually slipping her arm around her, "what do you think of Nigel Wynn?"

"He's so gorgeous!" Sela said honestly. "Hi, Nigel!"

"Hi, Sela," Nigel said from behind his blindfold. "You've got a great voice."

The crowd cheered and hollered some more.

"So, are you ready for his blindfold to come off…so that he can see you for the very first time?" Jazz asked.

"In person, you mean," Sela said eagerly. "I'm ready!"

Jazz went over to Nigel and, with great ceremony, yanked the blindfold off of his eyes.

"Sela Flynn," she announced, "meet Nigel Wynn!"

The crowd cheered loudly. But Jazz had been too slow. As soon as she had taken off the blindfold, Sela had made a quick move toward Nigel, enveloping him in her massive arms and pressing her body against him, even as Jazz got her last sentence out.

It was just what all the other couples had done.

Except, unlike the other couples, Nigel pushed Sela away.

Hard.

"What is this?" he sputtered. "Is this some kind of a joke? This isn't Sela Flynn. Who is this *thing*?"

Sela just stood there, now five feet away from Nigel, in complete shock.

What's going on? Chelsea wondered frantically. *What's happening? Of course that's Sela!*

"It's Sela Flynn," Jazz assured Nigel.

"No it's not!" Nigel exploded. "Sela Flynn has blond hair, and blue eyes, and high cheekbones. And she's slender. And tall. This girl is some...some...dog!"

The audience started whooping and hollering, and from the rear of the studio, some people started making barking-dog noises.

"You sent me her photo!" Nigel accused Jazz. "This isn't her! What kind of stunt are you people pulling here?"

Oh God, Chelsea thought, putting two and two together. *It's a setup. Trash sent Nigel a picture of some other girl—some beautiful girl—saying that it was Sela. Sela probably never described herself to Nigel on the computer. They did this—no, Barry did this—to embarrass this girl.*

This is the most horrible thing I've ever seen.

And there's nothing I can do about it.

"But...but it's me," Sela said miserable, her face red and blotchy with embarrassment. "You know, both with September birthdays, both of us like poetry."

"Look, I'm sorry," Nigel said stiffly. "You're not what I expected. I mean—"

"Why, Nigel," Jazz said mockingly, "I guess you're more shallow than you thought, huh?"

Jazz turned to the number-one camera as the cameraman, with Sky holding the cable for him, came in for a close-up of her face.

"So," she continued, "we see the truth. You think beauty is more than skin-deep? You think that we don't judge books by their covers? You think that looks don't count? Look again, everyone. Look again."

She glanced over at Nigel and Sela, both miserable. The camera pulled out to take in the two humiliated people, then came in tight on Jazz again.

"So, hey, guys, the next time you think of yourself as a real sensitive dude, you might want to think again," she said coolly.

"It's all image. It's all a game. You think you'll look like you do now forever? Even I won't look like this forever. It's disposable, we're all disposable. Poof. Bye-bye. Nothing lasts, know what I mean? But, that's what makes it *Trash*, doesn't it? So, until next time, may all your days—and especially your nights—be TRASHy."

The red light on the number-one camera clicked off.

The show was over.

The studio audience stood up and cheered as Jazz took a bow.

Slowly, Chelsea made her way onto the set, to collect Sela Flynn, who still hadn't moved.

"Come on," she said to Sela gently, putting her hand on the girl's arm. "I'll help you get a taxi back to your hotel."

Sela turned and looked at her, her eyes wounded and betrayed. "I thought you were nice...."

"I swear to you," Chelsea said, "I had no idea that Nigel didn't have your picture. I would never, ever have done that to you...or to anyone."

Sela just stared at her. Then, like a whipped dog, she let Chelsea lead her off the set of *Trash*.

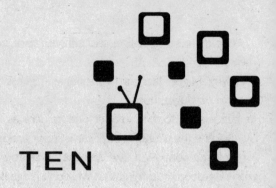

TEN

Chelsea just stood there in front of the *Trash* offices, staring at the taxi with Sela inside as it pulled away.

I can't believe it, she thought. *I just can't believe what Barry did with my show idea.*

"Wanna buy a pretzel? A hot dog?" The vendor standing next to her grinned a hopeful grin at her.

"No," she said tersely. She didn't want food. She wanted to wring Barry Bassinger's neck.

Chelsea turned on her heel, marched back into the building, where she took the elevator to the third floor, and marched right past Barry's new secretary—a voluptuous brunette version of Anna Nicole Smith—barging into his office.

"Barry—"

His back was to her. He swung around. He was on the phone, and he motioned for her to have a seat.

"Yeah, yeah, sounds cool," he was saying into the receiver. "Go with the guy whose mom shot up the shopping mall in Idaho, nix the babe whose brother poisoned the Jell-O at Fort Bragg—we'll do siblings of mass murderers another time, okay? Glad to see you're on top of it, Roxi."

He hung up the phone. "Chelsea, great to see you! Did you meet my new secretary, Olyvia? She just started this morning."

"No, I—"

"Listen, Roxanne told me that kids-of-mass-murderers idea came from a nine-hundred call off your tape," Barry said. "Lemme tell you, it's going to be killer—hottest show we've ever done."

"Barry, I—"

"I'm gonna tell Roxi you're free to help with the research now, okay? You're not all tied up with the marriage-to-Jazz thing, are you?"

"Barry, my show—"

"Oh yeah, it was great, wasn't it?" he said. He locked his hands behind his head. "You got your first one under your belt now, kid."

"How could you do it?" Chelsea yelled, jumping out of her seat. Her hands were trembling. She clenched them into two fists of rage at her sides.

Barry looked at her coolly. "You seem upset."

"How could you do that to my show idea?" she cried. "I worked my ass off, I haven't slept in five days, you told me you loved my idea, and then you . . . you—"

"And then I made it into something that would attract a *Trash* audience," Barry finished mildly. "You know, Chelsea, people are actually tuning in. Which is how we make money. Which is how we stay on the air. Or did you think this was social work?"

Chelsea took a deep breath. "No. I did not think this was social work. But you screwed me and you know it—"

"I don't recall getting any closer to you than a couple of drinks at the Empire," Barry said, a smug smile on his face.

Tears stung Chelsea's eyes. "You mean you did this to me

because I didn't...because I wouldn't go to your apartment with you?"

"Hey, don't flatter yourself," Barry said. "Sure. I wanted to get up close and personal with you, shall we say. But New York is full of pretty girls who are more than willing to spend time with me. You weren't interested—hey, that's the way it goes."

"But then why—"

Barry came around his desk and leaned on the edge. "Sit down," he told her.

"I don't want to sit down."

"Do it anyway," Barry said mildly. "I'm your boss."

She sat.

Barry folded his arms. "Let me explain the facts of life to you, Chelsea. TV is not some magical thing. It's not so complicated. We put on a show. If lots of people watch a show, the advertising time on that show is sold for more money. The show makes more money, the station makes more money, everyone makes money. It's really that simple."

"But...but what about *morals*?" Chelsea demanded. "What about *integrity*?"

"What about it?" Barry asked. "I happen to be very proud of what I do. It's great entertainment. What, you think everything Shakespeare did was so highbrow?"

"You set Sela up," Chelsea said, her voice low and tense. "You humiliated a perfectly innocent girl on national television—"

"Oh, come on," Barry interrupted. "It was at least as big a goof on that pompous jerk Nigel whatever-his-name-was. 'I don't care about looks, I love the real Sela,' " he mimicked with a fey British accent. "Please! What a *schmuck*! Guess we blew his little facade, huh?"

"But Sela—"

"Don't worry, Chelsea," Barry said. "I guarantee you that this experience will be the highlight of Sela Flynn's life. One day she'll tell her grandchildren about the time she was on national TV—"

"You're wrong," Chelsea said. "You just . . . you crushed her, Barry. I can't believe you don't see it. I can't believe that you can rationalize using people like this—"

"Let me ask you a question," Barry said. "How many TV internships did you apply for?"

Chelsea's face immediately blushed a bright red. "Wha . . . what do you mean?"

"I mean how many?" Barry asked.

"A few," she said, her cheeks burning.

"Give me a number," he said.

"Okay, a lot," Chelsea said, her voice low.

"And Chelsea Jennings, Queen of Integrity, picked *Trash*. My guess is, you didn't end up with a whole lot of options, am I right?"

The silence in the room was all the answer he needed.

"Right," Barry said, answering himself. "Hey, don't feel bad. The comp out there is a bitch. So, here you are at *Trash*, the only place where your nice-smart-girl-with-great-grades ordinariness made you stand out from the crowd." He smiled at her. "You knew exactly what kind of a show this was, right?"

"Right," Chelsea admitted tersely.

"So, why did you do it?" Barry asked, spreading his arms wide. "I'll tell you why. Because you wanted something and you wanted it bad—a chance to get into TV, right? Your only chance, is my guess.

"Well, everybody wants something, babe. You're no different than anyone else. You wanted to use *Trash* to launch your TV career, but now you want to go all holier-than-thou about the kind of stuff we do."

Barry brought his face close to Chelsea's. "Face it, Chelsea, it's all TRASH. That's the whole point. Everything and everyone is disposable. Including you. Including me. So we might as well ride the ride while the ride is good, you know?"

Chelsea stood up with what she hoped was a shred of dignity. "You're right, Barry. I knew what *Trash* was when I applied for this job."

Barry nodded. "I like you, Chelsea. You're a sweet girl. And you're smart. A little naive, maybe, but hey, that's kind of refreshing. So, you ready to go help with the mass-murderer research?"

"What I need," Chelsea said slowly, "is to get out of here."

"A little breather?" Barry asked. "Sure. Take a walk by the Hudson. I'll tell Sumtimes to expect you back in, say, forty-five minutes, okay?"

"I'm not coming back today," Chelsea said. "I have a lot of thinking to do. If you want to fire me, go ahead."

"Don't do anything stupid, okay?" Barry told her. "Don't blow your gig here—"

"I need to think about everything you said," Chelsea said. "And I need to figure out what kind of person I really am."

She turned and walked out the door.

"Mom? Hi, it's me." Chelsea sat on her bed, the phone cord wrapped around her pinky finger.

"Chelsea! Are you okay?" came her mother's concerned voice.

"Sure," she assured her mom. "I just wanted to call you."

"But it's six o'clock New York time," her mother said. "Didn't you tell me that you usually work until at least seven?"

"I got out earlier today," Chelsea said. "How's everything in Nashville?"

"Just fine," her mother said. "We started a summer choir at school, about twenty girls. We're going to put on a Fourth of July concert."

"That's really nice, Mama," Chelsea said softly.

"Honey?" her mother said. "You don't sound right."

"I'm fine," Chelsea said, trying to keep her voice light. She wrapped the phone cord more tightly around her pinky. "Mama, how come... how come we never talk about what happened with Daddy?"

Silence.

"Mama?"

"I can't talk about that now," her mother said quickly.

"But we never talk about it," Chelsea said.

"And I see no reason to start now," her mother said, her voice cold. "What's gotten into you?"

"It happened," Chelsea said softly. "You pretend like it didn't, but it did."

"Maybe it didn't," her mother said. Her voice sounded weird. "Sometimes I think it was just some terrible dream I had. And that's just the way I plan to keep it."

Chelsea shut her eyes. She was so tired.

"Now, honey, are you taking your vitamins?" her mother said, her voice back to normal. "Because you can get terribly run-down."

"I'm taking vitamins," she assured her mother.

"And get enough rest, Chelsea," her mother continued. "You don't do well if you get less than eight hours, sweetheart."

"I know, Mom," Chelsea said.

"Well, I don't want to run up a huge long-distance bill," her mother said. "You should wait and call me when the rates change, sweetheart."

"I'll call you again soon, Mom," she promised, and carefully hung up the phone.

Then she lay down on her back and stared up at the ceiling.

Who am I, really? she wondered. *What kind of person am I?*

Barry was right. I am just using Trash. *Maybe everyone really does use everyone. Maybe I'm just as bad as everyone else.*

There was a knock on the door.

She padded into the living room and opened the door without even checking to see who it was.

It was Nick.

"Hi," he said. "I was staring out the window in my apartment and I saw you walk into the building."

Chelsea sat on the couch. She put her head in her hands.

"Hey," he said, sitting down next to her. "What happened?"

"I hate my life," Chelsea said.

He put his arm around her. "You want to talk about it?"

She turned her head to look at him. "No. I want to talk about us. Did you break up with Jazz?"

"Is this an inquisition?" Nick asked uncomfortably.

"No," Chelsea said. "I didn't mean it to come out like that." She leaned her head on his shoulder. "Did you see my show today?"

"I haven't been in," Nick said.

Chelsea sat up. "Did Jazz fire you?"

"Nah," he said. His hair was loose, and he looped it behind his ear on the right side. "So, how did your show go?"

"Horrible," she said, and quickly told him what had happened. "I mean, this girl, Sela, was humiliated, totally humiliated. It was a horrible, cruel thing to do."

"Sounds like it," Nick agreed. "But you have to wonder . . . why would anyone agree to be a guest on *Trash*? I mean, Jazz pulls stuff like that all the time, you know?"

"I guess that's true," Chelsea agreed. "So, okay, people like the chance to be on TV. And they like the trip to New York, and the ritzy hotel and everything. But that doesn't make it right to exploit them, does it?"

"No," Nick said. "But they have some responsibility, too. It's like . . . like everyone is using everyone."

"Oh, God, that's what Barry says," Chelsea said with a sigh. "But I don't believe the world is like that—"

"Not everyone," Nick said, his voice low.

She leaned her head against his shoulder. "Not you," she whispered. He stroked her hair. "Well, at least now that my show is over, we'll be able to spend time together."

"Good," Nick murmured.

"That is, if you broke up with Jazz," she added.

"Didn't you just ask me that?"

"Yeah, but you didn't answer me." She lifted her head and looked at him. "You're afraid you'll lose your cushy job, is that it?"

"I was all set to break up with her, okay?" Nick said. "And she probably would have fired me. But this morning she broke up with me first."

"She did?"

"She met some French actor who's in town doing the new Richard Gere flick. She told me I could take the rest of the day off to lick my wounds."

Chelsea smiled and kissed his cheek. "We lucked out."

"Yeah," Nick said, but his voice sounded guarded, flat.

A feeling of dread tightened Chelsea's throat. "You don't sound happy."

"Look, Chels, I think you are fantastic—"

"Oh, God, this is the same talk I had with Alan—"

"No, no, I'm not blowing you off," Nick assured her. He pushed his hair off his face again. "I want to see you. I want to be with you. But..."

"But...what?" she asked, gulping hard.

Nick got up and paced to the window, where he stared out at the street. "I'm not ready for some...some big commitment or anything."

"Who said anything about a big commitment?" Chelsea asked.

"That's the kind of girl you are," he said, turning around and leaning on the windowsill.

"Oh, thank you for explaining that to me," she said sarcastically. "I don't recall our 'big commitment' conversation—"

"Come on, don't get all bent out of shape," Nick said. "I just mean we should be able to see who we want, and be together as much as we want—"

"In other words, we'd be free to see other people," Chelsea translated.

"Well, yeah," Nick said nervously. He walked back over to her and lifted her to her feet, then he stared into her eyes. "Can you go with that, Chels?"

"Can I go with that," she repeated. "Well, let me tell you how I feel.

When you really care about someone, you don't want to 'go with that.' When you really care, you want to only be with that person, and it hurts your heart if that person is with someone else—"

"Come on, Chels—"

"No, you 'come on,' " Chelsea said fiercely. "Can't you make a commitment to anything? You couldn't commit to college and you can't commit to a relationship, either."

"That's cold, Chelsea, don't be like that—" Nick began, reaching out for her.

Chelsea stepped backward, wrapping her arms around herself. "This is how I am, Nick. I'm not going to let you push me and pull me—like one day we're together and the next day there's some other babe. I didn't realize just how perfect you and Jazz really are for each other."

He reached out for her again. She moved away.

"Bye, Nick."

"But—"

"Bye. Have a nice life."

A muscle twitched in Nick's jaw. He opened his mouth to say something, then closed it again. Then he turned and walked out.

Chelsea dropped onto the couch. The only sound in the apartment was the omnipresent hum of life in New York City—sirens, taxis, buses on the street.

"Mama," Chelsea whispered under her breath. She began to rock back and forth, still holding herself, as if she was afraid she would dissolve into a million pieces if she let go.

And then the tears came.

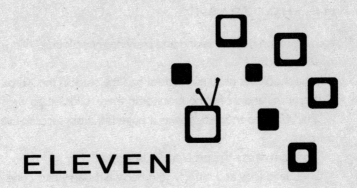

ELEVEN

Lisha walked into the apartment two hours later, and followed the sounds of sobbing to Chelsea's room.

The door was open. She was in there, crying, and flinging things into the open suitcase on her bed.

"Chelsea?" Lisha whispered from the doorway.

Chelsea didn't respond. She just kept crying and throwing stuff into her suitcase.

"Chels?" Lisha said, louder now. "What's going on?"

"I hate it here," Chelsea said between sobs. She pulled some T-shirts out of her drawer and threw them into her suitcase. "I can't stand it anymore. I'm going home."

Lisha walked over to her and gently pulled the denim shirt Chelsea was holding out of her hands. Then she sat her on the bed and sat down next to her. "What happened?"

"Everything happened," Chelsea cried. She plucked a Kleenex

from a box on her nightstand and blew her nose loudly. "Did you see my show today?"

Lisha shook her head no. "Bigfoot had me stuck in the Xerox room all afternoon, and there's no monitor in there. Didn't it go well?"

"Ha," Chelsea snorted. "It was a huge hit, a big success. Everyone loved it."

"So then, what's the problem?" Lisha asked.

Chelsea quickly and bitterly told her what Barry had done to her show. "I hate him," she finished, blowing her nose again. "I hate all of them—Jazz, and Roxanne, and Barry—Barry most of all. And then I came home, and—"

"We having a pj party?" Karma asked, coming into the room. She was carrying a grocery bag. "I bought a chicken to make you soup," she told Chelsea, then she saw the open suitcase and Chelsea's tearstained face. "Oh, God, someone died," she guessed, putting down her bag of groceries with a thud.

"Nobody died," Chelsea said. "My life died."

"What happened?" Karma asked, joining the other two on Chelsea's bed.

"Did you see her show this afternoon?" Lisha asked.

"Nah, I got stuck at the public library on Forty-second Street do-ing mass-murderer research. What, it was a disaster?"

Lisha filled her in.

"Why, that scheming low-life little twerp of a producer," Karma seethed.

"I guess we were right about Barry wanting to get into your pants," Lisha said dryly. "Not that I have any satisfaction in saying 'I told you so.' "

"But you know what?" Chelsea said. "He would have done what he did anyway. I could have been his new girlfriend and he still would have changed the show behind my back. That's how he is. I see that now."

"It's so underhanded," Karma said, shaking her head.

"I didn't even get to the worst part," Chelsea said, grabbing another Kleenex. "I got back here, and Nick stopped over and... and we broke up." Fresh sobs burst from her throat.

"Wow, that was the quickest torrid relationship in history," Karma said.

"What happened?" Lisha asked.

"Jazz dumped him," Chelsea said bitterly, her voice nasal from crying. "Lucky him—that meant he never did have to break up with her, and he got to keep his job at *Trash*.

"And then," she continued, "then he told me he really liked me, but of course he didn't want anything heavy, so we should both be able to see other people."

Karma and Lisha were quiet.

"So... so I broke up with him," Chelsea said. "Alan was right about him. He's a two-timing lowlife and I'm better off without him."

"Alan said that?" Karma asked, surprised.

"No," Chelsea admitted. "But he did tell me that he didn't think Nick was ready for a real relationship—same difference."

"But, Chels..." Lisha began carefully. "Don't get mad, but... I mean, what's so bad about starting out your relationship with Nick slowly?"

"Whose side are you on?" Chelsea demanded.

"I'm on your side, of course," Lisha said. She blew her feathered bangs out of her eyes. "But you guys don't even really know each other yet. I mean, what's so terrible about getting to know each other before you decide you and Nick are this big, exclusive thing?"

"He's just a big flirt," Chelsea said. "What, I'm just supposed to let him be with me on Monday, and some other girl on Tuesday, and maybe I'll see him one night of the weekend if he can fit me in—"

"But, Chels, you act like he has all this power," Karma said. "Like poor little you would be sitting by the phone dying for him."

"Well, I would be," Chelsea confessed.

"But you could be seeing other people, too," Karma pointed out.

"It's a two-way street. And in my experience, when the traffic is going both ways, the little guy car ends up wanting the little girl car all that much more."

Chelsea and Lisha just stared at her.

"Okay," Karma said, "maybe I didn't put it that well. The point is, if you act like you're all needy and desperate, that always drives a guy away, pronto."

"Needy and desperate?" Chelsea exclaimed. "Just because I'm mature enough to want a commitment?"

"Maybe you just need to give him a little more time," Lisha said. "Believe me, I know what happens when you let a guy be everything, the be-all and end-all of your life. I did it. It sucked."

"When?" Chelsea asked, wiping her eyes with her Kleenex.

"When what?"

"When did you do it?" Chelsea asked. "You act like you don't care about guys at all. You barely give Sky the time of day, and he's darling and smart and nice and crazy about you."

"Let's just say I…had a bad experience, okay?" Lisha said, her voice low.

"Here's what I suggest," Karma said, biting her lower lip thoughtfully. "You call Nick up, you tell him you want to talk. Then you tell him you've decided you really want to see other guys, so actually his idea is great, and—"

"But I don't feel that way!" Chelsea objected. "I don't want to play all these games! I don't even know how. All I want is a nice, normal, committed relationship between two people—"

"Well, if you ask me, Nick is too hot to throw away because his time frame doesn't fit yours," Karma said, folding her arms.

"It's more than that," Chelsea insisted. "He made it pretty clear he doesn't really care about me. It's over."

"But—" Lisha began.

"And *Trash* will be *Trash* if I never go back there," Chelsea continued. Her eyes swam with tears again. "And I can't. Go back."

"Oh, Chels—" Lisha tried again.

"No, listen," Chelsea said. "Barry was right. I'm a total hypocrite. I really did just take the summer internship because it was a way to get into television. I knew the kind of show *Trash* is. So I have no right now to bitch about it." She stood up and looked out the window, at the street scene below that she had actually grown to love.

Two African-American teenage boys were throwing a basketball back and forth as they walked along. A young couple walked hand in hand, laughing together about some private joke. The Arab hot-dog vendor on the corner, with his gold front tooth, handed a hot dog to a little girl as her elderly grandfather handed the vendor some money.

I'll miss that part of it, Chelsea thought, *all the different people and sights and sounds of New York.*

She turned away from the window. "I don't belong here," she announced.

"So, you're just...quitting?" Lisha asked. "Just like that? No notice, nothing, just walking out?"

"It's not like anyone will care." Chelsea sniffed.

"I guess you just couldn't cut it," Lisha said sharply.

"How can you say that to me?" Chelsea cried. "I did everything for that show today—everything! And then Barry—"

"So what?" Lisha asked. "And Nick didn't fall into line just the way you wanted him to—well, so what to that, too."

"Lisha, come on—" Karma chided her.

"No, she needs to hear this," Lisha continued. "When we were kids, I worshiped you. Do you know that? You were so much prettier than me, and so much more popular, so much cooler, that I was grateful every single day that you hung out with me.

"I always thought: Chelsea is going to have a really fantastic life. I just pretended that I was going to be a rock star because I thought it sounded so cool. But I knew it was never going to happen. But you... you really *were* going to be this famous journalist, and you'd live in all these exotic cities. You'd have romances and you'd win journalism prizes, and you'd be totally fearless."

Lisha cocked her head at Chelsea, then she laughed a short, cold laugh.

"Well, I guess I was totally wrong about you. You had me fooled. I never thought you were the kind of girl who would fold just because things got tough. But I was totally wrong. You're just a cute, sweet, ordinary girl from Tennessee, who wants a cute, sweet, safe, ordinary life—"

"You don't know what you're talking about!" Chelsea cried, jumping up from the bed.

"Oh, you guys, don't do this—" Karma began.

"If you only knew how funny that is—" Chelsea said.

"I have eyes, Chelsea," Lisha said. "I see the open suitcase—"

"There's nothing so terrible about wanting an ordinary life—" Karma tried to interject.

"The two of you know *nothing*!" Chelsea shrieked. She felt manic, crazed, out of control. "You are utterly clueless!"

"Look, all I'm saying is that everyone doesn't have to be Jessica Savitch," Karma said. "Remember her? She was this great investigative reporter and then there was this big scandal about her life—"

"Big scandal?" Chelsea echoed, her voice shaking. "*Big scandal?* I'll tell you what a big scandal is! I've lived with this big scandal my whole life, and neither of you know anything about it!"

Lisha and Karma stared at her, confused, waiting.

"Oh, right, Lisha, you thought you knew me so well." Chelsea sneered. "But you didn't know *anything*!"

She whirled around to face Karma. "Remember that guy that Roxanne is investigating? That mass murderer in 'some hick town in Tennessee'? The rich lawyer who shot up all those innocent people in a Burger Barn? And his wife who stabbed him with a kitchen knife to save the life of her baby?

"I'm the baby! That's me! That's who I really am!"

Lisha and Karma's jaws both fell open in silent shock.

Chelsea buried her face in her hands, sobbing so hard that she thought her heart would break.

Other than that, the room was deathly silent.

"Is this..." Karma finally began slowly, "is this a joke?"

Chelsea just kept sobbing into her cupped hands.

"My God, she's telling us the truth," Lisha realized. "You are, aren't you?"

Chelsea nodded yes into her hands.

"And I never knew a thing," Lisha marveled.

"No one knew," Chelsea said, still sobbing. "No one knows now, except me and my mother... and now the two of you. Oh, God, I'm gonna be sick."

Chelsea ran into the bathroom and heaved into the toilet. When she could lift her head she saw Karma and Lisha standing in the doorway.

"Go away," she moaned. "Please, just go away."

She bent over the toilet again, gagging and heaving.

And then she felt a soft, comforting hand stroking her back, so softly. "It's okay, Chels," Lisha said. "Let it all out."

Karma ran water from the sink into a glass and held it out to Chelsea. "Just take little sips," she cautioned.

"You don't have to be nice to me," Chelsea mumbled, her head resting wearily on her arms.

"That's true," Lisha said. "But we're going to, anyway."

"Here, drink," Karma said, making sure Chelsea took the water.

She took a small sip. "Are you... are you scared of me now?" she asked in a small voice.

"Oh, yeah," Karma said, her tone gently sarcastic. "Petrified."

"How could I ever be scared of you?" Lisha asked. "You're my best friend."

"Mine, too," Karma added. "What can I say?" she continued teasingly. "The three of us have bonded like sisters."

"You can't mean that—" Chelsea began.

"Of course we can," Karma said. "I've never had friends like you guys in my entire life. You think a little thing like a psycho-killer father is going to deter me?"

Chelsea laughed a little. "Don't make jokes about it."

"Why not?" Karma said. "It beats crying."

Chelsea got gingerly up from the floor of the bathroom. She rinsed her mouth with some Scope, then Karma and Lisha helped her back into her bedroom. She sat on her bed, Lisha on one side of her, Karma on the other.

"God, Chelsea, how did you and your mother keep it a secret all these years?" Lisha asked.

"She pretends it never happened," Chelsea said, reaching for another Kleenex. "I only know the details from the old newspapers up in our attic. I know Mom changed her hair color, and she got glasses—I guess so she wouldn't be recognizable. And of course she changed our last name—"

"Kettering," Karma recalled from her research. "That was your name, right?"

Chelsea nodded.

"The world is so bizarre." Karma marveled. "I mean, what are the odds that you'd end up working for *Trash*, and we'd be researching your family for a story?"

"Didn't you once tell me that you didn't move to Nashville until you were three?" Lisha recalled.

Chelsea nodded. "Mom told me that a long time ago. I don't know where we were, between the time I was ten months old and the time I was three."

"Relatives?" Karma guessed.

"There's my mother's sister," Chelsea said. "In Detroit. I don't know."

"And your mom won't talk about it at all?" Lisha asked.

Chelsea shook her head no. "You know my mom. You'd think she was the most 'normal' mother in the world."

"God, it's so hard to believe." Lisha shook her head in wonder. "Your mom, of all the people in the world, seems least likely to..." She let the rest of her statement trail off.

"What I want to know is how could you bear to carry this around by yourself all these years?" Karma asked. "I would have lost it!"

"I was afraid to tell anyone," Chelsea said, her voice low and ashamed.

"But you didn't do anything!" Lisha exclaimed. "You were an innocent little baby!"

"I know," Chelsea said. "I've told myself that a thousand times. But then I thought...my father seemed normal. Totally normal. That's what all the newspaper articles said. He wasn't crazy. He wasn't depressed. Just some weird chemical thing happened in his brain one day, and he turned into a monster." She gulped hard and twisted the Kleenex in her hand. "Sometimes...sometimes I have kind of a temper tantrum and I fly off the handle. And then I think..."

She was shaking so hard she could barely get the words out.

"And then I think," Chelsea managed, "what if it's genetic? And what if it happens to me, too?"

Tears streamed down her face. "Oh, God," she sobbed, "it's just so horrible."

Karma and Lisha both hugged Chelsea as she cried bitter, scared, pent-up tears. She cried and cried until she felt as if there was nothing left inside of her.

"I'm so sorry you felt like you couldn't tell anyone," Lisha said. "And I'm so sorry about what I said before."

"Forget it," Chelsea said. She took a deep, shuddering breath. "Well, anyway, I'm not sorry I told y'all now. I mean, it's scary, but I'm not sorry. Just promise me that you'll never, ever tell anyone."

"Promise," Lisha said.

"Double-triple promise," Karma added.

"So, I guess now you can see why I'm leaving," Chelsea said. "I'm not about to wait around for Bigfoot to slip the noose around my neck."

"We'll just have to make sure she doesn't find out who you are," Lisha said.

"But she's so relentless—" Chelsea began.

"Relentless, maybe," Karma cut in. "But, frankly, the three of us could outsmart her and only use half our brain cells. She's not nearly as hot shish kebab as she thinks."

Chelsea smiled at her. "Thanks, but...I'm still leaving. It's all over with Nick, and I'd be a hypocrite if I stayed at *Trash* and helped create *Trash* every day."

"Listen, I feel that way sometimes, too," Lisha admitted.

"You do?" Chelsea asked, surprised.

"Not at first," Lisha said. "I told myself this is a dog-eat-dog world, so I might as well be the big dog on the porch. But, I don't know, lately it's really been getting to me."

"Yeah, me, too," Karma agreed. "So what if this gig helps me become the next Ted Turner? I mean, my mother always says you lie down with dogs, you get up with fleas."

Chelsea laughed. "My mother says the same thing."

Lisha threw herself back on the bed and stared up at the ceiling. "Too bad we can't sabotage from within, huh? Or wait, even better, do something that exposes the true trash behind the public *Trash*—"

"Oh, my gawd, that's brilliant!" Karma cried, jumping off the bed.

"What?" Lisha asked, sitting up. "It was just wishful thinking."

"But it doesn't have to be!" Karma exclaimed. "What if...what if we made a film? Behind the scenes at *Trash*? A secret film—"

"Showing how ugly and backbiting it is," Chelsea continued, "how exploitive—"

"Time out," Lisha said, making a T-sign with her hands. "Just how are we supposed to accomplish this feat? 'Uh, excuse me, Bigfoot? Would you mind if I just film you while you lie, cheat, and sleep your way to the top?'"

"Not very subtle," Karma agreed, pacing Chelsea's room. "Here's how I see it. We get equipment from Sky—he's got great connections, right? We film secretly, we hide the camera. It can be done, I'm telling you!"

"You really think?" Chelsea asked slowly.

"Of course!" Karma insisted. "I'm telling you, the brainpower in the room could do just about anything!"

Chelsea smiled. "And you always claim you aren't smart."

"So sue me, I lied," Karma said. "It's a cute little affectation of mine."

"You know, we really could do it," Lisha realized. "It's so wonderfully underhanded... and so *just*! We just turn the tables on them—I love it!"

"And it's so much more satisfying than slinking home with your tail between your legs," Karma told Chelsea.

Chelsea smiled. "It's so, so... *Trash*!"

"And I've got the title!" Lisha cried, a huge grin on her face. *"My TRASHy Summer!"*

"It's perfect," Chelsea admitted.

"Brilliant," Karma agreed. She turned to Chelsea. "So, you'll stay?"

"You will, won't you?" Lisha added. "Come on, we'll be the three underground Musketeers, one for all and all for one."

"I just can't believe—" Chelsea began. She gulped hard. "I can't believe that now that you know the truth about me that you still... still want to be friends with me. I mean, I always imagined this scene where people would run away screaming."

"Chels," Lisha said, "everyone has secrets, you know? Stuff that they hide from the world, stuff that makes them afraid that if anyone knew, people wouldn't like them anymore."

Chelsea stared into Lisha's eyes. "Something happened to you in Europe, didn't it?" she said. "Something bad."

Lisha nodded. "And I will tell you—both of you—one day. I promise. I'm just not ready."

"Well, my life is an open book," Karma said in her nasal whine.

"Unless you count the fact that I was adopted from Korea when I was three, and I don't know anything about who I am or where I come from."

"So...I'm not the only one with secrets, huh?" Chelsea said in a small voice.

"Right," Lisha agreed. "Although admittedly yours is a whopper."

All three of them laughed.

"Okay, you guys," Karma said, reaching out a hand to Chelsea and a hand to Lisha, and trying, with all ninety-two pounds of her body weight, to lift them from the bed.

They both got up, and the three stood in Chelsea's room, hand in hand in hand.

"Now it's the three of us against the world," Karma announced. "Can I get an *amen*?"

"Amen!" Chelsea and Lisha cried.

"And here's to *My TRASHy Summer,*" Lisha said with conviction. "*Trash* is about to meet the enemy...and it is us!"

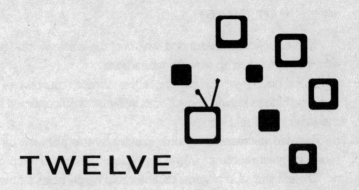

TWELVE

"It's show time," Lisha said laconically, taking the headphones off her head and rubbing her ears. "Man, these things hurt after a while."

The clock on the wall read four P.M. Lisha, Karma, Chelsea, and Alan had all been stuck transcribing 900-number phone calls for the past three hours.

"Time for today's *Trash*," Chelsea said, also pulling off her earphones.

"Monday, July first," Alan said with satisfaction. "Circle it on your calendar, folks. The first day of work on that soon-to-be infamous underground video, *My TRASHy Summer.*"

"Shhhhh!" Chelsea hissed, looking around nervously. "Someone could hear you!"

"There's no one here at Sicko-Central but us interns," Alan said. Sicko-Central was the name they had given to Room 401, where they seemed to spend half their time, transcribing the often bizarre 900-number phone calls.

"We diabolical, underhanded, wait-until-the-whole-world-sees-our-film interns," Karma added with satisfaction.

"Right now, right this minute, a tiny camera, courtesy of Sky, is running, hidden behind some books in Bigfoot's office, aimed right at her chair," Alan said smugly.

Alan had volunteered to come in extra early to plant the camera. It was a complete success. "Trash-cam in place," he'd reported proudly.

Chelsea smiled at her friends. She could hardly believe how much better she felt than she had felt on Friday.

For one thing, telling them my secret feels like this huge, heavy load has been lifted off my chest, she realized. *To think that they know the truth, and they still like me. It's...it's just so incredible!*

And then there's all the plotting we've been doing for My TRASHy Summer, she thought, a smile playing around her lips. *If we can pull this off, it will be the most satisfying thing I've ever been a part of in my entire life.*

The three girls had spent the weekend plotting their strategy for *My TRASHy Summer.* They had to have Sky in on it so that he could arrange to get them video equipment and editing space.

It wasn't hard to convince him, and on Sunday he had stopped over with a top-of-the-line video camera, which he showed them how to use. He also told them that a friend of his dad's with a studio in Brooklyn would let them use the editing room and equipment for free, providing the space wasn't booked by paying customers.

After that, they all agreed to tell Alan, and he had been just as enthusiastic as the other four of them.

Sunday afternoon, as they were all sitting around the girls' apartment, plotting just where and how to begin secretly filming the next day, and eating pizza, Nick had stopped over to see Chelsea. Everyone but her wanted to let Nick in on *My TRASHy Summer,* but she had been adamantly opposed and she had won.

Chelsea had gone out into the hallway to talk with Nick, but it didn't seem to her that he really had much to say. The conversation was terse and awkward, and finally Nick had just gone back across the hall to his own apartment.

I'm totally over him, Chelsea told herself. *I'm really glad it never went any further than it went.*

"I'd rather be here than on the set," Karma commented, interrupting Chelsea's thoughts. Karma took her headphones off. "Better company."

Nonetheless, she turned up the volume on the remote control so that the three of them could see what the *Trash* subject of the day was going to be.

To make their lives somewhat more pleasant, Sumtimes—whom Chelsea was actually, sort of, coming to like—had put a TV monitor in Sicko-Central so they could keep an eye on the show in the late afternoon.

"Okay, dudes and dudettes," Jazz was saying, after the audience had finally finished cheering her entrance. For some reason, she was dressed today, from head to toe, in black plastic garbage bags. The inflatable man and the inflatable woman were clad in the same material, and were sitting on the coffee table.

"So, guys," Jazz continued, "who here thinks that their after-school jobs totally suck?"

The audience went crazy.

"Big duh, right?" she asked. "I mean, flipping hamburgers, stuck in the stockroom, mowing people's lawns, taking care of their screaming kids, all for chump change. So what would you call it?"

"It's trash!" the audience yelled gleefully.

And that answer is written for all of you on huge cue cards that Demetrius is holding up right now, Chelsea thought cynically.

It was the truth. Chelsea had seen this drill before. When Jazz wanted the audience to respond as one in a certain way, she had Demetrius or Bigfoot drill them on their responses during the warm-up, and then had cue cards containing the appropriate response held up at the appropriate moments.

"You know it," Jazz agreed. "So today, we're bringing you six teens who all think their after-school jobs bite the big one. They're ready to tell their bosses, on nationwide TV, to take that job and shove it."

The refrain from the old country music song "Take This Job and Shove It" played for a few seconds on the studio sound system while the audience cheered again.

"But wait, there's more!" Jazz continued. "What are they going to do for money now, you may ask?"

What are they going to do for money? The audience chanted obediently, reading from another off-camera cue card.

"She's an artist," Karma said, watching Jazz on the monitor. "A sick and demented person, but an artist."

Jazz walked up a level on the set, to the three girls and three guys picked to be on the show. They sat there, grinning at her. One of them waved to the camera.

"What are they going to do for money, now that they're telling their bosses off?" she asked. "Well, these are six teens who'll do anything— and I do mean *anything*—for money! And we're gonna watch 'em do it! Why? Because we're all TRASH!"

"I can't take it," Karma said, snapping off the monitor with the remote control. "I'm going to get some coffee. You want?"

"I'll go with you," Lisha said.

Chelsea looked at the piles of cassette tapes she still had to transcribe and shook her head. "I'd better stay and work on these, y'all," she said, "or else I'll be here all night."

"Tell you what"—Alan got up and put his hands gently on the back of her neck—"I'll go get you some coffee and, say, a buttered bagel, and I'll bring it back here for you, okay?"

Chelsea smiled up at him. "You're nice."

"That's true," he said, smiling back at her. "Back in a flash."

"If you lose your mind, you come find us in the lounge," Karma called.

Chelsea turned back to her headset and computer keyboard. She put the earphones back on, faced the computer keyboard, and pressed the play button on the tape console.

"Hiya, Jazz!" a young voice with a definite California beach feel to it said. "I'm Lydia Lazinsky from Long Beach, California, and I think it would be too rad to do a show about teen girls who've broken up with their boyfriends, but now the girl wants to prove how much she wants the dude back, even if the guy, like, cheated on her or abused her, or something, because—"

Chelsea pushed the pause button.

"Lydia, you need two years of intensive therapy," she said, shaking her head. She rubbed her eyes, which burned from too many hours staring at a computer screen.

I guess I will just go join them in the lounge, she decided, getting up to stretch. *There's only so much I can take.*

Chelsea had just stepped into the hallway when Sumtimes came running up to her at full speed. There were beads of sweat on her bald head.

"Thank God I found you, thank God, thank God," Sumtimes said, the words rushing out of her mouth. She clutched at the sleeve of Chelsea's white cotton sweater.

"Are you talking to *me*?" Chelsea asked, totally bewildered.

"Come with me," Sumtimes demanded, and she pulled Chelsea with her down the hallway.

Oh, no, they found the video camera in Bigfoot's office and they think I did it, Chelsea realized with dread. *There goes my job, there goes My TRASHy Summer, there goes my professional reputation forever.*

"Come on!" Sumtimes screamed. "Move it!"

Maybe if I insist that I planted that camera all by myself, Chelsea thought, *maybe if they believe I acted alone, the others won't lose their jobs.*

"Look, I can explain—"

"Just shut up and run!" Sumtimes yelled over her shoulder. Chelsea followed her, thinking she would turn into Bigfoot's office, but to her surprise Sumtimes ran down three flights of stairs and into Studio C.

And when Chelsea finally, breathlessly, ran inside the studio, it was totally apparent what the problem was.

And it had nothing to do with a hidden video camera.

There was a teen girl on the set, but she wasn't one of Jazz's six take-this-job-and-shove-it guests.

She was an unattractive, overweight teen girl with a big nose and lank, greasy hair.

And she was holding a pistol to Jazz's head.

Chelsea recognized her immediately.

It was Sela Flynn.

"Okay, Sela," Chelsea said, her voice very shaky, her legs feeling like Gumby legs beneath her. "Here I come. Just take it easy, okay?"

"Get out here, Chelsea!" Sela yelled at her. "Get out here, now!"

"Just take your time, kid," a New York City hostage unit cop's voice said into Chelsea's earphone. "Take just one step at a time. And for God's sake, be careful!"

Chelsea gulped hard. "I'm coming, Sela," she repeated. "I'm coming out now."

Slowly, so slowly, with the encouraging voice of the cop from the hostage unit in her ear, she approached Sela Flynn.

The whole thing felt like a terrible nightmare.

Sela obviously hadn't gone back to New Mexico. Instead she had hung around New York all weekend, and then had managed to become a part of the studio audience of the day's show. She'd found a seat in the back row. And just as soon as the first commercial break ended, and Jazz had put the camera on the first teenager who was about to tell her boss to take her job and shove it, Sela had burst out of her seat and run down the aisle, waving her gun in the air. She ran onto the set, right up to Jazz.

At first, everyone had laughed, thinking that the whole thing was just TRASH.

But then, Sela had fired her gun at the ceiling, blowing a large hole in the acoustic tiles.

After that, it was pandemonium. People were screaming, crying, diving for cover under the seats of the studio.

There was a panicked run for the exits, but Sela had pulled the microphone off a white-faced guest and had yelled into it: "Lock the doors now, or I'm shooting Jazz! And I have five sticks of dynamite strapped to my right leg, under my jeans. I can blow this whole place up, and I'll do it, too!"

The doors had been quickly locked.

Then Sela made the rest of her demands.

She wanted twenty-five people from the staff of *Trash* brought in, and she wanted them to sit on the floor in front of her. This had to happen within three minutes. If there weren't twenty-five people sitting on the floor in front of her in three minutes, she'd shoot Jazz.

Staff members had quickly been dragged into the studio, among them Karma, Lisha, and Alan. Sky had already been in the room with a cameraman, and he, too, was sitting among the twenty-five hostages. While this was happening Sela yelled into the microphone that if one person who was already in the room tried to escape, she'd shoot Jazz.

She didn't want to see any police. If she saw a cop, she'd shoot Jazz.

She wanted everything that was going on to be broadcast live, and she wanted a TV set up within five minutes so that she could see that it was all being broadcast. If it wasn't live on the air, she'd shoot Jazz.

And she only wanted to talk to one person—one person to be the go-between, between her and the police who were sure to arrive soon.

That person was Chelsea Jennings.

"The only sane person around here!" Sela had screamed wildly into her mike, which she had clipped to her flannel shirt. "I want Chelsea!"

If Chelsea Jennings didn't show up within five minutes, Sela had sworn to shoot Jazz. And if anyone else tried to approach her, or talk to her, or even get within ten feet of her without her permission, she'd shoot them, too.

Right after that, Chelsea recalled as she walked slowly toward Sela, someone stuck an earphone in her ear so that she could hear from the police SWAT team that was set up outside the studio doors.

"Sela," Roxanne said, slowly getting up from her spot with the other staff members on the floor in front of the furious teen.

Chelsea froze, still twenty feet from Sela.

"I'm on your side, Sela," Roxanne said sweetly. "I know just how you feel, and I want you to know I'm going to arrange for you to be Jazz's special guest on a show next week—"

"Really?" Sela asked. She seemed to be considering the offer.

"Oh, yes," Bigfoot said, putting one large foot in front of the other as she approached Sela. "I can do it, too. I'll make sure that—"

Wordlessly, almost casually, Sela turned to Roxanne, aimed her gun, and shot her in the right foot. Bigfoot fell to the stage.

Everyone began screaming, but Sela screamed into her microphone loudest of all. "Just put a tourniquet on her foot and shut her up. I didn't shoot to kill. Believe me, I know how to shoot to kill."

She looked over at Chelsea, her eyes pleading.

Oh, God, please don't let her shoot me, Chelsea thought as Alan and Sky lifted Roxanne and carried her to the corner to apply first aid. "I'm right here, Sela," she said in what she hoped was a low, calm voice.

"She didn't follow directions," Sela told Chelsea.

"That's right," Chelsea said soothingly.

"You're doing great, kid," a cop said in her ear. "Talk to her calmly. You're the only one she'll talk to."

As she continued to walk sooooo slowly toward Sela, she saw Karma and Lisha looking up at her from their places on the floor. She saw the fear in their eyes.

Fear for her.

Please, God, she prayed, *don't let me die now. Now that I finally feel like I'm not alone anymore.*

Sela had her gun pointed at Jazz's head. Her hand was shaking. Chelsea was within five feet of her now.

"Take it easy, kid," the cop's gruff voice said in her ear. "Remember, she's nuts."

It was all Chelsea could do not to talk back to the voice in her ear, but she knew that would drive Sela absolutely wild—that she, Chelsea, had a direct line to a New York City Police Department SWAT team.

"That's close enough," Sela snapped.

Chelsea stopped walking. "Here I am, just like you asked for."

"Are we live?" Sela asked.

Chelsea pointed to the TV. "See for yourself. We're live," she said. "All across America."

Sela grinned a sick grin. "Good," she muttered. She leaned into the microphone clipped to her shirt. "Testing, one, two, three, testing." Sela grinned again at Chelsea. "That's what professionals say when they test their mikes.

"You want to know why I'm here?" Sela asked Chelsea, her voice reverberating through the studio.

"Yes," Chelsea said.

"I want her tied up, first," Sela said, nudging her gun at Jazz.

Chelsea spotted a couple of electrical cords a few feet away, lying in the aisle. She walked over and picked them up.

"You!" Sela yelled, pointing the gun at Alan. "Tie her up."

"Okay," Alan agreed. He took the cables from Chelsea and quickly bound Jazz's wrists and ankles. Jazz helped by holding her hands and feet out for him.

"Sit back down with the others," Sela barked at him.

Obediently, Alan found his place again next to Karma and Lisha.

"Get her talking," the cop said in Chelsea's ear. "Get her to confide in you."

Chelsea only prayed that Sela couldn't hear the cop, too.

"So," she said, "you're live on the air coast-to-coast. What do you want to say ... so that we can let some of these people go?"

"Good, kid!" the cop said in Chelsea's ear. "That's perfect. Keep it up."

"She humiliated me," Sela said, her voice low and hurt. "Jazz humiliated me. How can I go back home now? How can I? Don't you think everyone I know saw the show? Don't you think they're all laughing at me now?"

"I'm sure Jazz is sorry," Chelsea said, hoping that it was the right thing to say.

"Yeah?" Sela said. She pointed the gun at Jazz's ear. "Say it," she commanded Jazz. "Are you sorry?"

"I'm sorry," Jazz said.

Sela laughed hysterically, wiping her eyes, teary from mirth. "You must think I'm as stupid as you are. I know you're not sorry. Big duh, as you always say, Jazz. You're only sorry that now I have the power, and you don't."

"I really am sorry," Jazz said fervently.

"Sure." Sela sneered. "We'll see how sorry you are. We'll see how sorry you are when I keep you tied up here, for as long as I want." She swung her head to look at Chelsea, her eyes wild. "I want her humiliated like she humiliated me!"

"Tell her she's the boss," the cop whispered in Chelsea's ear.

"You're the boss, Sela," Chelsea said. "*Trash* is your show now. I'm here to help you run it."

The seconds stretched into minutes, the minutes into hours. It was now six forty-five P.M., and Sela was still holding the studio hostage. And the hostage drama was being broadcast live, coast-to-coast.

Not only was it on the stations that normally picked up *Trash* in syndication, but it was also on CNN Headline News, and large chunks of the drama were being shown on all the major-network nightly news broadcasts.

Sela had asked for a live hookup with one of the networks, and she'd received what she'd asked for. Now, Ted Masterson, the nationally known and very handsome news anchor, was asking her questions, which she was answering.

During all this, Jazz lay at her feet, bound, while Sela held court from the middle of the studio and Chelsea stood by her side.

"I mean, tell me, Ted," Sela was saying, "why is it that a girl like Jazz gets her own TV show, and all that money and fame? Why not me? Huh?"

"I don't know, Sela," Ted Masterson said, in his deep, sonorous tones. "Why do you think?"

"Because she's tall and thin and gorgeous, you moron!" Sela spat out. "Don't play dumb with me! What, you think you're a news anchor because you're so smart? Don't make me laugh. You look like a movie star, that's the only reason!"

"Uh-huh," Ted agreed gravely.

No one saw the trapdoor on the studio floor—which led to a crawl space full of cables and electrical equipment—open just a few inches behind the spot where Sela and Chelsea were standing.

Moments later it opened a crack more.

Then, so slowly, a few inches more.

That's when Chelsea saw, behind Sela, the top of Nick's head as he inched out of the crawl space.

Their eyes met. Sela didn't see him. She was too busy staring into the camera, ranting on.

Quickly, Chelsea turned her eyes back to Sela.

"I mean, that's all America cares about, right?" Sela ranted on. "Come on, Ted, try and tell me different!" She focused on camera number one, as if it were the news broadcaster himself. "You can't, you dumb-ass, because—"

She stopped suddenly and stood stock-still. Perhaps she'd felt a gust of breeze on her bare ankles from the slightly opened trapdoor behind her.

She whirled around. She saw Nick's head.

"No!" Chelsea screamed.

Nick lunged, reaching out to grab Sela's feet from behind, evidently hoping to trip her up and knock her to the floor.

"No!" Chelsea yelled again.

Sela fumbled a moment, then fired her gun at the trapdoor, as it slammed shut with a loud bang.

Some people were screaming, others crying, whimpering, and moaning.

"What the hell happened in there?" the cop was yelling into Chelsea's ear. "The angle of the camera sucks. Chelsea? Kid?"

Oh, God, she shot Nick, Chelsea thought, fear clutching her heart. *He's down in the crawl space, wounded, maybe dying, oh, God.*

I can't let Nick die.

And then, without giving herself time to consider the insanity of it, while Sela was still breathing hard, her gun pointed shakily at the trapdoor to the crawl space, Chelsea made her move.

Like a football lineman trying to deliver a vicious sack to a hapless quarterback, she took a flying leap, and landed on Sela's back.

The two of them fell to the studio floor, and the gun flew harmlessly away from Sela, skittering across the floor like a hockey puck.

In an instant fifteen people converged on Chelsea and Sela as the two of them wrestled on the floor of the set.

Thirty arms held Sela down.

Bedlam reigned on the set as the doors to the studio burst open and three dozen policemen, wearing flak jackets and helmets, ran through the open doors and onto the set. Quickly and efficiently, they handcuffed Sela and hustled her away.

Wordlessly, Lisha and Karma hugged Chelsea tight.

"Get me out of these damn cords," Jazz yelled. She was still helpless, tied up in the electrical wires. Sumtimes quickly began to untie her.

"Wow, is all I have to say," Alan said, grabbing Chelsea up in his arms. Sky came over and hugged her, too. "You're a hero, Chels."

Just then, Barry, who had made sure he was nowhere in sight of the studio during the ordeal, entered and ran over to Chelsea. "You were fabulous!" he cried, hugging her hard. "So fabulous!"

It felt as if a zillion people were surrounding Chelsea, and flash cameras were going off. It was pandemonium.

"I have to find Nick!" Chelsea yelled, tears streaming down her face. "We need an ambulance! She shot him! He's down in the—"

And then she felt warm lips on the back of her neck.

She turned around.

Nick.

"I thought you were—"

"She missed," he said, and enveloped Chelsea in his strong arms, pressing her face into his chest.

"You were an idiot," Chelsea said softly.

"The thought of something happening to you . . ." Nick said gruffly. "For two hours I was stuck under the stage, in the crawl space. I was running wires down there when all this started. So I waited. Then I saw the trapdoor. Then I waited some more, until her foot covered a hole in the floor by the trapdoor. Then—"

"I thought she shot you," Chelsea said, holding him so tight that her knuckles were white against his flannel shirt.

"Chels," he murmured. "Chelsea . . ."

They just held each other, their eyes closed, realizing what they meant to each other, realizing what they had almost lost, before it had ever really begun.

"Hey, Chelsea?" Barry Bassinger said, sticking his head in between hers and Nick's. "Listen, Larry King's office is on the phone. Can you do his show live at nine tonight? With Jazz? His office just called, and they say they'll send Ted Turner's jet—"

Chelsea just stared at him. More camera flashes went off in her face.

"And then can you do *Good Morning America* tomorrow, six-thirty?" Barry continued. "You and Jazz? The *Today* show? *CBS This*

Morning? Jesus, kid, take your pick! The phone's ringing off the hook already!"

"Snap ratings are in, Barry," Demetrius called from the wings. "We just beat the O.J. verdict!"

Barry punched the air in triumph. "Chelsea," he said, "I'm a genius for bringing you in with us. A genius!"

Someone tapped Chelsea on the shoulder.

It was Jazz.

"I wanted to thank you," she said softly. "You saved my life."

"Thanks, Jazz," Chelsea said. Nick's arm was still around her shoulders.

"No," Jazz said, "thank you, uh... Chutney." She looked from Nick to Chelsea, and back at Nick. "You make a cute couple," she added.

Jazz walked away, adjusting her clothes and her hair, and went over to the number-one camera, which apparently was still broadcasting live.

"Okay, Jazz," some producer called from the wings. "We go live again in five, four, three...!"

Chelsea and Nick watched, astonished, as Jazz automatically counted off the last two seconds silently and looked into the camera, turning on her charm.

"Well, well, well, gang," she said lightly, looking into America's living rooms, "where were we before we were so rudely interrupted?"

Everyone in the studio just stood and cheered.

THIRTEEN

"Well, well, well, gang, where were we before we were so rudely interrupted?"

A close-up of Jazz's face filled the TV screen in the girls' living room. The six friends sat there, along with Belch the dog, rapt, and watched a replay, on a late-night network news special, of the drama that they had lived out earlier in the evening.

"This is truly the weirdest experience of my life," Karma said, her eyes riveted to the screen.

The camera went to Darla Dunnings, a reporter, who was standing on the street, just outside the *Trash* studio. "So, there you have it, Ted. The alleged perpetrator, Sela Flynn of Gallup, New Mexico, is now in police custody. This is Darla Dunnings. Back to you in the studio, Ted."

The camera went to Ted Masterson and his coanchor, Kate Pride.

"What an incredible story," Kate said, looking over at Ted. "I'm sure our viewing audience would like to know what it was like for you, Ted."

"Well, as you know, Kate, Sela Flynn specifically requested that I speak with her on the air, which I did, for an hour," Ted intoned, his voice filled with self-importance. "I found her to be a surprisingly intelligent young woman, actually. But clearly deeply troubled."

"Big duh, Ted!" Lisha yelled at the TV.

"Just incredible, Ted," Kate said again. She looked at the camera. "This is Kate Pride—"

"And Ted Masterson—"

"Wishing you good night."

Alan reached for the remote control and clicked off the set.

They had all been watching TV for the past two hours—ever since they'd managed to get home from *Trash*. Over and over again, on station after station, they had seen their lives played out on TV, with Chelsea making her flying leap at Sela to save the day.

Every station was calling her a hero. Every station was trying to get more information about who she was, where she lived, and just why it was that Sela Flynn had asked for her in the first place.

Chelsea had turned down all the offers to appear on the news broadcasts.

In fact, after calling her mother to assure her that she was all right (Lisha and Karma had called their parents from the guys' apartment), she had unplugged the phone so that no more reporters could get through. Nick had given Antoine the doorman twenty dollars to keep the reporters out of the building, and for once Antoine seemed to be on top of things.

Outside the window, Chelsea could still hear the noise on the street, where hordes of reporters were gathered, waiting for her to come out so they could interview her.

Sky got up and peered out the window. "Yep, they're all still out there, all right," he said. "Like ants at a picnic."

"You realize I can never leave this apartment," Chelsea said.

"They'll move on to the next instant, trashy scandal soon," Alan promised.

"I wish they'd just leave me alone," Chelsea said.

Lisha and Karma caught her eye, and both nodded with sympathy.

They know what I'm worried about, Chelsea thought. *What if some enterprising reporter really digs deep and finds out who I am?*

"I wonder if the Trash-cam got anything good in Bigfoot's office before all hell broke loose," Sky said.

"Sky!" Lisha cried, tilting her head toward Nick, who was sitting on the floor next to Chelsea, holding her hand.

"Oops," Sky said, chagrined. "I forgot he didn't know."

Nick scratched at his chin, and Belch leaped up and licked his face. "Hey, Belch," he told the dog, "I got a feeling there's a secret going on that we didn't get let in on."

"I'm sorry, man," Sky said. "We should have told you." He looked over at Chelsea. "I'm sorry, but we should have. We're all in this together, okay?"

Chelsea looked over at Nick. "Okay," she finally said. "He earned it today." And then she told him about *My TRASHy Summer,* and the Trash-cam that they had planted in Bigfoot's office.

"Whoa," Nick said. "Diabolical."

"We like to think so." Karma smiled.

Nick scratched his chin again. "So, the idea is, we take the very medium that they're using to make a mint by humiliating people, and we use it against them and expose them for the petty, ugly, little despots they really are."

Chelsea grinned. "What a smart guy."

"A smart slacker," he corrected her, kissing her cheek. "I think it's great. Count me in."

Chelsea kissed him back, on the lips. "Cool," she whispered.

"Of course, we're stuck in this apartment forever," Nick added. "I don't know how any of us is going to get to the office in the morning to get the camera."

"It's still in Bigfoot's office, even as we speak," Alan said smugly. "Although I guess it ran out of tape by now."

"So, tomorrow I leave really early," Sky said. "I don't think I was on camera enough for the vultures downstairs to know I work for *Trash*. And I'll get the camera, reload 'er, and set it up in, say, Jazz's office?"

"Perfect," Lisha said.

They all agreed.

"You realize," Sky continued, "that if we get caught, we'll lose more than our jobs. I mean, forget a career in TV for any of us, because our reps will be shot."

They were all quiet for a moment.

"You know, sometimes you just have to stand for something," Nick said slowly.

"I thought you didn't believe in anything," Chelsea said.

"Guess you don't know me all that well yet, after all," Nick said softly.

Chelsea stood up and, reaching for Nick's hand, she led him into her bedroom and closed the door, to the good-natured catcalls of their friends and yelps of protest from Belch. Then she turned to him.

"I want to tell you something." She took a deep breath. "You were right. I...I pushed too hard for some kind of big commitment from you when we barely knew each other. There's a lot about me you don't know...things that made me afraid—"

Chelsea stopped. *Am I ready to tell him my big secret?* she wondered. *No, not yet. I need time. And he needs time. But maybe someday...*

"Anyway," she continued, "I know that sometimes I kind of...fly off the handle. I kind of have a temper," she admitted.

"I noticed," Nick said, a smile playing at his lips.

"The thing is," Chelsea continued, "I really do care about you. And...and I want us to get to know each other. So if you still want to be with me—"

"Oh, Chels," Nick murmured. And then his arms were around her, and his lips were on hers, and he kissed her until she felt breathless and giddy with happiness.

"Hey, celebrity!" Karma called from the living room. "If the two of you still have your clothes on, get back out here! Bigfoot is on TV, live from her hospital bed. It's a scream!"

Chelsea and Nick ran back into the living room. There was Roxanne, propped up in a hospital bed, her makeup perfect, her huge cast sticking out of the bottom of the bed.

"...and I always knew that Chutney was the perfect intern for *Trash*," Bigfoot was saying. "We really value her. She's smart and fearless—everything that *Trash* is all about."

"Get me the hurl sack!" Karma squealed.

"Will you be back at *Trash* soon?" the reporter asked Roxanne.

"Oh, yes," she replied, turning on a photogenic Sharon Stone smile. "I'll be back on my *feet* in no time!"

This sent gales of laughter around the room. In fact, the six of them laughed so hard that they were crying.

"Stop, stop," Lisha cried, holding her stomach. "I can't take any more!"

"You guys," Karma finally managed, "I don't want to get too mushy about this, but you guys are incredible. And this TRASHy summer is turning into the best summer of my entire life."

"And it's only just begun," Chelsea said, her eyes shining. She took in the faces of her five friends, who had become so dear to her, in such a short time.

I am so lucky, she thought. *I am the luckiest girl in the world.*

She smiled at all the faces in the room, all of whom were smiling back at her, in friendship, in love.

It was going to be one unbelievable, incredible, and totally trashy summer.

LOVE, LIES, and VIDEO

For Lisa Hurley,
world's greatest teen

ONE

"Chutney Jennings, America's newest teen sex symbol!" Karma Kushner cried dramatically, her nasal, New York accent very apparent. She pushed open the door to Chelsea's room. "How did lowly me get lucky enough to be *your* roommate?" Karma fluttered her eyelashes comically, then rushed over to Chelsea's bed.

"Please, allow me to serve you your morning bagel and cream cheese in bed, O Famous One," Karma said, plunking a tray with coffee and a bagel down on Chelsea's nightstand.

Chelsea opened her eyes wearily and blinked a few times. "Huh?"

"Brilliantly put. May I quote you to the press?" Karma asked eagerly.

"Have you lost your mind?" Chelsea croaked, fumbling for her beeping alarm clock. "What time is it, anyway?" Then she remembered, and her head jerked toward the window. "Are they still out there?"

"Let's see, in order of your questions, that would be: I don't think so, seven-fifteen, and yep," Karma answered.

Chelsea eyed Karma through puffy, sleep-filled eyes. "You're dressed."

"Oh-mi-gawd, famous *and* observant, folks," Karma intoned, as if she were speaking to a crowd of reporters. "On top of that, the girl looks like Hilary Duff. So I ask you, America, what more could you want?"

"I could want to go back to sleep," Chelsea said, pulling the covers over her head.

"No such luck," Karma said. She pulled the covers off of Chelsea's face. "Feel free to compliment me on how incredible I look, by the by," she added.

"How would I know, I can barely see yet," Chelsea replied.

"Sip the coffee, then tell me," Karma suggested, lifting Chelsea's coffee cup.

Chelsea sat up and took a sip, eyeing Karma, who twirled around for her.

"Whaddaya think?" Karma asked expectantly.

Karma, a petite Korean-American girl who, ironically, sounded just like Fran Drescher on *The Nanny,* stood barely five feet tall. Adopted from her native Korea as a baby, she had been raised by a wonderful Jewish former-hippie couple who now owned a health-food store and bookstore on Long Island.

Karma's gentle, nonmaterialistic parents loved her dearly, but they were chagrined to have raised a daughter who lived for designer fashions, played the stock market, and planned to become a multi-millionaire CEO of a major TV network as soon as possible.

Karma, quite accurately, considered herself something of a fashion genius. She put together incredible outfits—combinations of expensive designer pieces (she knew all the best places in New York City to get them on sale) and thrift-store chic. Today, for example, she had on a very expensive BCBG tangerine-colored cropped sweater with a Betsy Johnson lemon-yellow miniskirt, over a thrift shop crinoline, and $1.99 yellow fishnet hose from Kmart. Her shoes were shiny orange patent-leather loafers with three-inch chunky heels, while a row of three tiny orange-and-yellow fish-shaped plastic barrettes held her waist-length hair off her face.

"You look like a mobile dish of sherbet," Chelsea decided.

"Drink more coffee, I'll get cuter," Karma suggested.

Chelsea threw her head back down and pulled her pillow over her face. "I don't want to be famous. I mean I do, someday, but not like this!"

" 'Morning," their third roommate, Lisha, said in her throaty, sexy voice. She padded into Chelsea's room sipping a cup of coffee. "I just looked outside. It's still a zoo."

" 'Cuz Chutney here is the flavor o' the day," Karma said. She walked over to the grimy window and looked straight down, five stories, to West End Avenue. "Wow, you guys, look."

Chelsea got out of bed, and she and Lisha walked over to the window.

"You see what I mean," Karma said, looking down at the crowd. "Boy, do we have to plan a cute getup for you today, or what?"

"I don't want to face them!" Chelsea cried, wrapping her arms around herself.

Karma put her hand on Chelsea's arm. "Chels, remember, they don't know anything about . . . you know."

"But they could find out," Chelsea pointed out, her voice tense.

Karma nodded with understanding. She knew what her roommate was afraid of. Even though Chelsea seemed to be the most normal person in the world—all-American, cute, blond, an honor student from Nashville, Tennessee—she had a big dark secret, which she had only recently shared with Karma and Lisha.

Chelsea's dad was an infamous mass murderer.

Yes, her dad was Charles Kettering, who had gone berserk one day eighteen years or so before, and shot and killed an entire restaurantful of people. Then he'd rushed home to kill Chelsea's mom and their baby, but his wife had stabbed him to death to protect her child.

And that child was Chelsea.

Karma knew that Chelsea's mom had changed her appearance, changed their last name, and moved to a new town. And she knew that Mrs. Jennings never talked with her daughter about what had happened. But Chelsea lived in constant fear that someone would find out. Other than herself and her mom, only Karma and Lisha knew the truth.

Amazingly enough, the press knew nothing about that part of Chelsea's life. No, she had become world-famous the day before for something else entirely.

Something equally incredible.

And I thought it was weird to be Korean and not know anything about my birth family, Karma thought. *I can't imagine what it's like to be Chelsea.*

"No one is going to find out," Lisha assured her friend.

"Really?" Chelsea asked hopefully.

"Really," Karma confirmed. She peered out the window again. "Gawd, they're like a flock of vultures down there. You think they've been out there all night?"

When they had finally fallen asleep the night before, at about two in the morning, there had still been a huge crowd of magazine, newspaper, radio, and television reporters camped out at the entrance to the Upper West Side apartment building where she, Chelsea, and Lisha shared an apartment. All three eighteen-year-old girls were summer interns on the phenomenally popular and hip teen television talk show *Trash.*

And right across the hall from them lived the three eighteen-year-old guy interns. Very convenient.

"I wouldn't camp out there all night for a story about me," Chelsea said.

"But, *Chutney,*" Karma teased, "you're big news!"

Chelsea sighed and shook her head. "How did my name get changed from Chelsea to a condiment?"

"Because Jazz Stewart, teen-babe hostess of *Trash,* is more famous than you are," Karma explained, "and she called you Chutney on the air, so now you're Chutney, forever. Anyway, I count five."

"Five what?" Chelsea asked her friend.

"Satellite trucks," Karma explained. "Waiting to do live reports with you. Last night we only counted four."

"They're multiplying," Lisha said, blowing her shaggy brown bangs out of her eyes. "Like bacteria."

"Just for a while," Karma said reassuringly. "There'll be another big scandal soon to take their minds off you."

"You think?" Chelsea asked anxiously.

"I know," Karma insisted confidently.

And I hope I'm telling the truth, she added to herself.

"Anyway, the Pope's coming to New York tomorrow. You just have to last twenty-four hours, and they'll all be following him around instead of you," Karma continued.

"You think?" Chelsea asked again. She walked across the room and picked up her cup of coffee.

"I remember the last time he came," Karma began. "He's, like, bigger than Mick Jagger when the Rolling Stones were everything."

"I met Mick Jagger once," Lisha put in.

"Get out of here!" Karma shrieked.

"I did," Lisha affirmed. "When I was in Europe."

"So what was he like?" Chelsea asked.

"Skinny," Lisha said, sipping her coffee. "And old."

"You promised to tell us about Europe, you know," Karma reminded Lisha.

Lisha shrugged coolly, which was her patented gesture that meant she wasn't going to give you any information.

"I swear, you look just like Demi Moore when you do that," Karma said. She had a habit of comparing everyone's looks to those of someone famous. "I suppose you met *her* in Europe, too."

Lisha laughed. "Nope, can't say that I did."

"Come with me, I wanna hear more about Mick," Karma insisted. She turned to Chelsea. "So drink your coffee and get dressed—wear something fabulous. I'm gonna plug the phone back in now, in the living room."

"But I don't want to talk to—" Chelsea began.

"Don't worry," Karma interrupted, "if the White House calls, I'll pretend I'm you."

Karma and Lisha went into the living room, and Karma reached for the phone cord. "Here goes."

"I'm surprised none of the reporters down there tried to fly into our apartment by helicopter," Lisha said wryly, scratching a mosquito bite on her shapely, tanned leg.

"Five," Karma said.

"Five what?"

"Seconds until the first call after I plug the phone in. Wanna bet?"

"Against a Wall Street whiz like you?" Lisha asked. "No shot."

Karma sat down on the couch next to Lisha and took the telephone cord in her right hand and the small, white phone in the other. She had unplugged it the night before, at ten P.M., after the calls from reporters had begun to pour in, one after another. Since Chelsea didn't want to do any interviews, it seemed like the best policy.

With great ceremony, Karma plugged the phone cord into the telephone and started counting backward.

"Five, four, three—"

Ring, ring.

"Gee, we both lose," Karma said, picking up the receiver. "Hello?"

She listened for a few seconds, then put her hand over the receiver.

"*Access Hollywood,*" she whispered to Lisha. "They want to talk to Chutney."

"Tell them she flew to Tibet last night to study with the Dalai Lama," Lisha suggested.

"Chutney's not available now," Karma said into the phone. A voice droned on and on in her ear, all about how important *Access Hollywood* was and how they would treat Chutney with total respect (*yuh—right,* Karma thought) and whoever was on the phone, would she please answer a few questions.

"Sure, I'll answer a few questions," Karma agreed. "Her name is *Chutney* Jennings—"

Lisha nudged Karma hard in the ribs.

"Gosh, I don't know where she got such an unusual first name," Karma said innocently into the phone. "Yes, she's the girl from *Trash*. Yes, she's the one that the other girl, the one who held the whole show hostage yesterday, asked for. Yes, she's the one who saved the day by tackling the girl with the gun while it was all being broadcast on national TV. You want an interview with her? For how much money?"

"Karma!" Lisha hissed.

"Five thousand for an exclusive?" Karma repeated for Lisha's benefit. "I'm not impressed. Seven? Maybe ten?"

"You know Chelsea isn't going to—" Lisha began.

Karma just grinned. "Ten thou? Lemme think about it," she said into the phone. "Okay, I thought about it. We're blowing you off. Bye." She hung up the phone. "Oh, that was so much fun!"

"Don't play games at Chelsea's expense," Lisha warned.

"I would never!" Karma insisted. The way she said *never* sounded like *nev-uh.* She cocked her head at Lisha. "It's so weird, you know?"

"What?" Lisha took a sip of her coffee.

"That you guys actually were best friends in junior high, and then you moved to Colorado, and then out of, like, ten thousand applicants you both got picked to be *Trash* interns."

Lisha shrugged. "Sometimes truth is stranger than fiction."

Karma looked over Lisha's curvy figure, clad at the moment in a long T-shirt and a pair of bikini panties. "And you really used to be fat?"

"Mega," Lisha replied.

"So how did you lose it?" Karma asked.

"You're asking *me* for dieting tips?" Lisha laughed. "You wear a size one on your fat days."

"I just want to know more about you," Karma said. "You're very secretive, you know."

Lisha jumped up. "And I'm also going to be very late for work if I don't go get dressed."

"Okay, then," Karma said, "I'll just invent an entire past for you. You were Mick Jagger's love slave in Europe. He only fed you bread and water—"

"You're a sick girl," Lisha called as she hurried toward her room.

"I prefer to think of it as imaginative," Karma called back. "Hey, dress fast and the three of us will sneak out the freight entrance, okay?"

Karma poured herself another cup of the very strong coffee that she practically lived on and wandered back into the living room. The decor was very bizarre—old-fashioned furniture, with bad erotic art on the walls. *Trash* had rented it for them furnished, and the art was by the landlord's son, a student at the Kansas City Art Institute—and evidently not a very talented one.

In a small mirror, framed with cartoon-like drawings of neon-hued bikinis, Karma looked at her reflection.

Different, she thought. *Having Asian features in America automatically makes you different.* She smiled ruefully as she thought about the current trend toward Asian chic, and how so many guys of every possible ethnicity seemed to find it oh-so-hip to have a cute Asian girlfriend.

It's hard to see myself as pretty, even though everyone tells me I am, Karma realized. *I mean, pretty is supposed to mean blond Chelsea, or sexy brunette Lisha, not Asian me.*

At her Long Island high school, Karma had been fairly popular, but she mostly kept to herself. She was already reading *BusinessWeek* on a regular basis, and she spent the money from her after-school job on fashions and stock options.

Incredibly, she had actually earned thousands of dollars in the financial markets. In fact, her record was better than some of the best investment analysts on Wall Street.

I guess that helped me get picked for Trash, Karma thought idly.

When *Trash* had announced, way back in January, that it was going to select six just-graduated high-school seniors—three girls and three guys—from around North America to work as interns on the hit show, Karma had made a snap decision: she would apply. The contest had gotten tons of press—it was even bigger than getting picked to be on *Survivor*. But Karma had hoped she would stand out from the crowd.

And she did.

She made sure that her application would be unique. Not only did she send in the normal application, but she also sent her financial records, as well as several full-length photos of herself and an audiocassette, in which her unusual, nasal voice sounded off in all its glory.

She'd been quickly accepted. Which was good, because Karma had a limitless supply of energy, and she'd wanted a gig besides her part-time night job tending the juice bar at the ultra-hip East Village teen nightclub Jimi's.

After all, designer fashions are pricey, Karma thought to herself. *And a girl doesn't become rich and famous sitting at home and dreaming about it.*

"Hey, Karma, can I use your toothpaste?" Lisha asked, sticking her head into the living room. "I'm out."

"Sure," Karma replied.

She smiled, pulling her brush out of her patent-leather backpack, and brushed through her beautiful, perfectly straight, glossy hair.

I totally lucked out in getting Lisha and Chelsea as my roommates, she thought to herself. *They are the best friends I've ever had. If it wasn't for Trash, I never would have met them. And I would never, ever betray Chelsea's secret, no matter what—*

Knock-knock-knock at the front door.

"Who is it?" Karma called cautiously. Antoine, the doorman, hadn't announced anyone through their staticky intercom system, but since Antoine often suffered from sleep deprivation caused by his staying up all night to bet on the trotters at Yonkers Raceway, no announcement wasn't proof of anything.

"It's Sky," the voice through the door called.

Sky Addison was one of the three guy interns who lived directly across the hall. Karma had pegged Sky as Keanu Reeves, since that's who he resembled. He was from Brooklyn, his dad was some bigwig in the TV tech union, and he was interested in following in his father's footsteps. He was also totally in love with Lisha, who, for some mysterious reason, treated him more like a brother than like the hot guy he was.

Karma quickly undid the multiple locks and chains on the door. "'Morning," she said.

Sky thrust a copy of the morning tabloid *New York Post* at her. "Read it and weep."

The headline was gigantic. WHO'S CHUTNEY? it proclaimed, above and below a full-page picture of Chelsea, on the set of *Trash,* standing next to Sela Flynn, the girl who'd taken the whole show hostage at gunpoint the previous evening. In the photo, Sela was pointing her gun directly at the head of Jazz Stewart, *Trash*'s nineteen-year-old host.

Karma read the photo caption.

All New York (and America) wants to know—who is Chutney Jennings, the teen intern who saved the day yesterday on *Trash*? *Trash,* America's hottest (and most outrageous!) teen talk show, got ratings that *beat* the O.J. Simpson verdict. But this was no stunt, this was live drama, and this Hilary Duff–esque girl brought

the deadly crisis to a safe conclusion. Single-handedly. So, who
is the girl to whom Jazz said, "Thanks, Chutney"?

"I wore my normal boring clothes," Chelsea told Karma as she
hurried into the living room, wearing a short, straight khaki skirt and
a sleeveless white blouse. "Oh, hi, Sky," she added, when she realized
he was there.

"You're famous," he said.

Karma handed Chelsea the newspaper.

"Oh, no!" Chelsea cried, staring at the huge photo of herself on
the front page.

"What is it?" Lisha yelled, running into the living room. She was
naked under a white towel. Sky's eyes lit up when he saw her.

"I'm on the front page of the paper," Chelsea moaned.

"Is that all?" Lisha asked. "I thought someone died."

"Are you wearing *that* to work?" Karma asked Lisha.

"I could," Lisha replied. "In our office, weirder is better." She turned
around and headed back to her bedroom.

"She looks great in a towel, you have to admit," Sky said with a
sigh, his eyes following Lisha down the hall.

I wish some guy would look at me that way, Karma thought. *Correction. Not just "some" guy. Some incredible guy. Sky is in love with Lisha,
and Chelsea's in love with one of Sky's roommates, Brad Pitt look-alike
Nick Shaw, and I'm in love with no one. Of course, there's someone at
Trash I have my eye on... not that he's ever noticed me at all.*

"How am I ever going to get out of here?" Chelsea asked, peering
out the window at the street below. "I'll never get through that gauntlet."

"Never fear, my diabolical little mind is working overtime," Karma
said. She ran to her room and came back with a shoulder-length,
wavy blond wig.

"You don't actually wear that thing, do you?" Sky asked, incredulous.

"You have a problem with a blond Asian girl?" Karma asked archly. "It's a kick. I happen to own a red curly wig with hair that goes down to my butt, too."

"So what do we do with the wig?" Chelsea asked. "Don't tell me you're going to wear it and pretend you're me, because it won't work."

At that moment Lisha came into the living room.

"Big duh, Chels," Karma remarked, imitating Jazz Stewart's favorite phrase. "Lisha will wear the wig and pretend she's you."

"I will?" Lisha asked, grabbing the wig from Karma.

"Sure," Karma said. She turned to Sky. "You and Alan and Nick take Lisha out the front. Pretend you're trying to hide her. They'll all think it's Chelsea and they'll follow you. Meanwhile I'll sneak Chelsea out the freight entrance in the back."

"You sure you didn't get good grades in high school?" Sky asked with a laugh. "Because you're kinda brilliant."

"Chelsea's the straight-A girl, Miss fifteen-sixty on her SATs. Me, I'm your basic underacheiver. Hey, I ought to tell the vultures downstairs all about your academic brilliance!" Karma teased.

"Don't you dare!" Chelsea cried.

"You know, it might actually work," Lisha said slowly, fingering the blond wig.

"It *will* work," Karma said firmly. "Oh, you guys will have to wear each other's clothes," she added, eyeing Lisha. "No one would expect America's Sweetheart, Chutney Jennings, to wear that slutty outfit."

Lisha looked down at her short midriff-baring black vest, and her black hip-hugger jeans. There was a slender gold chain wrapped around her taut, tanned waist, and you could see the heart-with-a-dagger tattoo on her shoulder.

"Ha," Lisha barked. "This could be the real Chutney Jennings— rock-and-roll downtown diva. I see recording contracts—"

"That idea has possibilities...." Karma mused.

"Y'all cut it out!" Chelsea admonished them. "You're supposed to be helping me!"

"You're right," Karma agreed. "I just get carried away when I hear a great money-making concept. So, you two go swap clothes," she urged them.

"And hurry," Sky added, "or we'll all be late for work."

"I must really love you," Lisha said, heading for her bedroom with the blond wig, Chelsea close behind. "I'm about to go out in public in preppie clothes from The Gap, just for you."

"And I'm about to go out on the street with a chain around my naked waist and my navel showing," Chelsea said with a laugh. "Gosh, my mama would just die!"

"Welcome to Sin City!" Karma called to them. "Now let's get this show on the road!"

TWO

"Hey, I heard how you got Chelsea to work today," a deep, male voice said to Karma as she sat in the tiny cubicle that passed as her office. "Impressive."

Karma looked up from the mountains of faxes and telegrams of congratulations to *Trash* that had come in from around the country.

It was Demetrius Raines, or as Karma thought of him, twenty-year-old Hispanic Olivier Martinez–look-alike-to-die-for-gorgeous-fellow-*Trash*-employee-to-whom-she-had-not-previously-said-more-than-a-dozen-words Demetrius Raines.

But even though Karma hadn't talked to him much, she had talked *about* him, prying information about him out of anyone and everyone. She knew he had worked as an intern on *The Real World* during the summer between his senior year of high school and his first year of college, and he was now a full-time employee of *Trash* and part-time student at the School of Visual Arts.

She also knew that more than half the women who worked at *Trash* were after him, and that he hadn't dated any of them. Which had led to a rumor that Demetrius was gay, but nobody knew for sure.

It's probably true, Karma mused. *No guy in New York City that gorgeous is ever straight.*

Demetrius had glossy brown hair that flowed halfway down his back, and golden skin stretched over six feet four inches of muscle. And Karma, who was never shy around anyone, could barely talk in his presence.

"Oh, hi there," Karma said, striving for nonchalance. "Word got around, huh?"

"It sure did," Demetrius replied, smiling at her. He strode over to her desk. "Hey, I don't think we've actually ever really introduced ourselves to each other. I'm Demetrius Raines." He stuck a large hand out for Karma to shake. She took it. Her own hand felt like a toy in comparison.

"Whose is bigger?" she joked, looking at her tiny hand, dwarfed in his. "I'm Karma, Karma Kushner."

Demetrius laughed. "I know," he said. "Word got around."

"Really?" Karma asked, flattered.

"I'm teasing you," Demetrius said.

"I knew that," Karma said with dignity.

"No, seriously," Demetrius told her, "I've been wanting to get to know you. And I was wondering . . . if you'd like to have lunch with me today? It's really nice out. We could walk over to Lincoln Center."

He just asked me out to lunch, Karma thought. *That did just happen. I didn't dream it.*

"I'll have to check my daily planner," she replied coolly. She closed her eyes for a moment. "Okay, it's fine."

Demetrius laughed. "It's all in your head?"

"Well, I could lie and tell you I'm booked for lunch for the next two months, but I'd rather just tell you the truth—I'd love to go to lunch with you!"

"Great," Demetrius said. "I just have to tell Paul in accounting that I won't be going for pizza—"

Paul in accounting. He had a date with Paul in accounting. Oh God, he really is gay, and he's just being friendly.

"Hey, listen, if you and Paul have a thing going, it's cool," Karma insisted. "I mean—"

"A 'thing'?" Demetrius repeated.

"I mean, if you're, like, seeing him, you could invite him along, too—"

Demetrius laughed. "Seeing him? As in, am I gay?"

Karma scrunched up her nose. "Too personal a question?"

"Karma, we work for *Trash*. If I were gay, it'd be a big yawn around here."

"True."

"But the fact of the matter is, I'm not," he said, his voice low and sexy.

"Oh," Karma replied. "Good."

He grinned at her. "So, is say, eleven forty-five okay for you? I've only got till twelve-thirty."

"Yeah," Karma agreed. "Sumtimes told me I could take lunch whenever I want today. I guess I'm in her good graces for a very short period of time." Sumtimes was one of Karma's many bosses.

"Well, then," Demetrius said, reaching over to tug gently on a lock of her hair, "I suggest we take advantage of it. See you."

He turned and walked out of Karma's cubicle, leaving her openmouthed with shock and glee.

"Karma Kushner," she said out loud to herself, "you are about to have lunch with Demetrius Raines. And he's straight! *Yes!*"

"So, what do you want for lunch?" Demetrius asked Karma as the two of them searched out a place to sit together on the short stone wall surrounding the immense fountain in the middle of Lincoln Center for the Performing Arts. It was another gorgeous, if hot, summer day, and the plaza was filled with people on their lunch break. "A knish?"

Karma shook her head. "The only knishes I eat are my mother's, which are to die for. Of course, she only makes vegetarian ones."

"Your parents are vegetarians?" Demetrius asked as they strolled slowly along.

"Big-time," Karma replied. "They don't even wear leather, much less fur. Now, me, I love a good cow sandwich."

Demetrius laughed. "Cow sandwich?"

"You know. Hamburger," she explained. "Or hot dogs—love those additives—I suck up every carcinogen known to humankind."

"So you want a hot dog, then," he guessed.

"Yeah, with everything," she agreed. "And coffee, please. I live for black coffee, the stronger, the better."

"Double espresso," Demetrius said, "coming right up."

He bounded off to get their lunch while Karma hopped up onto the ledge. She watched as Demetrius made his way over to the line of pushcart vendors who assembled every day along Broadway in front of Lincoln Center. From these pushcarts, you could buy basically anything you wanted for lunch, from a simple hot dog or hamburger, to a Middle Eastern falafel sandwich, to—and this astonished Lisha and Chelsea the first time Karma showed them—all manner of Japanese, Chinese, and even Thai food.

Six-foot-four Demetrius towered over most everyone else in the crowded Lincoln Center plaza as he walked.

He moves like a cat, Karma thought happily. *A really big cat.*

And every girl's eyes in this entire plaza are on him right now, she realized. *It's that Hispanic Olivier Martinez thing. With a little younger Antonio Banderas thrown in for good measure.*

Karma leaned back and closed her eyes, enjoying the feeling of the hot sun on her face. She thought about what Demetrius had told her as they'd walked along.

He told me that his mother is from Greece and his father is from

Madrid, Spain, she recalled. *They met on some Greek island, fell in love, and then came to New York in the early 1970s to open a business together.*

She opened her eyes again and watched Demetrius heading back toward her with their lunch. *So fine,* she thought to herself again. *So why did he ask teeny-tiny Asian moi to lunch?*

No, stop that, Karma, she scolded herself. *That is negative thinking. Just because this is America doesn't mean you have to be tall and blond to be a babe. He asked you to lunch because you are utterly fabulous.*

And maybe if I keep telling myself that, I'll actually start to believe it.

"One hot dog with everything, one double espresso," Demetrius said, handing her the food. He balanced a cardboard container of sushi on his lap and glanced at his watch. "But eat quick, because we've got to be back in the *Trash* can in twenty minutes."

"On a day like this there should be no time limits," Karma said, biting into her hot dog. "Mmmm, dee-lish."

"I agree," Demetrius said. "Let's stay outside and play all afternoon."

Karma eyed the sushi he dropped into his mouth. "You're eating raw fish."

"True," he replied.

"Do you know how polluted the ocean is? And fish go to the bathroom in it. So how can you eat the little darlings raw?"

Demetrius picked up another piece of sushi. "Because I like it," he said easily. He closed his eyes and put his face up to the sun. "Sun feels good, huh?"

"Yeah," Karma concurred. Demetrius was wearing a denim shirt with the sleeves rolled up, and she could see the massive muscles in his arms. "So, do you, like, live in the gym?"

He opened his eyes and looked at her. "What prompted that?"

"This," Karma said, putting her tiny hand on his biceps. "It's huge. And like a rock."

"I train two hours a day, every other day," Demetrius said. "It's not all that much. I guess I just have lucky genes."

"I'll say," Karma agreed, sipping her coffee. "So, between that, and *Trash,* and college, when do you breathe?"

"How do you know I go to college?"

Karma blushed. *Oops. I can't very well tell him I was pumping everyone in the office for information about him.*

"Oh, someone must have mentioned that you go to Visual Arts," she said casually.

"Yeah, it's true," he confirmed. "I'm pretty much booked up every hour of the day, except for Sundays. I like to spend Sundays with my family."

"Every single Sunday?" Karma asked him, surprised. "I'm always trying to figure out ways of getting out of going back to Long Island, myself."

"That's where you grew up?"

"What, the voice wasn't a clue?" Karma whined.

Demetrius laughed. "I have friends from Long Island, and they don't sound like you do."

"You hate my voice?" she asked.

"Not at all," he replied, popping another piece of sushi into his mouth. "Somehow on you, it's very cute."

"Oh, please," Karma groaned. "Don't call me cute. When you're as little as I am, you spend your whole life getting called 'cute.' "

"I'll keep that in mind," he said, smiling.

"So what's this Sunday thing with the family?" she asked.

"It's kind of a holdover, I guess, from when my parents lived in Europe," Demetrius explained, "and they'd spend Sundays with their families. Now, me and my younger brothers do it with them. Don't your parents mind that you don't want to come see them?"

"I suppose they do," Karma admitted. "And they're really nice, so now that you mention it I feel really guilty." She took another sip of coffee. "Mom and Dad are former hippies. They own a health-food store—which could explain my diet. And no, they aren't Korean. They're American. And Jewish. And no, I wasn't born here. They adopted me from Korea when I was a baby."

"That's cool," Demetrius said. "Although I wasn't planning to ask you about that now."

Karma cocked her head slightly in surprise. Demetrius was right. He hadn't asked her about how she, obviously Asian, had come to get the name Karma Kushner and live in the New York metropolitan area. She was just so used to fielding the question from nearly everyone she met that she'd automatically volunteered the information.

"Hey, check that guy out," Demetrius said, pointing to a guy dressed up as a clown who had just dipped a big bucket into the water in the fountain and was sneaking up on a group of maybe five businessmen who were standing together, munching hot dogs, about fifteen feet away.

Together, Karma and Demetrius watched as the clown stealthily approached the businessmen. All around them, office workers and secretaries who had seen the clown fill the bucket were pointing and tittering.

"I can't believe he's going to soak them!" Karma exclaimed.

As Karma and Demetrius watched, the clown tiptoed up to the businessmen and tapped one of them on the shoulder. The man—he was in his fifties—saw the clown, saw the bucket, and obviously put one and one together.

The clown held out his hand and made some motions as if to tell the businessmen that if they'd give him a dollar or two, he'd relent.

One man objected, but the others clearly talked him into it, and then they all took out dollar bills and handed them to the clown. The clown ostentatiously shoved the money into his giant back pocket, bowed to the businessmen, and took some exaggeratedly proud steps away from them. The businessmen all grinned, as did everyone else watching the clown.

"Fun way to earn a living," Demetrius commented admiringly.

"You think?" Karma asked.

"Sure," he said. "Making people smile is a great thing to do, don't you think?"

"He's not finished yet," she noted as she—and the crowd—watched the clown tiptoe like a cartoon character right back toward the businessmen, putting one finger over his lips ostentatiously, as if to tell the crowd not to make a sound.

"His bucket's still there," Demetrius said, chuckling.

The businessmen were back in deep conversation, absolutely oblivious.

"You think he's going to soak them anyway?" she asked.

The clown silently hoisted his bucket, stealthily approaching the knot of businessmen, until he was mere inches away. Then he brought the heavy bucket back along his side with two hands . . . and let 'er fly.

The crowd gasped.

A bucketful of multicolored confetti flew into the air, and then landed, like snowflakes in a winter storm, on top of the businessmen.

The crowd cheered, and the businessmen, once they'd figured out what had hit them, grinned good-naturedly, brushing confetti out of their hair. The clown bowed to the applauding crowd, and then put his bucket on the ground, reached into his big back pocket, and dropped the five dollar bills into the bucket.

Demetrius was the first person in the crowd to reach into his own wallet and take out a dollar for the clown, then several other people followed suit.

"I love New York," he said with a grin to Karma, after he'd put the dollar in the clown's bucket. "Where else can you see something like that?"

"Not on Long Island, that's for sure," she said.

"You really hated it there, huh?" he asked as they dropped their paper into the nearest litter basket.

"Well, I wouldn't call it hate, exactly," Karma said. "But it was so not me. I mean, I didn't fit in with the beauty-queen-cheerleader crowd, and I didn't fit in with the Birkenstock-sandals-let's-overthrow-America crowd, either."

"So who did you fit in with?"

"Oh, with my sister Jewish Asian-Americans who love designer fashions and worship the stock market," she quipped.

Demetrius laughed. "Do you really play the market?"

"Yeah," she said. "It's fun. My dream is to make a million and own a network before I'm thirty. What's yours?"

"Smaller. To own my own restaurant," he said.

"For real?" she asked.

"Yeah," he replied. He held out his hand. "Come on, I'll tell you about it on the way back to the *Trash* can."

"Deal," Karma said, and she put her hand in his.

And even though she only came up to the middle of his chest, and his hand could wrap around her hand three times with space left over, it felt terrific, perfect, and absolutely right.

"So," Karma said to Lisha and Chelsea, "we walk back to *Trash* together, talking about everything, and he's holding my hand, and I've got a stiff neck now from looking up all the way to talk to him."

"What's this restaurant he wants to open?" Chelsea asked.

"Spanish-Greek," Karma said, reaching for a tangerine from the small bowl of fruit Chelsea had put on the table. "He wants to call it 'Hola Zeus!' "

"That means 'hello, Zeus!' in Spanish," Lisha said.

"I know," Chelsea told her. "I took Spanish in high school."

It was later that evening, and Karma, Lisha, and Chelsea were all home, after work, in their apartment. Karma had a rare night off from Jimi's, so she was enjoying it with her friends. The guys from the apartment across the hall were supposed to come by, too, at any minute. And so far, to everyone's relief, the phone had only rung a couple of times since they'd come home from work. Karma, on "Chutney's" behalf, had turned down the offer from both TV shows. The crowd outside their apartment had diminished to a few straggler print reporters, and no one had noticed when the three of them had snuck in the freight entrance.

As Karma had predicted that morning, most of the media had moved on to the next sensation, in this case the Pope, who was fly- ing in to Newark Airport in New Jersey the next day.

"I guess your fifteen minutes is just about up," Lisha told Chelsea.

"Fifteen minutes?" Chelsea echoed.

"She's quoting Andy Warhol," Karma explained. "He was this pop artist—hung out with the rich, beautiful, and heavily drugged during the disco scene. He said everyone in the world would be famous for fifteen minutes."

"Well, I'd rather be famous for saving Jazz's life than for . . . you know," Chelsea said.

Than for being the daughter of a mass murderer, Karma filled in mentally. But she didn't say anything. She just nodded at Chelsea in sympathy.

"You know what amazes me?" Lisha said, peeling a tangerine. "How everything really *is* trash. I mean, what's permanent anymore, anyway? Not fame, not love—"

"Hey, wait a minute," Karma protested. "Love can be permanent."

"Oh, right," Lisha snorted. "Half the marriages end up in divorce. Every guy I've ever known has cheated on his girlfriend—"

"Did your boyfriend cheat on you?" Chelsea interrupted.

"I didn't mean me, necessarily," Lisha said carefully.

"Yes, you did," Karma said. "Some guy hurt you bad, is my guess."

"Welcome to the real world." Lisha blew her feathered bangs out of her eyes. "That's what guys do."

"Oh, come on, you don't mean that," Chelsea chided her.

"I do, too," Lisha maintained. She looked over at Karma. "If you want my advice, don't get too crazed for Demetrius. Because no way is a guy who looks like that going to be any good for you."

"Well, I just totally don't believe that at all," Chelsea said.

Lisha gave her an arch look. "No? Take Nick, the Canadian slacker, for example. You're crazed for him, right?"

"Kind of," Chelsea said.

"He's gorgeous," Lisha said. "He likes you, but he wants to be free to see other girls, too. So . . . I rest my case."

"But you're the one who told me I shouldn't be so quick to expect a big commitment from him!" Chelsea reminded her.

"Because I don't want you giving him all the power in the relationship," Lisha explained.

Chelsea popped a section of tangerine in her mouth. "Too complicated for me. All I want is love and happily-ever-after with one great guy. I don't think that's too much to ask." She turned the conversation to Demetrius. "So, you really like him?"

"I don't know him very well," Karma admitted.

"But you like him," Chelsea coaxed.

"Yeah," Karma said with a grin. "I mean, I haven't even kissed him yet. It was just lunch—"

"There'll be others," Chelsea assured her. "The two of you make such a cute couple!"

"Pardon me while I barf up my sleeve," Lisha said.

"Something really, really awful must have happened to you in Europe," Chelsea began. "And that's why you—"

Just then the guys gave the special quadruple knock they'd recently worked out for the two apartments so they wouldn't constantly have to call out "Who's there?"

"I'll go," Chelsea volunteered, scrambling to her feet. She opened the door and let Alan, Nick, and Sky in. Alan and Sky hugged her, and Nick gave her a soft kiss.

"Wow, great hello," she murmured.

He kissed her again.

"No more mush!" Lisha commanded.

"I love mush," Karma said. Smiling, she eyed the three guy interns.

How did we get so lucky? she thought. *They are really nice, terrific guys. Nick's just like Brad Pitt, except with slacker clothes and a slacker attitude. And Alan, who wants to be a writer, could pass for Johnny Depp. Can you imagine having a father who owns a National Football League franchise, and not being interested in football yourself? He's so crazy about Chelsea, but Chelsea is too in love with Nick to see it. And Sky, he's such an all-American guy, and it doesn't hurt that he looks like Keanu Reeves. So why is it that Lisha treats him like he's her brother, and—*

"Hey, guys," Sky said, pulling Karma out of her musings. He tossed a videotape up and down in the air. "Guess what I've got, right in my hot little hands."

"Our tape!" Karma cried. "Oh-mi-gawd, it's our tape!"

"We haven't watched it yet, either," Alan told them.

"So, stop talking and pop it in!" Lisha exclaimed.

"*My TRASHy Summer* rules!" Alan laughed.

As Alan put the tape into the VCR, Karma thought about what they were about to see.

The six friends had a big secret project. They were making a clandestine videotape that they called *My TRASHy Summer*. Disgusted by the low-down dirty tricks that *Trash* played on its guests and by the sordid shows that Jazz and her staff concocted, they had decided to make, in secret, a video film that would document their summer as interns and blow the cover off the hottest show on television.

To kick off the *My TRASHy Summer* research, Sky, whose dad was an official in the TV technicians' union, had borrowed a tiny video camera and hidden it in the office of Roxanne Renault the day before. Roxanne, also known as Bigfoot because of her nasty personality and gigunda feet, was one of the show's young producers.

So what if she looks like Gwyneth Paltrow with red hair, Karma thought. *She's still a total bitch.*

"We won't have anything if Bigfoot's dawgs get in the way of the camera," Karma joshed, settling down on the rug to watch the tape.

Everyone laughed.

"Here goes," Sky said, pushing the ON button. The TV screen was illuminated.

"She's not at her desk," Chelsea said, noting the camera focused on an empty desk.

"What do you want?" Sky said, settling back against the couch where the six of them were sitting. "The tape runs for four hours."

"Fast-forward it, man," Nick suggested.

"Good idea," Lisha echoed.

Sky fast-forwarded the tape for several minutes.

"Something's happening," Chelsea said. "Slow it down."

The tape changed to normal speed.

Bigfoot was at her desk now, going through some papers. The phone rang.

She stopped and picked up the phone.

"Renault," she said.

"Turn the sound up," Alan suggested to Sky, who then fiddled for a moment with the remote control.

"Okay," Bigfoot said, and then listened as someone was talking to her.

"Right now?" Bigfoot asked.

"What's she talking about?" Chelsea asked Karma.

"Who knows?" Karma hissed.

"Okay, I'll be ready," Bigfoot said, and then put the phone down. Then she sighed.

Moments later, the door to her office opened, and the camera moved to it automatically, following the sound.

"Barry!" Chelsea said. "It's Barry!"

Barry was Barry Bassinger, the slight, brown-haired senior producer of *Trash*, a guy in his mid-thirties who had actually put the moves on Chelsea not long after she began work at the show. She hadn't realized what he was doing at first, but when she did, she turned him down, flat.

"What's he doing in there?" Lisha wondered out loud. "I wonder if—"

"Shhhhh!" Karma shushed.

Barry strode right over to Bigfoot at her desk, leaned down, and gave her a passionate kiss.

"Bingo!" Lisha laughed. "I called it! She's doing him."

"Yowza," Alan murmured as Barry's hands went to the buttons on Bigfoot's blouse, unbuttoning them one by one by one, until the blouse opened up to reveal that Bigfoot hadn't worn a bra to work that day.

"God, how scummy are these people?" Chelsea asked rhetorically.

"I guess we don't need to guess why Bigfoot has so much power anymore, do we?" Lisha snorted.

"I think," Karma said as a torrid scene unfolded on their television set, "that *My TRASHy Summer* just earned itself an NC-17 rating." She turned to her friends. "I also think this is only the beginning of exposing them for the lowlifes that they really are."

THREE

"Good morning, Roxanne," Karma said, trying to keep a straight face and mostly succeeding. "How's your, uh, foot feeling?"

"Foot? What foot?" Bigfoot laughed as if she had made the world's greatest joke.

"Your foot that was shot," Karma explained carefully.

Bigfoot grinned hugely. "To tell you the truth, with these pain pills, I don't even know I have feet!" She laughed again, throwing her head around. "I am so funny, aren't I?"

"Oh, yeah," Karma answered. "I'm falling on the floor, here."

Those pain pills she's on must pack a serious punch, Karma thought. *She is in la-la land.*

Of course, I'd be on pain pills, too, if I'd been shot in the foot one day and had returned to work two days later. She probably hurried back to work because she's scared Jazz might learn she's not as important as she thinks she is.

Or because Jazz, who demands total loyalty, might find out that she's doing it with Barry Bassinger.

It was the next morning, two days after Sela Flynn shot Roxanne in the foot on live television. Now that foot—the right one—was propped up on Roxanne's desk, inside a humungous cast. In fact, from where she sat, Karma could barely see Bigfoot's face, because the cast mostly blocked her view. She glanced at the clock on the wall; it was barely nine-thirty in the morning.

Karma edged her chair unobtrusively a bit to the right so she'd have a better view of her boss.

"So, how long do you have to wear the cast for?" she asked politely.

"Eight weeks, at least," Roxanne replied. "The bullet broke a bone."

With your dawgs, Karma quipped to herself, *I can't imagine how the bullet could have missed a bone.*

"Well, it's a, uh . . . nice cast," she said lamely.

"I'm having cast covers made to match all my outfits," Roxanne said.

"Oh, yeah, great," Karma replied.

"But enough about me," Roxanne said blithely, her voice really weird from the pain pills. "How's the ol' research going?"

"Research?"

"Kids of mass murderers," Roxanne explained. She got a glint in her eye that told Karma that even if she were on pain pills, the idea of the *Trash* story about the children of mass murderers was enough to temporarily focus her mind.

The week before, Bigfoot had assigned Karma a heavy chunk of the research for her pet show idea. So far they'd decided to do a segment on the teen children of postal workers who'd killed their colleagues, and on the teen son of the guy in Chicago who killed and then ate all those people.

Meanwhile Karma was supposed to be researching the case of a certain Charles Kettering, who had shot everyone in a Johnson City,

Tennessee, Burger Barn eighteen years earlier. And then was stabbed to death by his wife.

Kettering's daughter would now be eighteen.

Of course, what Roxanne didn't know was that Chelsea Jennings, whose last name had been changed from Kettering, was the kid that Roxanne wanted on *Trash*.

And she's not going to find out, either, Karma thought.

"Pretty good," she reported. She pushed a pile of papers and clippings over at Bigfoot, who picked up a couple of them and leafed through them.

"How about the rich lawyer—what's his name—who shot up the Burger Barn?" Roxanne asked suddenly.

"Kettering?" Karma asked innocently.

"Yeah. Find anything?"

Yeah, sure, Karma could almost hear herself saying to Roxanne. *I know just where she is. Her name is Chelsea Jennings, although you tend to call her Chutney, and she's just down the hall. You want me to go get her for you?*

"Gosh, Roxanne, not really," she lied. "His family just seemed to, uh, drop off the face of the planet."

Roxanne tossed the papers Karma had given her across her desk, scattering them everywhere. "Kettering is my number-one priority, dammit! Do you understand me?"

"Number-one priority," Karma repeated.

"I just said that!" Roxanne yelled.

"I think maybe your pain meds are wearing off," Karma suggested.

"When I want your opinion I'll ask for it!" Bigfoot thundered. "Get me my pain meds!"

"Where are they?" Karma asked.

"On top of the filing cabinet," Roxanne said petulantly.

Karma crossed the room and brought Roxanne the vial of pills. Bigfoot swallowed two without water, then leaned toward her summer intern.

"Where were we?"

"Uh, Kettering."

"Right," Roxanne said. "Find his kid. I want her found and I want her found yesterday!"

Then, tired from the effort, Bigfoot sat back in her chair and closed her eyes.

Later Karma couldn't explain what made her say what she then said. If Roxanne hadn't been so spaced out on pills, she might not have suggested it.

But, she thought later, *it was a brilliant stroke.*

"Roxanne?" she said. "I've got an idea about how to find Kettering's kid."

Bigfoot looked up with interest.

Karma looked at her directly. "Let me get another one of the interns to help me," she suggested. "Like...Chutney Jennings. She's perfect. She's from Tennessee, just like Kettering's daughter. They'd be the same age. They'd talk the same way...probably. She could help me with the interviews and—"

"Fine," Bigfoot said dismissively. "If you want Chutney to help you, you tell her I said she should help you."

"Gee, thanks, you're a peach," Karma whined sweetly.

"I know I am," Bigfoot snapped. "Now get out of here."

Karma got up.

"Oh, one more thing. Call Barry and tell him I want to have lunch here in the office instead of going out. My foot is killing me."

"Well, the meds should kick in soon," Karma said. "And I'll call him."

"Tell him to order deli," Roxanne continued.

And here I thought the two of you would be too busy with each other to actually eat, Karma thought with a smirk.

"Deli. Got it," she said.

Roxanne reached for the telephone and punched in some numbers. "Oh, Karma?"

"Yeah?"

"Now your butt and Chutney's butt are both on the line." Roxanne smiled sweetly. "Deliver for me on this, okay?"

"You got it," Karma said cheerfully.

"Or else," Bigfoot added, her eyes glittering malevolently. "Or else."

"Oh, shish kebab," Karma muttered. It was her favorite anticurse, trying as she was to cure herself from swearing.

By mistake, she had pushed the MESSAGE button on the console in front of her. She sighed. Once the intro message got started, there was no way to cut it off until it was over. So she listened to it again.

"Hey, this is Jazz," Jazz's voice said coolly. "Thanks for calling 1-900-I'M *TRASH*! That's right, it's your chance to be with me, Jazz, live on TV, coast to coast, and now in Holland, Argentina, and Australia, too! Just tell me why you should be on my show, your TRASHY show idea. Leave your name, address, and phone number, too! If you're under eighteen, get your parents' permission—big duh. This call costs you just a buck ninety-nine a minute. Go for it at the tone!"

Sicko-Central, how do I love thee? Karma thought glumly.

It was later that morning, and Karma was sitting in Sicko-Central. Sicko-Central, which was what Lisha had nicknamed the room, was the control room for the special 1-900-I'M TRASH phone number. The 900 number allowed *Trash* viewers, for the price of a dollar ninety-nine a minute, to call in to the show with their best show ideas.

All the interns spent an inordinate amount of time listening to and transcribing the thousands of phone calls that poured in every week. They dutifully wrote down each idea, no matter how weird, and passed them on to the senior producers, usually either Lydia Sumtimes (whose first name changed every week—last week she'd been Julia) or to Bigfoot Renault.

They were also supposed to highlight what they considered great show ideas, which was exactly where Bigfoot had found her kids-of-mass-murderers show concept.

For the moment Karma was at Sicko-Central alone. Chelsea was out picking up Barry Bassinger's dry cleaning and special-order Jamaican coffee beans, and Lisha was out walking Jazz's two matching dalmatians. As for the guys, Karma had no idea, though she had seen Nick disappear into Jazz's private office as soon as he'd arrived that morning.

And I'd thought she'd broken it off with him, Karma had thought. *Of course, it might be nothing. Jazz might not even be in there. I hope it's nothing....*

Karma reached over and pushed the PLAY button.

"Hi, Jazz!" said a male voice. "This is Kenny Bright, I live in Mankato, Minnesota, and I really want to talk to Chutney Jennings. Hey, Chutney, did anyone ever tell you that you look just like Hilary Duff? You could be her sister! I'd love to get a date with you. Maybe Jazz can set it up or something. If you like farmers, that's great, because my dad raises corn and I sometimes help him. I'm eighteen, and here's my number. I'd sure like it if you'd call sometime."

Karma typed quickly as she listened. It was the third call that morning asking for a date with Chelsea. For the moment it seemed as if Chelsea was as popular as Jazz herself, who'd received only one marriage proposal so far that morning.

Karma went on to the next call.

"Hello, *Trash,* this is McCloud Crichton, the rock-and-roll manager. Listen, one of of my clients—I'm sure you'd recognize who—wants to book Chutney Jennings to be in their next video. They think she looks just like Hilary Duff, and Hilary is asking megabucks these days. Listen, these guys won't take no for an answer. My butt is on the line here! So if you have a shred of human dignity, you'll return my call. Please?"

So what do I do with this one? Karma wondered as she transcribed the call. *Who knows? But I'll jot the number down for Chelsea, in case she wants to make some extra money. Although I don't think rock videos are exactly her thing. Maybe I'll give the number to Lisha, instead.*

Karma went on to the next call. For a change, it wasn't about Chelsea.

"Hello, *Trash,* here's why I should be on your show," another male voice said. "Because I have a foolproof method of ripping off the phone companies, and I want to give it to every teen in America. But I'll only appear with a mask and a wig on. If you're interested, call my—"

A pair of hands covered Karma's eyes. Big, sexy hands.

"Your hand is bigger than my entire face," Karma said, turning around.

Demetrius grinned his easy smile and looked down at Karma. She felt even tinier than usual, with him standing and her sitting way, way down below him. She was looking straight at his belt buckle.

"That's better than the greeting you gave me last night," he told her, sitting down next to her. "Though not by much, I'd have to say."

"Uh, Earth to Demetrius," Karma said. "I didn't see you last night."

"Oh, come on," he said.

"Come on, what?" she asked, bewildered.

Demetrius laughed. "One of the many things I like about you is your sense of humor. But you could have said hello to me last night."

Karma blinked slowly. "This is a very strange conversation, big guy. Let's review, shall we? We had lunch together yesterday. It was really fun. But last night I was at my apartment giving myself a manicure. See?" She held out her freshly manicured pale nails.

"Pretty," Demetrius commented. "But obviously it didn't take you all night."

"Why am I not tracking this conversation?" Karma asked.

He laughed again. "You're good."

"True," she said. "I always agree when someone says I'm good, but I still have no idea what you're talking about."

"Last night?" Demetrius asked, his face amused. "I came up behind you on Broadway, about nine, when you pretended you didn't know me? Ring any bells?"

"Not a one," Karma replied.

"In fact, you told me that you're used to being approached by guys, but usually they take no for an answer."

Karma reached out and touched his hand. "That wasn't me. I wasn't on Broadway last night."

"Come on...."

"I swear!" she insisted.

"Right," Demetrius said. "I believe you. No, I don't. If it wasn't you, who was it?"

Karma shrugged. "You know us Americans," she quipped, "we all look the same."

Demetrius cocked his head at her. "Is this for real?"

"Yeah. It must have been some other Asian-American fox with a great personality and a fantastic sense of fashion."

"Hmmmm," Demetrius mused. Clearly he still didn't believe her. "Well, what I wanted to ask you last night was when I could see you again."

"You're seeing me now," she told him with a grin.

And to think I was afraid to even open my mouth around him, she thought. *Now I'm even flirting with him!*

"You know what I mean," Demetrius said with a look of exasperation.

"Is this a charming Greek-Spanish way of asking someone out?" Karma asked.

"Something like that," he said.

"Here in America, we usually call a person up on this thing called a telephone," she explained.

"Yeah, but somehow asking you here in Sicko-Central seems more appropriate," he said with a laugh.

"How did you know we call it that?" Karma asked.

"Nothing stays hidden for long here at the *Trash* bin," Demetrius replied.

Ha. Shows what you know, Karma thought. *We're making the exposé video of all time about this place, and it's going to stay a big, fat secret until we're ready to show it to the world.*

"Does it ever bother you, working here?" Karma asked suddenly.

"Where did that come from?"

"All thoughts are connected in my head," Karma explained. "So, does it?"

"I don't think this is the time or the place to talk about it, actually," Demetrius said. "I mean, we're on their dime, right?"

"You have a point."

"Anyway, are you trying to change the subject? Wasn't I just asking you out?"

"No, you were asking some other girl who looks like me," Karma said.

Demetrius groaned and started to get up, but Karma stopped him. "Wait, wait, I'll be serious. Yeah, I'd love to go out with you. I consider it my patriotic duty, what with tomorrow being the Fourth of July and everything."

Demetrius looked at his watch. "I've got to get back downstairs. We're having a meeting about new show warm-ups. So, how about tonight?"

"Tonight?" Karma asked. "Isn't that a little rushed? What if I already have a date?"

"Do you?"

"No," she admitted.

"Good," Demetrius answered, shaking his long hair off his face. "That means yes?"

"You know Jimi's?" Karma asked.

He nodded. "Who doesn't?"

"I work there until one-thirty."

"How about I meet you after work and we go to Around the Clock?" Demetrius asked. "Over on Third Avenue?"

"I know it," Karma said. "Their coffee is beat but it's a date. It *is* a date, right? Or is it too late?"

"Hey, tomorrow's a holiday," he said easily. "And I have a feeling you're worth waiting for. I would have asked you last night on Broadway, if you'd been kind enough to acknowledge that you knew me."

"Mistaken identity," Karma suggested. "Maybe you've been reading too many mystery novels or something."

"I don't read mysteries," Demetrius said. "I think you were just playing hard to get."

"Moi?" Karma asked. "I'm telling you, it wasn't me."

"Oh yeah, right," Demetrius said with a laugh as he headed for the door. "Believe me, Karma, there couldn't possibly be two of you in this world." He waved.

"I'm going to take that as a compliment," Karma called to his retreating form.

She put her hands behind her head and smiled. "Yeah," she said out loud to the empty room. "Like I would really play hard to get with Demetrius Raines."

She pushed the ON button on the computer and got ready to type. But a niggling thought stayed with her.

If he really likes me so much, how could he possibly mistake someone else for me? she thought. *How?*

FOUR

"Thirty-six hours *Trash*-free!" Sky chortled as he put his video camera down on the girls' living-room table. "Enjoy it!"

"We will," Karma said, "although some of us have to work tonight and tomorrow night."

"Some of us, meaning you," Alan said. "Two full-time jobs. You are the hardest-working human I know."

"Not to mention the best-dressed," Karma added.

It was about eight o'clock that evening. Nick, Sky, and Alan had come over to the girls' apartment because Sky had some filming that he wanted to do for their video project, *My TRASHy Summer*. All the girls were there, too, and Karma didn't need to leave for Jimi's for another hour. Then, the rest of them were going together to see Vanessa Carlton, who was doing a concert at the Beacon Theater on Broadway.

Nick and Alan had brought over a couple of take-out Ray's Original extra-cheese pizzas, and they put them on the living-room coffee table. Everyone reached for slices.

"Karma's got a date with Demetrius later," Chelsea told the guys as she bit into her pizza.

"Down, Belch," Chelsea said as Nick's dog jumped up and down, begging for pizza.

"Go, Karma," Nick said, giving Belch a slice of pepperoni. "A date with the guy they call Mr. Studly!"

"Who calls him that?" Chelsea asked. She sat cross-legged on the floor, her head leaning against Nick's knees.

"You should sit in the control room sometime," Sky replied, licking some tomato sauce off his finger. "They've got nicknames for everyone."

"So what's mine?" Lisha wondered.

"My lips are sealed," Sky said. He sat on the rug next to her.

"Come on, I really want to know," Lisha pressed, nudging her shoulder into his.

"Okay, you asked for it," he said with a sigh. "It's . . . Luscious Lisha."

"*Luscious Lisha?*" Lisha repeated incredulously.

"Take it as a compliment," Sky suggested.

"Yeah, I'll try," Lisha said dubiously.

"Demetrius is a really nice guy," Alan told Karma. "He's one of the few people at *Trash* who doesn't seem to belong there."

"So how'd you get the date?" Nick asked, his voice teasing. Belch jumped up and licked his face, and Nick scratched the dog behind his ears.

"Overwhelming charm and scintillating personality," Karma said, chewing her pizza. "Oh yeah, plus exotic beauty and hypnotic appeal as a sex goddess."

She padded to the refrigerator and took out a pitcher of lemonade. "Lemme ask you guys something. If you were, like, really into a girl, do you think you could mistake someone else for her?"

"No chance," Nick said, looking down at Chelsea, who smiled up at him.

"Why do you ask?" Alan asked her.

"Demetrius saw someone on Broadway last night he seriously thought was me." Karma poured glasses of lemonade and handed them out.

"Does the guy wear glasses?" Sky suggested, reaching for another slice of pizza.

"Not that I know of," Karma replied.

"I'm sure it was an honest mistake," Chelsea said.

"Yeah," Karma said, sipping her lemonade, "I guess."

"So, Sky," Lisha asked, reaching for a second slice of pizza, "what's this video thing you want to do tonight?"

"I want to try some segments in the video that we'll call 'My *Trashy* Moment,' " Sky explained.

"They'll be stand-ups," Alan chimed in, "where we each get to talk about something trashy that happened to us at *Trash* recently."

"Or something like that," Sky continued. "Or something we heard or saw."

"I've got a million *Trashy* moments," Lisha said.

"We all do," Sky agreed. "That's the whole point."

"Hey man, let's go do it on the roof," Nick suggested, getting up from the couch. His hair was loose, and he looped it behind his ears. "Belch misses that clean Canadian air, eh, Belch?"

Belch barked.

"Honestly," Chelsea said, getting up from the rug, "sometimes I think you love that dog more than anyone or anything else in the world."

"Hey, man's best friend," Nick said easily.

They all picked up some of the pizza and followed the seldom-used staircase one flight up, to the door that opened onto the roof of their apartment building.

"Whoa, *quel* atmosphere," Lisha said dryly, almost tripping over a broken beer bottle.

Sky caught her arm. "You okay?"

"Sure," she replied, brushing her hair off her face with a shake of her head. "But it sure is trashy up here."

"*Trashy,* perfect," Sky said with a laugh.

"Wow, the view is incredible," Chelsea breathed, staring out at the brightly lit buildings of midtown Manhattan.

"You ain't in Tennessee anymore, sugar," Nick said with an exaggerated Southern accent.

"Hey, don't rag on Tennessee," Chelsea told him, defending her home state.

"You're right," Nick agreed. "After all, it did produce you."

Chelsea laughed and kissed him, which made Belch bark.

"Do you think Belch is jealous?" Karma asked.

"I think that you guys need to lock lips a lot less," Lisha said.

"Or we need to lock lips a lot more," Sky suggested hopefully.

Lisha just gave her patented Lisha shrug, and reached for a slice of the now-lukewarm pizza that Alan was carrying.

Karma shook her head. *What is it with this girl?* she wondered. *Someone must have broken her heart big-time. And I hope someday soon she trusts me and Chels enough to tell us what happened.*

"Okay, you *Trashites,*" Sky called to them, hefting the camera on to his shoulder. "Who's gonna go first?"

The other five gathered around him.

"How about you?" Chelsea suggested. "I'll film you."

"Yeah, go for it," Nick urged him.

Sky shrugged, and handed the camera to Chelsea. "You know how to use this, right?"

Chelsea nodded. "You showed us over the weekend. It's the same camera?"

"The same."

"Hey, over here," Alan called, pointing to a spot near the edge of the roof of the building. "You'll get the best background."

They all moved over to where Alan was pointing. He was right. If

Sky stood at that spot and Chelsea aimed the camera at him, there'd be a terrific mass of tall buildings behind him.

"Take a piece of pizza with you," Karma told Sky, who was looking at Lisha. He turned a little guiltily toward Karma.

He's crazed for her, Karma thought with a sigh. *Completely and totally crazed. And she barely pays attention to him. And he's such a sweetheart. And so is she, really, it's just that she's so secretive and... scared. Yeah, that's it. She's scared. But I don't know why.*

Chelsea focused the video camera on Sky's handsome face, which was clearly illuminated by the setting sun. "Go for it," she said.

"I'm Sky, tech intern," Sky said self-consciously.

"Loosen up, man," Nick urged him.

"Yeah, relax," Lisha added.

"Thank you, friends and critics," Sky said with a half grin.

"You look great on camera," Chelsea told him as she looked through the lens.

"Okay, let's see, it's July third, and here's my most recent *Trashy* moment," Sky said. "Today I was supposed to talk to a group of teen guys who claim they get drunk every single night. Serious alcoholics, right? So I was supposed to make them feel comfortable. All these guys were underage. So I'm getting Cokes for them, like a good little intern, and Bigfoot—that's Roxanne Renault—tells me that the Coke bottles have been filled with dark ale, and a hidden camera is going to record how they react."

"That's sleazy," Alan said disgustedly.

"And stupid," Lisha put in. "Obviously they would know that they were drinking ale and not Coke."

"But, see, I was supposed to keep insisting that it was Coke," Sky continued. "Then, day after tomorrow, they'll have these same guys back and they drink plain Coke, and I'm supposed to tell them it's heavily spiked with vodka. It's a big mind game."

"Stupid," Nick commented, standing next to Chelsea.

"Not to mention illegal," Chelsea added. "Who's next?"

Lisha calmly slid into the spot where Sky had been standing. She took a contemplative bite of her pizza and then brushed her hair off of her forehead.

"Lisha Bishop, intern," she said calmly. "*Trash*iest moment of the day? This big guest for today's show made a pass at me in the green room."

"But it was a woman!" Chelsea exclaimed.

"No kidding," Lisha agreed. "She wrote this tell-all book about her experiences as a teen hooker in L.A. and how all these movie stars were her clients. I told Barry Bassinger, senior producer, that she was coming on to me big-time, and he asked if he could film it for *Trash*."

"Ugh," Chelsea grunted. "Next?"

Alan jumped in and bowed to the camera. "Alan Van Kleef, wannabe writer of dubious talent, the only Texan who doesn't like football, and *Trash* intern." He smiled self-consciously. "So, my *Trash*y moment of the day: reviewing videotape of the last year's shows, looking for the best punch thrown by a female guest at a male guest, and finding videotape of Jazz doing an impromptu striptease for the camera guys. And I do mean guys. There are exactly zero female techs working at *Trash*. Next!"

"Karma Kushner, nice Jewish girl from Long Island, *Trash* intern," Karma intoned. "*Trash*iest moment of the day? I was supposed to take notes during this senior staff meeting, and they were laughing at the photos sent in for the So You Want to Be Made Over into a Teen Slut Contest. It was so disgusting."

"Why were they laughing?" Sky asked.

"You know, making fun of them, putting them down," Karma said. "Like one was fat, and one had bad skin, and they dished on them mercilessly."

Nick walked into the spot as Karma exited. "Yeah, Nick Shaw, intern," he said in his usual laid-back tone. "My *Trash*iest moment? Having to clean up Jazz's office after Her Trashiness's dalmations had another of their accidents this morning. They've got some kind of intestinal thing—disgusting in a major way."

Oh, so that's what Nick was doing in Jazz's office, Karma thought. *I'm so glad he isn't two-timing Chelsea. Boy, before Jazz broke up with him she would never have made him do something menial like that. I wonder if he's sorry.*

"Her Trashiness," Lisha said. "I like that."

"I guess it's my turn," Chelsea said, looking for someone to hand the camera to. Nick took it from her as she walked over to the edge of the building. Nick focused on her.

"Chelsea Jen—"

"Chutney," Alan called out, interrupting her. "Get it right. Your name is *Chutney.*"

"Chelsea," Chelsea repeated firmly. "My *Trashiest* moment today? Waking up this morning, knowing I had to go to a job where I don't respect the people or the work they do."

"So why do you work there, then?" Sky called out to her.

"Sky!" Alan objected.

"No, this is good for the video," Sky insisted. He turned back to Chelsea. "Why do you work there? Why do you take a stipend from them? Aren't you being kind of hypocritical?"

"I'm working underground," Chelsea said firmly. "I can't change anything if I quit."

"Good for you!" Karma exclaimed.

"Hey, we need to get Belch on tape," Nick said, aiming the camera at his dog. "Belch, belch!" he commanded.

Obediently, the little dog let out a loud burp.

"Good dog!" Sky said with a laugh.

"Hey, man, I told you, never call him the D-word," Nick said. "He doesn't know he's a different species."

"Hey, look, someone on the next roof has one of those giant bubblemakers," Lisha said, pointing.

Huge bubbles were drifting through the air toward them. It was almost dark now, and they could barely make out two figures on a roof across the street, blowing three-foot transparent bubble circles into the fading evening sky.

"Great bubbles!" Karma called over to them.

"Yeah!" a voice called back. "Don't you just love New York?"

No one answered. They just smiled happily and watched the bubbles floating upward, against the spectacular New York skyline.

"So," Karma asked Demetrius as soon as the waitress had brought them their dessert, "how come a guy who looks like you doesn't have a girlfriend?"

Demetrius, who'd been drinking a glass of iced tea, actually spit up.

"Have you ever heard of the word tact?" he asked her, reaching for a napkin to wipe his face and grinning at the same time.

"Yeah," Karma said. "My mother told me once that I don't have much of it."

"I'd like to meet her sometime," Demetrius said. "I bet we have a lot in common."

"I'm so sure," Karma snorted. "Since you're both forty-year-old former hippies with gray hair down to your waists, and firm believers in past-life regression."

It was two-fifteen A.M., and Karma and Demetrius were sitting together at a table in Around the Clock, the very hip twenty-four-hour-a-day restaurant/bar located just off Third Avenue near St. Mark's Place, in Manhattan's oh-so-trendy East Village.

Even though it was past two in the morning, the place was hopping. In fact, a line had begun to snake out the door and up the street. The crowd was mostly young, and very, very hip.

Jimi's had closed at one-thirty—early, by New York standards, but the owners of the club had turned that into a selling point for the young clientele. Demetrius had come to the club at about one and patiently waited at the juice bar until Karma closed up. Then they'd walked around the corner to Around the Clock, where the hostess, who knew Karma, immediately gave them a table.

The two of them fit right into the downtown crowd. Karma had changed from her hot-pink Jimi's T-shirt into a tiny, lime-green, open-crocheted, and cropped silk T-shirt by her favorite designer, Todd Oldham, over her faded jeans. Her shoes, three-inch-high platforms from the sixties with plastic goldfish swimming in the Lucite plat-forms, had been a real find at a thrift store on St. Mark's Place. Demetrius was wearing a simple black T-shirt and black jeans.

Very simple and very hot, Karma thought, eyeing him. Per usual, he was getting a tremendous amount of attention from all the girls in the restaurant, just as Karma had noticed girls checking him out in Jimi's.

And he's with me, she thought, with some astonishment. *He could be with any of them, but he's with Karma Kushner. And if it's only be-cause of some Asian-chic thing, I will personally kill him.*

"So," she said, taking a sip of her coffee, "do I get an answer?"

"Doesn't all the caffeine keep you up?" Demetrius asked her curi-ously.

"I'm always up," Karma said. "It's a perpetual state with me." She took another swallow. "So?"

"So what?"

"I'm waiting."

"Yeah," Demetrius said, scratching his chin. "Your question. Actually your question makes me . . . kind of uncomfortable."

He took a quick swallow of his fresh-squeezed juice and looked at Karma. "The truth is that I've only had one girlfriend in my life," he admitted. "We were together a long time. Her name is Mindy Moscow, and we broke up about six months ago."

"*The* Mindy Moscow?" Karma asked, astonished. "No way."

She had heard of her. Everyone had heard of Mindy Moscow.

Mindy was this very hip alternative singer-songwriter, who accom-panied herself on piano. She was rapidly acquiring a die-hard New

York following, even though, to Karma's knowledge, she didn't have a record deal yet.

And she's very pretty, Karma recalled glumly. *A waif. Long, straight blond hair. Big eyes. Very Kate Moss.*

"That's her," Demetrius confirmed. "We actually met in sixth grade. I fell in love with her when she dumped a Coke on my head. And we were together ever since."

"How romantic," Karma said skeptically. "And that's it?"

"That's it," Demetrius replied.

"I'm finding this hard to believe," Karma said, draining her coffee. A young waitress with a nose ring and buzz cut poured more as she hurried by the table.

Demetrius shrugged. "You can't judge a book by looking at the cover. I wouldn't want to have a million girlfriends. For one thing, there are scary diseases going around. And for another, well, who'd want to wake up next to someone new every morning?"

"About two thirds of the male population of the planet," Karma pointed out. "And quite a large portion of the female half, too, come to think of it." She took a spoon and stirred her coffee contemplatively.

"So, how about you?" Demetrius asked. "Which portion of the population do you fit in with?"

"Well, after I was crowned homecoming queen at South Long Island High School, I decided to devote my life to dating football players," Karma responded blithely.

"Seriously," Demetrius said.

"Seriously, huh," Karma echoed. "Well, I dated in high school. You know, the Asian-chic thing." She studied his face for a reaction.

"What?" He looked confused.

"Like, it's very cool to have an Asian girlfriend these days. Next year it'll probably be cool to have a Native American girlfriend, but for the last few years I have been *sooooo* popular."

Demetrius eyed her contemplatively. "They think it's cool to date you?"

"Yeah," Karma said. "Like, all okay-looking Asian girls look alike, like we're interchangeable or something."

"That's ludicrous," Demetrius commented.

"You think so?" she asked bitterly. "I mean, look at you. You thought some other teeny little Asian girl walking down Broadway last night was me."

"It *was* you!" he insisted.

"Well, see, this is exactly my point," Karma said, running her finger around the rim of her coffee cup. "It *wasn't* me. Which means even sensitive, politically correct you can't tell us apart."

Demetrius shook his head. "Not fair. It was a legit mistake."

"Whatever," she said. "The point is, once I figured out I was the trophy of the moment, I didn't date very much."

"Well, a lot of girls would think it's cool to go out with me because I'm quote-unquote ethnic," Demetrius said with a shrug. "It's all the same stupid thing."

"Yeah, stupid," Karma agreed, relieved.

Demetrius drained his juice and stifled a yawn.

"You're tired?" she asked.

"I'm not used to these kinds of hours," he admitted. "Not like someone I know."

"Then let's get the check," Karma suggested. "You live uptown?"

"Near Columbia University," Demetrius told her. "We can share a cab?"

Karma nodded and scanned for their waitress. As she did so her eye caught the two girls at the next table staring at Demetrius. She gave them a little wave with her fingers to show them that she saw them, and they audaciously waved back at her.

"Why don't they just come over here and throw themselves at your feet?" she wondered out loud.

Demetrius looked over at the table, and the girls waved to him, cocking their heads at him to invite him over. He smiled and shook his head no.

"That stuff happens to you all the time, doesn't it?" Karma realized.

"Not all the time," he replied, clearly embarrassed.

The waitress brought the check, Karma and Demetrius split it, and the two of them went out to Third Avenue to hail a taxicab uptown.

"So, how come you asked me about whether I had a girlfriend?" Demetrius asked as they slowly strolled along the sidewalk toward the street.

"You can't be too careful," Karma said lightly.

"True," he answered. "It's a drag to get your hopes up if a person you like is already involved with someone else."

"Who said I was getting my hopes up?" Karma asked quickly.

"I didn't mean you," he said gently. "I meant me."

Demetrius stopped, turned, and gently lifted Karma up, as if she were no heavier than a piece of paper. He carefully set her down on a foot-high stone ledge in front of the hardware store they were passing.

"Now we're the same height," he whispered to her.

"Almost. Hey, I could get used to this," Karma replied.

"And this," Demetrius said softly. Then he leaned forward, and kissed Karma so sweetly, his long hair brushing against her long hair, beautiful waterfalls rippling against each other in the moonlight.

She pulled her head back and looked into his eyes.

"Nice," she managed, feeling giddy with happiness. "But since you only ever had one girlfriend, how'd you learn to kiss like that?"

"We practiced a lot," Demetrius admitted. "But I'm not thinking about her right now."

"Me, neither," Karma agreed.

And then, wordlessly, with the sounds of downtown New York at night buzzing around them, their lips met again.

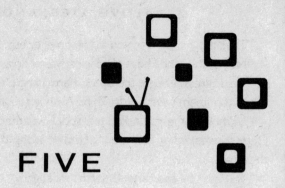

FIVE

"Hey, yo, dude, look!" A sixteen-year-old guy wearing a Bergen Catholic High School varsity football jersey with the sleeves cut off, a backward New York Giants baseball-style cap, and plain blue jean cutoffs nudged his bud. "It's Chutney, that babe from TV! Hey, it's Chutney!"

His friend swiveled around, bumping into one of the people in the crowd who was pressed up against him; the person barely seemed to notice the impact.

"Far out," his friend said. He wore an identical outfit to his bud's. "That's definitely her." He waved in Chelsea's direction, then cupped his hands around his mouth and called, "Yo, Chutney! Did anyone ever tell you that you look just like Hilary What's-her-name? I love you!"

Other people standing on the roadway also noticed Chelsea, and started to point, stare, and wave.

"Nice tackle on the crazy chick, Chutney," one guy called out. "You should try out for the Jets!"

"She's too good for the Jets!" someone yelled. "She should *coach* the Jets!"

A whole group of people cracked up.

"This is so embarrassing," Chelsea muttered to her friends.

"It's the price of fame," Karma said to her as they weaved their way through the enormous crowd that had gathered on the closed-to-traffic FDR Drive, overlooking the East River.

"Chutney! I love you!" another guy yelled, his hands placed dramatically over his heart.

"Wave," Lisha instructed her friend. "You're a star, girl."

"But I don't want to be a star," Chelsea protested.

"Yeah, yeah, you want to fall in love and live happily ever after," Lisha said, "but meanwhile, wave."

Chelsea managed a sick wave to the high-school guys, who made kissing noises in her direction. The people standing around them laughed some more.

"I should have worn a mask," she lamented.

Nick, who had been a few paces behind the girls, talking to Alan, with Belch jumping around at their heels, caught up with her. "Don't get bent out of shape," he advised, draping his arm around her shoulders. "I mean, think about it—you're a hero."

"I'm not—" Chelsea began.

"Chutney! Hey, Chutney! Can I have your autograph?" a teenage boy yelled from the crowd.

"Forget the autograph, I want you to have my baby!" his buddy cried dramatically.

"No, *my* baby!" another guy yelled.

"No, mine!" shouted another.

"Oh, this is ridiculous," Chelsea said, burying her face in Nick's shoulder.

"You might as well enjoy it," Karma said.

"But she doesn't enjoy it, that's the whole point," Alan interjected. As usual, he was acutely sensitive to Chelsea's feelings.

"Excuse us, excuse us," Karma said loudly, weaving her way through the thicket of bodies on the roadway.

"They should just leave me alone," Chelsea said crossly. "Can't they just get a life?"

"Chutney, sweetheart, you *are* their life," Nick teased, but Chelsea didn't even crack a smile.

She's acting weird, Karma thought. *Something's wrong. I just know it. And it's not just all these guys glomming onto her.*

It was the evening of the Fourth of July, almost time for the enormous fireworks display that was shot off every year from barges anchored in the East River, under the sponsorship of the famous department store Macy's. Karma had returned to the apartment at three o'clock in the morning, but it had taken her until five to actually fall asleep.

She kept replaying those two amazing kisses from Demetrius over and over again in her mind.

And the third one, she remembered, *just before I got out of the taxicab. The third one.*

She'd awakened at around one in the afternoon, had a very, *very* late breakfast, and then spent the rest of the afternoon in Central Park with her buds—everyone but Sky, who was attending a family picnic in Brooklyn.

I can't believe I asked Demetrius to come to see the fireworks with us, Karma thought, *and I can't believe he said yes.*

She looked down at the outfit she'd chosen—a daisy-patterned minidress from Mary Quant—very retro—with lace-up yellow sandals with her usual three-inch heels.

I hope Demetrius likes the look, she thought, *'cuz it's always weird the first time you see someone after you've gotten romantic with them.*

She looked over at Chelsea and Lisha. Chelsea had on jean overall shorts over a white T-shirt, and Lisha wore hip-slung black jeans and a black crocheted vest, with nothing underneath.

The three of us couldn't look any more different from each other if we tried, she thought, smiling to herself.

"Man, it is so crowded," Nick said as a big guy bumped into him without offering an apology.

"I can't see a thing," Karma whined, trying to make herself taller. She gave a glum look at the enormous crowd.

I told Demetrius we'd be right at Thirty-fourth Street, she thought. *But he'll never find us in this mob.*

And it *was* a mob. It was a spectacular summer night in New York City—the temperature about eighty-two degrees, the evening sky cloudless—with an easterly breeze off the nearby Atlantic helping to keep the crowd cool. So the throng for the fireworks display was enormous. Judging from the people who were set up all around with barbecues, lawn chairs, and binoculars, many of them must have arrived just after the normally busy highway had been closed to traffic early that afternoon.

"Whoa, Chutney!" a young guy yelled. "Hey, let's get her autograph!"

"She's popular," Nick said to Karma as the same group of high-school-age guys pushed their way over to Chelsea, this time holding out pieces of paper for her to autograph.

"Very," Karma agreed, leaning over to see what Chelsea, though very embarrassed, was writing on the scraps of paper.

"Hey," one guy said, looking at the autograph. "This says Chelsea Jennings."

"My name is Chelsea," Chelsea told him.

"Yo, Ricky," the guy called to one of his friends. "She says her name is Chelsea, not Chutney."

"It's Chutney," Ricky called back. "I saw it on TV!"

Chelsea sighed, and took the next scrap of paper from the next guy. On it, she wrote CHUTNEY JENNINGS in big letters.

"If you can't beat 'em, join 'em," Karma said to Nick.

"I think she looks cute surrounded by guys," Lisha added wickedly, eyeing Nick. "Don't you?"

"Sure," he said easily, shaking his hair out of his eyes.

"You're not jealous?" Karma asked him as her eyes halfheartedly scanned the crowd, looking for Demetrius. It was basically a lost cause. Even with her three-inch heels, she was so short that she could barely see three people away, let alone spot Demetrius in the press of the crowd.

"Jealous of what?" Nick asked.

"Her fan club," Lisha said. "Those guys would give anything for a date with her."

"They don't even know her," Nick replied. "Besides, jealousy is a total waste of time."

"Hey, let's go look at the water," Alan suggested to Lisha. "Too many people here to think."

"Fine with me," Lisha agreed. She turned to Karma. "We'll be right back."

"You'll never find us again," Karma objected.

"We'll find you, we promise," Alan said.

"If you see Demetrius, tell him where I am," Karma called to them as they wended their way through the crowd.

Meanwhile even more guys came up to Chelsea as word spread through the crowd that the heroine of the *Trash* hostage crisis was in their midst.

"Honest to God, that doesn't bother you?" Karma asked Nick.

"Hell no," Nick said. "She's the one with the problem."

"I have a feeling you're about to tell me what her problem is," Karma said, folding her arms.

"Down, Belch!" Nick commanded as Belch jumped up against his leg. He turned to Karma. "I told Chelsea that Jazz invited me to be her escort to the Rock of Ages Awards in three weeks," he explained.

"Yeah, and...?" Karma prompted.

"And she just stood there and *breathed* at me."

Bingo, Karma thought. *That's it. That's why Chelsea's acting weird. She's mad at Nick, again, and she's also mad probably because he doesn't even care that right now she's surrounded by guys.*

"It's no big thing," Nick continued, "but try to tell Chelsea that. Maybe you should—"

Boom!

The first big blast of the fireworks display was set off from the barge directly in front of the friends.

All around them, people turned up the portable radios they all seemed to have brought, and simultaneously tuned to one of the New York City rock-and-roll stations. That station was playing rock music synchronized to the fireworks.

Boom! Boom! Boom! Boom! A fantastic array of fireworks exploded overhead.

Boom! Boom! Boom! Boom!

Gee, it's so much fun to be short, Karma thought as she craned her neck, trying to see something—anything—overhead. *There are so many advantages, like, like...*

She couldn't think of a single one as the fireworks continued to blast off.

Boom! Boom! Boom!

And then, suddenly, she felt herself lifted up, up, up, as if she were one of the fireworks rockets blasting toward the sky.

"Hey, what the—" she began.

"Tall guy, at your service," a deep, amused voice said.

Demetrius.

When she looked down, she was on Demetrius's broad shoulders, and she could see just fine.

"This is an interesting greeting," she called down to him. "How'd you find us, anyway?"

Boom! Boom!

"I followed the crowd to Chelsea," he told her, motioning with his head to his right. Karma followed with her eyes.

Chelsea was surrounded by about twenty guys, all of whom seemed to be content to stand near her as she watched the fireworks.

Boom!

Karma planted a big kiss right on the top of Demetrius's head as spectacular fireworks went off above her.

"Nice," he called up to her. "What did I do to deserve it?"

"I just realized," she called back. "Thanks to you, these are the first fireworks I've ever actually been able to see!"

"So, what have you got?" Bigfoot asked pointedly, her cast-enclosed foot up on her desk in the identical place it had been two days before. The only difference was that now the cast was draped in orange material, which matched Roxanne's sixties retro orange-and-hot-pink minidress.

Karma and Chelsea sat opposite her, each angled so that they could see past the enormous cast.

It was the day after the fireworks display, and they were back at *Trash.* The two of them had been summoned to Bigfoot's office as soon as they arrived, but Jazz's newly hired male secretary, a Jamaican guy named Winston who had dreadlocks down his back (and who, Karma had heard through the grapevine, had gone to Harvard) had kept them waiting in her outer office while she finished a phone call. Winston was doing double duty and working for both Jazz and Roxanne while Roxanne's foot was out of action.

"How's your foot feeling?" Karma asked, stalling.

"It hurts like hell and the doctor won't give me any more pain meds," Bigfoot snapped. "You have any other stupid questions?"

"No, no, I'm all out of stupid questions," Karma assured her.

"I could get any drug I wanted off the street and self-medicate," Roxanne went on, "but I need a clear head at this job."

"Right," Chelsea agreed.

"I didn't get where I am by being drugged out of my mind," she added superciliously.

No, you got where you are by doing Barry Bassinger, senior producer, Karma thought.

Her face, however, betrayed nothing.

"So don't waste my time," Bigfoot continued. "Report."

"Well, yesterday was a holiday," Chelsea reminded her, "and it was only the day before that you told Karma that she should have me be involved in—"

A rubber band came zooming across Bigfoot's desk, scoring a direct hit on Chelsea's chest. Karma and Chelsea both looked at Bigfoot.

"Did you just fire a rubber band at me?" Chelsea asked, shocked.

"Oh, lighten up," Roxanne grumbled. "It wasn't a spit wad." She moved her leg around on the table. "So, Chutney, let's review, shall we? What's your job here at *Trash*?"

"Intern," Chelsea managed to say.

"How many people do you think applied for your job, the job *we* gave you?" Bigfoot continued.

"Lots," Chelsea said.

"That is why you don't *take* holidays!" Bigfoot yelled. "You are an intern. Interns do not take holidays! Am I understood?"

Yes, sir, very well, sir, aye-aye, sir! Karma wanted to say, but she was busy thinking.

"Yes," Chelsea replied, gritting her teeth. "Whatever you say."

"You can always quit," Roxanne goaded her.

Chelsea looked her straight in the eye. "You'd like that, wouldn't you?"

Karma flashed Chelsea a look that said shut up, but Chelsea's eyes were glued to Bigfoot's.

"You think I'm not a big Chutney fan, is that it?" Roxanne asked, her voice dripping venom.

"I don't think you like me very much, no," Chelsea admitted, trying to control her shaking voice.

"Well, guess what?" Roxanne asked. "I don't have to like you. And I could care less if you like me. I'm your boss. So if you want to keep your internship, you'll do what I say, when I say it. Got it?"

"Got it," Chelsea said, her voice low.

Roxanne turned her attention to Karma. "I hope you have something to say for yourself."

Well, here goes nothing, Karma thought. *No reason to have Bigfoot ticked with both of us.*

"Uh, I did some research yesterday," she improvised, making it up as she went along as she saw Chelsea's eyes widen in surprise. "It was mostly on the telephone, to England and to . . . other foreign countries!"

"Yes, go on," Bigfoot said, wincing as she repositioned her foot.

"Well, I think I found her," Karma said. "Kettering's daughter, I mean."

Chelsea's jaw fell open in shock, and Karma prayed that Bigfoot didn't notice.

"Where?" Bigfoot demanded.

"I understand from my sources," Karma said slowly, giving herself time to think, "that the girl and the mother moved to . . . Australia! That's right. Australia. Uh . . . years after the incident! They changed their name, and the teen daughter is now a student at . . . the University of . . . Melbourne!"

"Isn't she a little young to be going to college?" Bigfoot asked sharply.

Karma froze momentarily. "She's . . . supposed to be, like, supersmart," she managed. "She was valedictorian of her high-school class. And then she . . . uh . . . skipped a grade."

"How come no one ever found her before?" Bigfoot demanded.

Karma didn't dare look over at Chelsea. "I, uh, found the mother's death certificate on the Internet," Karma invented. "She just died. The mom, I mean. And of course we aren't going to want to dig this girl up in Australia, right? But there was this other mass murderer—the one in Florida who killed the people from the tour bus—and he has a son who is—"

"Time out," Bigfoot interrupted. "I'm still on the Australia thing. It could be quite the juicy story. The kid is real smart. No one else has been able to track her down. And now she's an orphan. I'd say if this works out, we're going to have ourselves—I mean *I'm* going to have myself—quite a story, won't I?"

Karma snuck a peek at Chelsea. Her face was the color of chalk.

"Well, what are you two waiting for?" Bigfoot asked. "The Pope? He left New York early this morning. Get to work! Bring me this girl!"

Karma and Chelsea walked out of Bigfoot's office together and into the main hallway. As soon as they turned the corner, Chelsea whirled on Karma.

"Have you completely lost your mind?" she exploded.

"Well, I—" Karma began.

"She's in *Australia*? Her mother just *died*? You found the information on the *Internet*?" Chelsea yelped.

"I was trying to steer her away from—"

"Hi, interns," Sumtimes sang as she hurried by, her shaved head wreathed with a garland of pink flowers that matched the pink in her short, crocheted jumpsuit. "What are you guys doing?"

"Just came from a meeting with Roxanne," Karma reported.

Sumtimes waggled her fingers at them and sailed on by. As soon as she was out of earshot, Chelsea turned back to Karma. "How? How could you tell Roxanne that—"

Karma quickly pulled an out-of-control Chelsea into the nearby ladies' room. She took a quick look under the stalls to see if anyone was in them. No one was.

"Okay, now we can talk," Karma said. "The walls have ears in the *Trash* bin."

"I just can't believe you—"

"But think about it, Chels," Karma said to her friend. "Better to give Bigfoot something and then not have it work out, don't you think?"

"But she wants to bring Kettering's daughter in from *Australia!*" Chelsea cried. "All you did was whet her appetite!"

"I have a plan," Karma said defensively, hoping she could invent one really fast.

"What is it?" Chelsea asked dubiously.

"We lead Bigfoot on this wild-goose chase," she improvised.

"And then?"

"And then...the girl just...isn't available. Or something. It'll buy us time," she explained. "And then finally it'll be too late for Bigfoot to do anything. Gawd, I hope there really is a University of Melbourne."

Chelsea winced. "You don't *know?*"

"I guessed," Karma said brightly.

Chelsea folded her arms. "This won't work."

"It will," Karma insisted. "Now, you've got to play along. Okay?"

Chelsea sighed and bit her lower lip. "Okay," she said finally. "But if Roxanne finds out that this whole thing was a smoke screen—"

Just then Barry Bassinger's new secretary, who looked like a brunette version of Anna Nicole Smith, walked into the ladies' room.

"Hi, y'all," she said to them in a thick Texas twang, going straight to the mirror to check out her makeup.

"Hi, Olyvia," Karma and Chelsea said at the same time.

They both knew the conversation was over. And they both knew as well that if Bigfoot found out that Karma had been leading her down the garden path with her made-up story about Charles Kettering's daughter, life at *Trash* for the two of them was going to be very, very short.

SIX

Karma let herself into the apartment, unlocking all three locks on the door, working methodically from top lock to bottom lock.

"How did you find me?" Lisha was saying into the phone, her voice low and intense.

Karma tiptoed into the kitchen, an open space off the living room divided by a counter and some high stools, and poured herself a cup of coffee from the Mr. Coffee.

"Well, my mother shouldn't have given you my number," Lisha snapped into the phone. "She doesn't know you for the true low-life scum-sucking dog turd that you are."

Who could she be talking to? Karma wondered. *Whoever it is, she hates them a lot.*

"No, I don't want to see you," Lisha continued. "I mean it, Harley. If you show up here, I'll call the police and your butt will be in prison so fast... or did you forget that you told me you're wanted by the FBI?"

Wanted by the FBI? Karma thought. *Lisha knows a criminal who's wanted by the FBI?*

"Look, forget you have this number, Harley," Lisha said, pacing with the phone. "Forget you ever knew me. In fact, you can just drop dead." She slammed the phone down and stared at it, breathing hard.

"Just a wild guess on my part," Karma said, sipping her coffee, "but I have a feeling you don't like whoever you were just talking to."

"Forget it," Lisha snapped.

"Forget that you know a criminal named Harley?" Karma asked.

"Used to know," Lisha corrected. "As far as I'm concerned, he doesn't exist anymore." She turned to Karma, her face tense. "Listen, if he ever calls here, tell him I moved, okay?"

"Yeah, but who is he?" Karma was dying to know.

"Someone dangerous," Lisha said.

Karma put her coffee down on the counter. "Like, how dangerous is dangerous?"

"Happy Fifth of July," Chelsea called out to them as she came into the living room from her bedroom. She saw the intense looks on their faces. "What happened?"

"Some felon just called for Lisha," Karma reported.

"If a guy named Harley ever calls here, I moved," Lisha told Chelsea.

"Who is he?" Chelsea asked.

"I don't want to talk about it," Lisha stated firmly.

"But—" Chelsea began.

"Please, you guys," Lisha interrupted. "Just . . . just leave it alone."

Karma and Chelsea exchanged looks. Finally Karma shrugged. "Okay," she agreed. "But we care about you, you know. I mean, if there's anything we can do—"

"Thanks," Lisha said, finally allowing herself a small smile. "I appreciate it. And I'm fine. So let's just change the subject."

"Your mother called," Chelsea told Karma. "She and your dad are in the city. They want to stop by and take you out to dinner."

"Did you tell them not to?" Karma asked, plopping down into the overstuffed chair. "Did you tell them that I took the A-train subway and never returned?"

"Nope," Chelsea said. "I told your mom you'd be home in five minutes. Which you are."

"Gee, thanks so much," Karma said, slipping off her chunky heels. She picked up the clicker and turned the TV on, to the PBS *Nightly Business Report*. She studied the stock ticker running across the bottom of the screen for a moment. "Cool."

"What's cool?" Chelsea asked.

"I bought call options on Compaq last week," she said. "The stock's up three points today. Anyway, did they at least say when they're coming? I doubt it, that would be a departure for them."

"They're in the neighborhood, so they said they'd come in a half hour," Chelsea informed her.

"They're probably out buying vitamins," Karma commented. "They only buy vitamins in the city at one special store in SoHo. Don't ask me why."

"They said you're probably abusing your body with pizza and MSG-laced Chinese food—" Chelsea said with a grin.

"I live for additives," Karma agreed, her eyes still watching the stock report.

"Your mom also said there's a new health-food restaurant on Ninth Avenue they wanted to check out," Chelsea went on. "You can call them on their cellular if you want, your mom said."

"Sounds like the two of you had a delightful little chat," Karma said, muting the sound on the TV.

"She sounded really nice," Chelsea commented with a shrug.

"If they're here in the city," Lisha asked Karma, "who's running their store?"

"Some huggie-veggie person or other wearing drawstring pants and Doc Martens," Karma replied. "Put up a health-food store, they come around like flies. It's really amazing."

"So, we get to meet your parents, finally," Lisha said, sitting on the couch.

"They're unforgettable." Karma lifted one foot and rubbed it gingerly. "Someone tell me why footwear can't be great looking *and* comfortable?"

"You should just get over this high-heel thing of yours," Lisha advised. She picked up the clicker for the TV and changed to MTV. "Try flat boots. Much hotter, and your feet won't kill you at the end of the day."

"In flat boots I could play the eighth dwarf in the Snow White story," Karma said tartly.

"Oh, come on," Chelsea chided her. "You're so cute! It doesn't matter that you're short!"

"And it doesn't matter that Kevin Costner is going bald," Karma said, "since he wears a rug."

"Kevin Costner wears a hairpiece?" Chelsea asked, shocked.

"You're so naive." Karma grinned. "It's kind of sweet."

"Hey, look," Lisha said, her eyes on the TV. "Our Fearless Leader is in this video."

Lisha was right. The video was for a new female rap artist named Wet Tee, who was performing her number in front of a giant, blown-up, movie-screen-sized photo of Jazz Stewart.

"Jazz is a publicity goddess," Karma stated.

"I wonder how she managed that," Chelsea mused.

"Demetrius told me," Karma said. "He said Wet Tee just came up to Jazz while she was walking her dalmatians and asked her, and Jazz said yes."

"That's amazing," Lisha said, admiration in her voice. "I mean, I must open a hundred mailed requests like that every day."

"Demetrius told me—"

"That's two sentences you've started with those magic words." Lisha smiled. "Sounds like someone has fallen for Mr. Studly big time."

"Yeah, I like him," Karma said casually.

"Like him?" Lisha repeated. "No, I like you. You want to jump his bones."

"Not, like, instantly." Karma stuck to her guns.

"Yeah, you never go for it on the first date!" Lisha teased.

"Frankly, I've never gone for it at all," Karma admitted.

Lisha's jaw dropped open. "You're kidding."

"No," Karma confessed. "I've never had a really serious boyfriend, so who was I supposed to 'go for it' with?"

"Me, neither," Chelsea admitted. Her eyes got dreamy. "Maybe I was just waiting for Nick."

"Meaning you love him again?" Karma asked.

"Meaning he drives me crazy but I want him bad," Chelsea said with a sigh. "Is that sick?"

"Wait a second," Lisha said, bringing her knees up to her chin. "Are you two honestly telling me that you're both still virgins?"

Karma and Chelsea nodded.

"We could put the two of you on Trash!" Lisha said. "Only no one would believe it!"

"It's not like it's a crime," Karma protested.

"I'm not saying that," Lisha explained. "It's just...unusual. Anyway, I'm giving up sex, myself."

Karma looked at her. "Forever?"

"Who knows?" Lisha said. "Let's just say right now I am not into guys."

"Does Harley have something to do with this?" Karma guessed.

"I don't want to talk about it," Lisha said quickly.

"Lish, we're your best friends," Chelsea said. "I told you the biggest, darkest secret of my life—"

"I know," Lisha said. "I'm just...I'm not ready." Her eyes searched Karma's and Chelsea's. "I'm not blowing you guys off, I swear. Please don't be mad at me."

"We're not mad, we're insanely curious," Karma admitted. She reached into her backpack, pulled out a candy bar, unwrapped it, and took a huge bite.

"Won't you spoil your appetite for dinner?" Chelsea asked.

"That's the idea," Karma replied, washing the candy bar down with some coffee. She turned to Chelsea. "Are you really ready to have sex with Nick?"

"Maybe." Her arms wrapped around her waist, Chelsea shook her head. "Did you know he's taking Jazz to the Rock of Ages Awards?"

"He told me," Karma admitted, finishing her candy bar. "He says it's no biggie, and that you're jealous for no reason."

"So I'm jealous," Chelsea confessed. "But only because I care about him so much."

"He cares about you, too," Karma assured her.

"You think?" Chelsea asked. "Then why's he going to that thing with Jazz?"

"Because Jazz asked him to," Lisha interjected. "Of course, she might have asked Demetrius first, and he might have said no."

"Did she?" Karma asked, concern in her voice.

Just then, the doorbell buzzer sounded. Karma went over to the wall speaker, through which Antoine the doorman announced that she had some guests. Per usual, she could barely make out what he was saying.

"Yeah, send them up," she told Antoine, pushing the talk button as she did so. Then she turned back to her friends. "Prepare yourselves," she said ominously.

A few moments later the apartment doorbell rang, and Karma looked through the peephole.

"It's them," she announced, unlocking the three locks and opening the door.

Karma's parents stood in the doorway.

"Hi, Mom. Hi, Dad," Karma greeted as each of them embraced her. "Come on in."

"Hey, sweetie," Karma's father said, his voice warm and loving.

"I'm so glad you could come out with us!" Karma's mom told her. "We haven't seen you in, what, two weeks?"

Marty Kushner was in his late forties, very slender and tall—maybe six-foot-one, with wire-rimmed glasses that framed his blue eyes. He had a scraggly brown beard, and long, scraggly brown hair that fell to his shoulders. He was wearing a Filipino dress shirt and jeans. On his feet were open-toe water-buffalo-style sandals.

Wendy Kushner had the same nonapproach to style as her husband. About five-four, with long, straight, gray hair, she wore a peasant-style embroidered white blouse with a gauzy multicolored skirt. On her feet were sandals identical to her husband's.

"Mom, Dad," Karma said, "I want you to meet my roommates, Chelsea Jennings and Lisha Bishop."

"Great to meet you!" Karma's dad went over and shook the girls' hands. "I'm Marty Kushner, Karma's dad." Karma's mom waved to the two other girls.

I just said that, Karma thought.

"And I'm Wendy Kushner," her mom said. "Please call me Wendy."

"And me Marty," Marty said. "I don't answer to anything else, really."

"You answer to 'hey, you, I want seconds on tofu!' " Karma corrected dryly.

"Well, yeah, that, too, but never to you!" Marty smiled good-naturedly.

Dad may look strange, Karma thought, *but he's always had a great sense of humor. Mom, too.*

"It's really warm out, huh?" Wendy said, lifting her gray hair to fan the back of her neck.

My mother screams "makeover," Karma thought for about the millionth time in her life. *She could look just like Anjelica Huston. But she'd never do one for as long as she lives. She's going to dress like this when she's a great-grandmother.*

"Sit down," Lisha offered. "Can I get you anything to drink?"

"Everything we have has artificial everything in it," Karma warned them.

"Oh, we're fine," Marty assured them as he and Wendy sat down on the couch. "So, what do you girls think of working on *Trash*?"

"It's ... interesting," Chelsea said carefully.

"It's trashy," Lisha added.

"Well, you wouldn't have become a national heroine without it, would you?" he asked Chelsea, a broad grin on his face.

Chelsea smiled ruefully. "I guess not."

"You know, Wendy and I knew Andy Warhol when he was still alive, and I remember when Andy made that remark about how everyone would be famous for fifteen—"

"Dad, don't you think we'd better go?" Karma asked, edging toward the door.

"Don't you want to put on some shorts?" Wendy asked her daughter. "It's hot outside."

"I'll change later," Karma said, wanting to get her parents out of the apartment as quickly as possible. She glanced at Chelsea and Lisha, who didn't even notice her.

They're charmed by my dad! Karma realized. *He looks so geeky, but this always happens.*

"So, what were you saying about Andy Warhol?" Lisha prompted her father.

And the next thing Karma knew, Wendy and Marty were engaged in a deep discussion with Lisha and Chelsea about what it had been like in New York in the late 1960s, when they'd both been students at Columbia University during the student uprisings.

It took Karma forty-five minutes to get them to go to dinner, and even then Lisha and Chelsea didn't want them to leave. In fact, the four of them got along so well that before her parents left, they invited Karma to bring Chelsea and Lisha out to their house on Long Island that Sunday.

"And Karma," Wendy added warmly to her daughter, "you bring anyone else you want, too. Those guys from across the hall you told us about, and anyone else, too."

"Sure," Marty said. "We'll have a barbecue!"

Karma groaned. "You haven't lived till you've enjoyed barbecued tofu."

"Sounds good to me," Chelsea said.

Lisha nodded in agreement. Both girls knew that Karma's parents lived just minutes from Atlantic Beach, which they'd heard was a great beach, and they were both up for a good beach day.

"Are you sure?" Karma asked them dubiously.

They were sure.

It was a date.

Maybe it'll be fun, Karma thought warily. *We can fill up on junk food before we go. Now all I have to do is to decide if I have the nerve to invite Demetrius.*

"Your friends are great," Wendy said to Karma as she, her daughter, and her husband all strolled on West End Avenue toward the new health-food restaurant about twenty blocks south.

"Aren't they?" Karma agreed with enthusiasm. "Am I lucky or what?"

"They're lucky, too," Wendy said, hugging her daughter's shoulders quickly.

"They're so interested in what it was like for us when we were teens," Marty chimed in. "You don't find that very often. So many kids today are completely apolitical. They only care about making money."

"You mean like me," Karma said sharply.

"Not at all, honey," her father assured her. "You have a spiritual side. I should know. I'm your father." He smiled lovingly at her.

A middle-aged couple walking their poodle glanced at Karma's parents, who both had their arms around their daughter. A look of mild surprise crossed their faces, then they looked away.

My parents are really nice, Karma thought, *and I really love them a lot. But it's the same thing every time we come into the city.*

People stare at us.

And not because I'm an Asian girl with two Caucasian parents. This is New York City, so no one really cares about that.

It's that people are thinking, "What're those two people dressed like that doing with a girl dressed like her?"

"So, anyone else you want to invite Sunday?" Marty asked.

"Maybe," Karma said slowly.

"A guy?" her mother asked impishly.

"Yeah. His name's Demetrius."

"Is it serious?" her mother asked.

"No, it's not serious, and no, he's not Jewish," Karma said with sigh.

"I wasn't even going to ask!" her mother protested.

"You thought it, though," Karma replied.

"Guilty," Wendy said with a grin.

"I might invite him," Karma said, "but he spends Sundays with his family, usually."

"Well, that's unusual, these days," Wendy commented.

"He's an unusual guy," Karma replied.

"How'd you meet him?" Marty asked his daughter as they came to a "Don't Walk" sign on the corner of West End Avenue and West Seventy-second Street. Like most New Yorkers, Karma and her parents waited in the street close to the curb for the light to change or for the traffic to abate before they would cross. A big city bus, its diesel engine grinding, rolled in front of them.

"I met him at—"

Karma froze, unable to finish her sentence.

That's impossible, she told herself.

But Demetrius said...

"Karma, are you okay?" Wendy asked her daughter.

"Sweetheart?" Marty asked, putting his arm around Karma again. "You're all pale."

"I'm . . . fine," Karma said, taking a deep breath. "Fine."

It was . . . my reflection, that's all, Karma told herself. *It was just my reflection in the window.*

But try as she might, Karma couldn't shake the feeling that she'd just seen a ghost in the window of the crosstown bus as it passed by her.

And the ghost looked exactly like Karma Kushner.

SEVEN

"I'm telling you, this wasn't just my imagination," Karma insisted to her friends. "I saw someone on that bus who looked just like me."

"Lish, toss me the sunscreen," Chelsea said without opening her eyes. "I'm frying."

"You are such a white girl," Lisha teased as she heaved the sunscreen at her friend. It landed in the sand next to her blanket.

"Hel-lo, are you guys listening to me?" Karma called. "I'm having a serious identity crisis!"

It was the following Sunday, and as Marty and Wendy Kushner had suggested, all the interns had decided to make a day of it at the beach. The fact that the temperature the day before had hit ninety-five in Manhattan, and that the forecast for Sunday was for hot, humid, and ninety-eight-degree weather, made it an easy decision.

They'd all taken a bus from the downtown Port Authority Terminal to Atlantic Beach, which was right near Kennedy Airport. There,

Marty had picked them all up in the health-food store's van, and had deposited them at the beach. He was going to pick them up at dusk and bring them to the house for a tofu barbecue. Then he was going to drive them all back into Manhattan.

On the trip to the beach, Karma had told them about seeing someone who looked exactly like her in a crosstown bus. But even though it was driving her nuts, no one else seemed to be taking it very seriously.

"Hey, don't get crazed about this, okay?" Nick said, settling his hands underneath his head. "Man, this is the life, eh?"

"I'm sure all you saw was a reflection of yourself in the window of the bus," Lisha told Karma.

"I don't think so," Karma maintained. "I was on the sidewalk. The bus window was way up there. How could I have been seeing my own reflection?"

"So maybe there's some girl in Manhattan who looks kind of like you," Chelsea suggested as she spread sunscreen on her pale legs. "Dang, my legs are the color of typing paper. I need to get out more."

"Good thing there's a slight breeze," Sky said as he looked up at the kite that was flying from the string in his hand. "Or else this puppy would be grounded."

"That kite was a stroke of genius," Alan said, turning over on to his back.

Karma looked up at the dalmatian-print black-and-white kite with the hot-pink *Trash* logo that flew above them. It was one of the many, many items that *Trash* sold through the mail with its logo on it. In fact, *Trash* merchandise alone was a multimillion-dollar profit source.

"See, aren't you glad I liberated that kite from the storage room at work?" Nick asked.

" 'Liberated' sounds better than 'stole,' " Alan said dryly.

The kite had been Sky's idea—a way for Demetrius to find them on the beach.

Demetrius said that he'd come find us around this time, Karma thought, looking at her watch. It was three-thirty. *He was going to have lunch with his brother and his parents, then he was going to drive out here on his motorcycle. I told him to look for the Trash kite. And it's a good thing it's flying up there, because this beach is so packed, it would be tough to find anyone.*

The beach was absolutely jammed. People were lined up blanket to blanket, and there were so many of them in the ocean that it was hard to find an empty few feet of water without a body bobbing in it.

"Hey, did I mention how cute you look in that bathing suit?" Sky asked Lisha playfully. He staked the kite, and then poured some hot sand over her arm.

"Thanks," Lisha said. "It feels funny wearing the top part, though. In Europe, girls only wear the bottom half of their bikini."

"I've clearly been living in the wrong country," Sky replied.

"Not me," Karma said. "Like I'd really walk around on the beach naked in front of the entire world. Ha!"

"Yeah, what good is fashion sense in a nudist colony?" Alan teased her. "Oh, I love this song." He reached over and turned up the radio they had brought with them, and the sounds of Sheryl Crow filled the air.

Karma looked over at Lisha, who wore a tiny black bikini, with her skinny gold chain wrapped around her waist. Then she looked at Chelsea, who had on a yellow-and-white daisy-print two-piece that wasn't too revealing. Then she looked down at herself, in her hot pink one-piece with very high-cut legs and a halter top. Alan and Sky both had on baggy swim shorts, and Nick wore cutoffs that were frayed at the bottom. The only one missing was Belch—although Nick had wanted to bring him along, the others had vetoed the idea.

These guys look really cute without shirts, Karma thought. *But I bet Demetrius shirtless puts them all to shame.*

"Hey, think about it," Nick called to Karma, pulling her from her thoughts. "Now you can't rag on Demetrius for thinking some other girl on the street was you. I mean, *you* thought some other girl was you!"

"Maybe," Karma admitted. She looked at her watch again. "I hope Demetrius sees our kite."

"Relax," Nick told her. He sat up and looked down at Chelsea. "You wanna go in the water, pretty girl?"

She opened her eyes. "I just gunked myself up with sunscreen."

"So?" Nick said, standing up. "I'll rub it all over you again when we get out."

Chelsea reached out her hand and he pulled her up.

"In a few," Nick called to the group as he and Chelsea headed for the water hand in hand.

Karma wrapped her arms around her knees and looked out at the water, and the image of the face she'd seen on the bus came to her again. "I'm not crazy. I saw someone who looked just like me."

"I read somewhere that everyone has a double," Alan said easily. "Maybe you just saw yours."

"Alan, this is not an episode of *The Twilight Zone*," Karma whined. "This is my life."

"What's *The Twilight Zone*?" Lisha asked.

"Only the best old TV show in the world," Sky replied. "I can't believe you never heard of it! Rod Serling? He was scary way before Stephen King—the show comes on cable late night."

"Whatever," Lisha said, adjusting the strap of her bikini.

I know I'm not losing my mind, Karma thought, staring out at the ocean but not really seeing it. *And I don't believe everyone has a double. I'm going to go nuts if I don't try to find that girl I saw. But how could I—*

"Nice kite."

Karma looked up.

Demetrius stood above her, like some kind of Greek statue, looking down at her. He had on nothing more than a pair of shorts and some sunglasses. His golden skin shone, in sharp contrast to the whiteness of his shorts.

"Lost in thought, huh?" he said gently. "You were looking right at me as I walked over, and you didn't even see."

"You found us!" Karma said happily. She scooched over on the blanket so that Demetrius could sit down next to her.

"Only *Trash* kite on the beach," he said.

"Don't tell me you rode your motorcycle out here in bare feet and no T-shirt," she said accusingly. "You're not that tough."

"You're right," Demetrius said with a laugh. "I put my helmet and other clothes in a locker back there." He cocked his head in the direction of the entrance to the beach.

"How you doin'?" Sky greeted Demetrius.

"Great," Demetrius said. "What a day, huh?"

"Unbelievable," Lisha murmured. "I may live my whole life on this beach. I may never move again."

"Where are Nick and Chelsea?" Demetrius asked.

"In the water," Karma said.

"Great idea!" he said. "Want to go for a swim?"

"With a guy who looks like an ad for suntan lotion?" Karma quipped, scrambling up from the beach. "Why not?"

They threaded their way through the maze of towels and bodies and then waded into the water, until the cold ocean water was up to Karma's neck and to the middle of Demetrius's chest.

"Good thing it's calm today, or a midget like me could drown," Karma said, riding a small wave as it came toward her.

"You shouldn't down yourself for being short, you know," Demetrius said quietly.

"I'm only joking," Karma explained.

"Maybe," he said. "But I think it bothers you, too."

"Thank you *so* much, Dr. Freud," Karma said. "What, like nothing about yourself bothers you?"

"Oh, yeah," Demetrius said. "Lots of stuff." He let his body ride gently into another small wave. "Nice, huh?"

"Salt water is great for the skin," Karma replied. "I read about it in *Vogue*."

"Did you read about this?" Demetrius asked. He eased over to her, bent down, and kissed her slowly and deliciously.

"Yep, there was an article about that, too," Karma said. "*Vogue* covers everything." She pushed off the sandy bottom and Demetrius caught her legs, his arms secure under her knees and behind her neck. She bobbed gently, cradled in his strong arms.

"I can't say I read it often," Demetrius replied, smiling down at her.

"I have a lifetime subscription," Karma confided. "I got it when I was ten. When I was twelve I also got one to *BusinessWeek*."

"You are one unique woman," he said.

"True," she agreed. "Although someone else looks just like me, right?" She squinted up at him, the sun bright in her eyes.

Demetrius frowned. "That really bothered you—"

"Yeah, kind of," Karma admitted. "But then this weird thing happened to me the other day."

She quickly told him about the girl she'd seen on the bus.

"So there really *is* someone in this city who looks like you!" Demetrius marveled.

"Who knows?" Karma said. "But if she's out there, I'm going to find her."

"How?"

Karma righted herself in the water. "It just came to me!"

"I can see the wheels turning in your head," Demetrius said.

"I really just thought of a way to find this girl!" She was ecstatic.

"Do you plan to tell me what it is?" Demetrius asked.

"Absolutely," Karma told him happily.

Demetrius pulled her to him, holding her weightless against him. "Are you going to tell me now?" he asked gruffly. Clearly his mind was not on the mystery of Karma's look-alike.

"Later," she murmured, putting her arms around his neck and wrapping her legs around his torso. "Much later."

"Okay, gang," Jazz called out to her studio audience, "let's give our *Trash*iest welcome to our favorite teen girl currently awaiting trial on multiple felony charges, Miss Seeela Flynn!"

The studio audience went absolutely bonkers, cheering and applauding. Jazz, who was sitting on a stool in the center of the studio, her arms and legs tied up in electrical cord, shook her mane of thick blond hair off her face, a smug glint in her eyes.

"She's an artist," Karma said, from where she was standing in the back of the studio, monitoring one of the exit doors. "She's sick, and she's demented, but she's an artist."

"You've said that before," Lisha, who was standing next to her, pointed out.

"Well, it's true," Karma said. "Just look at her. This crowd would do anything for her."

"Mass hysteria," Lisha said bluntly. "Groupthink can be real dangerous, you know."

It was Monday, exactly one week to the day after Sela Flynn had held the entire show hostage, on live television, with the whole thing being broadcast coast to coast and around the world.

And now Jazz had outdone herself.

She'd invited Sela to be her main guest, via live television hookup, from the Manhattan Women's House of Detention, where the girl was currently being held without bond pending her trial on attempted murder, kidnapping, assault, and weapons-possession charges.

Sela, who hated Jazz's guts, had agreed to do the live hookup on one condition—that Chelsea, whom she'd designated live-on-the-air a week before as her envoy to the police, be part of the camera team that was transmitting the live pictures back to the studio.

So Chelsea's down there with Sky and a whole camera crew, and

Lisha and I are up here watching. Who knows where Nick and Alan are, but they really shouldn't miss this.

With Jazz's words, a huge image of Sela Flynn, looking as unattractive as ever—her hair stringy, her massively overweight body straining the confines of her all-orange prison garb—was projected on a gigantic screen over to Jazz's right.

"Sela, you're gorgeous, will you marry me?" some guy in the audience called out as the rest of the audience hooted and catcalled at him.

"This is disgusting," Karma whispered to Lisha.

"Yeah, that's the whole point," Lisha whispered back.

"Hey, chill out," Jazz called to the heckler in the audience. "A little respect for our guest, here."

This is sick genius at work, Karma marveled. *Jazz is turning Sela Flynn into a pop-culture star. I can't wait to see what the ratings are for this show. I heard Barry Bassinger thought of it. But it seems like pure Jazz to me.*

She looked to the right side of the stage, where Barry stood, his arms folded, a happy grin on his face. Next to him stood Bigfoot on crutches, with red silk voile material that matched her red silk pantsuit wrapped around her cast.

"Hey, Sela," Jazz said, "what's happening, how you doing?"

"Okay, Jazz," Sela replied. "I guess."

"How's the food?" Jazz asked earnestly.

"It sucks," Sela answered. "No Pepsi, either."

"Yo," Jazz called, to someone offstage. "Make sure that Sela gets sent five cases of regular Pepsi, on me."

"I heard that, Jazz," Sela said sullenly. "I guess you expect me to thank you."

"Not really," Jazz said coolly.

"Good," Sela replied. "Because I'm not going to."

Jazz nodded. "So, you've been in jail for six days now?"

"Something like that," Sela said, scratching absentmindedly at her scalp.

"Have you had a chance to think about what you did?" Jazz asked. "I mean, what would you do if you had it to do all over again?"

"I'd have aimed higher at the bitch with the big feet," Sela growled.

The audience went wild, screaming, yelling, catcalling. From the wings Bigfoot waved and took a small bow, Barry helping to steady her on her crutches.

"Another thing," Sela went on. "I would have made you cut off all your hair on camera."

"Oooooh," the studio audience went, prompted by cue cards being held up by Demetrius.

"How come?" Jazz asked. "Because you hate me?"

"No, becáuse I love you," Sela said sarcastically. "Of course I hate you! All you do is humiliate people. You make millions by making fun of people. You suck."

"Oooooh," the studio audience went again, prompted by another cue card. Sela smiled with satisfaction.

"You know, Sela," Jazz suggested, "I think it's a question of power."

"What is?" Sela asked suspiciously.

"All this." Jazz waved her hand dismissively. "I think you hate my guts because I've got the power, and you don't."

"As you would say, big duh," Sela snorted.

"So, what that means is," Jazz said, "you'd feel better if you had the power."

"Big duh again," Sela said.

"So, I think what we need to do, gang," Jazz continued, turning to the audience, "is give Sela Flynn some power. What do you say?"

Unbelievable, Karma marveled. *Really unbelievable.*

"Yeaah!" everyone cheered.

From the back of the room, a chant of "Sela, Sela, Sela!" went up, until Jazz made a motion with her chin to tell them to hold it down.

"Sela, the audience agrees with you," Jazz said. "And since I can't make you host of the show for a day, I'd like to do the next best thing."

"What's that?" Sela asked dubiously.

"Make you judge for a day!" Jazz exclaimed. "Sela Flynn, you are now the judge of today's *Trash* live event: the Ex-Con Model Challenge! And honey, you have all the power!"

Here, a voice-over, which Karma recognized as being supplied by Demetrius, announced how the Ex-Con Model Challenge would work. Ten girls aged eighteen to twenty-five, who had recently been released from prison, would model designer women's fashions from such houses as Azzedine Alaia, Donna Karan, and Betsy Johnson. And it was up to Sela to pick the winner, who'd get to keep all the clothes she'd modeled.

"Sorry you can't be in on this," Jazz said to Sela, "but we'll put you on in twenty or thirty years, okay?"

Sela glowered at Jazz. "And what do I get out of this?" she asked her.

"A lawyer who isn't a public defender, courtesy of *Trash*!" Jazz replied.

Sela took a few moments to think.

"Okay," she said, "I'll do it."

"Forget our underground video," Karma hissed to Lisha. "Jazz goes so low in public that there's nothing about her left to expose!"

"And she's proud of it," Lisha added, shaking her head with disgust.

"Okay," Jazz said, "we'll be back with our first ex-con model, Ms. Champagne Jones, in a moment. Ms. Jones, recently released from New Jersey's Rahway State Penitentiary after doing five-to-fifteen on a felony charge, will be showing us the latest from Keith Hartley's spring collection. But first, these commercial messages!"

The studio audience cheered, as the cue cards told them to cheer, and the lights went down on the set suddenly.

"This is it!" Karma cried, grabbing Lisha's hand. Her eyes were riveted to one of the television monitors in the studio.

She'd had the idea for this yesterday, in the ocean, standing with Demetrius. She'd discussed it with Sumtimes, who cleared it with Roxanne (who'd approved it not because she had any great affection for Karma, but because she thought it might just lead to a theme for a great *Trash* show). And then, they'd filmed it right after lunch.

Now, will they actually put it on? Karma thought. *Knowing Bigfoot, she could change her mind at any time.* She hoped that it would air, and at the same time hoped it wouldn't. The whole thing was so crazy, anyway.

It aired. The whole thing took five seconds, as they were showing the logo for *Trash* right before the commercials began.

Karma's picture appeared on the screen.

"Are you this girl?" a voice-over, again Demetrius, read. "Because if you are, *Trash* wants to find you! We promise to make it worth your while, too. Send your photo to Department K, *Trash,* P.O. Box 150326, Grand Central Station, New York, New York 10015, with a name, address, and phone number. Do it today—it'll be kind of like finding Cinderella—only, hey, this is *Trash,* so it'll be even better!"

The address flashed on the screen.

Then a commercial for an acne remedy began.

There it is, Karma thought. *It's done. And if my look-alike is really out there, and I'm not totally out of my mind, maybe she'll see it. And then I'll find out who she is.*

And maybe learn why she looks just like me.

EIGHT

"Hey, I heard you got tons of mail," Nick said, sticking his head into Karma's tiny cubicle.

"Already?" Karma said. "But the spot only aired two days ago. Who said?"

"Lisha," Nick replied. "I just ran into her. She's bringing it down to you." He stepped closer to Karma's desk and leaned toward her. "Hey, guess where I managed to put the Trash-cam this morning?"

"Jazz's office?" Karma guessed.

"Right on the first guess," Nick agreed. "I can't wait to see what we end up with."

"Hey, there's something I don't get," Karma said, cocking her head at Nick. "How come you're willing to hide the Trash-cam in her office if you're also willing to go with her to the Rock of Ages Awards?"

"What does one have to do with the other?" Nick asked, shaking his hair off his face.

"Well, what I mean is, are you into her, or not?" Karma asked.

"I'm not into her," Nick said.

"So then why are you—"

"Did Chelsea put you up to this?" Nick asked.

"No," Karma said. "I'm Little Miss Curiosity all on my own."

"Look, it's not such a big—"

"Is it that you just want to hang with the beautiful people," Karma asked, "the rich and famous, like that?"

"Not my style." Nick scratched at his chin. "Look, Jazz and I had a . . . a thing for a little while, right? I've stayed friends with every girl I was ever involved with. I don't see why Jazz should be any different."

Karma shook her head. "I totally don't get you, Nick. And you're hurting Chelsea."

"Let's not turn this into some big thing, okay?" Nick asked. "Chelsea needs to learn to trust me."

"Yeah, but how can she when—"

"Mail call," Lisha called out as she lugged a huge canvas mailbag across the floor, depositing it with a thud in the middle of the floor. "Love letters for Karma."

"All this is for me?" Karma asked, regarding the heavy bag with shock.

"You're Department K, right? Unless there's another Karma Kushner, this is all routed for you from the mailroom downstairs."

"Looks like a lot of people think they look like you," Nick said.

"Hi, y'all," Chelsea said, sticking her head in the door. She looked down at the mail sack. "Wow!"

"Wow is right," Karma agreed. "It'll take me a lifetime to go through all this."

"We'll help you," Chelsea offered.

"What is this, some kind of convention for the underworked?" Bigfoot asked suddenly, appearing in the doorway balanced on her crutches.

"Karma got a lot of mail," Lisha explained.

"And?" Bigfoot asked. "What does that have to do with all of you in here wasting time?"

"We thought we could help her—" Chelsea began.

"Oh, really?" Roxanne interrupted. "Is that because you and Karma have found that Kettering girl in Australia and arranged for her to be on the teen-kids-of-mass-murderers show? Because I don't remember that info being delivered to my office."

"We're still...working on it," Karma told her.

"I expect it done by the end of this week," Bigfoot snapped. "Or heads will roll around here." She turned awkwardly on her crutches and limped away.

"Man, that wench is in a permanent bad mood," Nick grumbled. He turned to Chelsea. "What girl in Australia are you supposed to find for her?"

"Never mind," Chelsea said quickly, her cheeks reddening.

"Hey, great response to the spot!" Sumtimes stuck her head in the door. "There must be a thousand letters there!"

Sumtimes—whose first name changed weekly depending on her mood, therefore they all called her Sumtimes, which was her last name—was the hardest-working person on the *Trash* staff. She was also almost, kind of, human. In fact, the interns were actually starting to like her.

"Can we help Karma go through this stuff?" Lisha asked Sumtimes.

"Oh, yeah, sure," Sumtimes said. "I can't wait to see what you guys come up with. Just make sure you get the latest *Trash* tapes transcribed this afternoon, okay?" She disappeared down the hall.

"Well, you heard her," Lisha said. "We get to help."

"But Bigfoot—" Chelsea began.

"Forget Bigfoot," Lisha snapped. "Let her duke it out with Sumtimes."

The four of them plopped down in the tiny space in front of Karma's desk and emptied the mail onto the floor.

"Geez, a lot of people think they look like you," Nick said, marveling.

"Dig in." Karma reached randomly for an envelope.

The postmark is from Mary, Kansas, she thought, looking at the address. She tore the envelope open and pulled out a letter and a photo.

She looked at the photo.

It was a girl, with hair as blond as Chelsea's, sitting on the back of a horse.

"You won't believe this." Karma turned to her friends. "Look who thinks she looks like me."

She held up the picture of the girl for her friends to see.

"Look at this one!" Lisha said. She held up a photo of a small, red-headed girl in a white bathing suit. The girl in the photo held up a little sign that read HI JAZZ!

And then, one by one, Chelsea, Alan, and Nick each held up their first pictures.

None of the girls looked remotely like Karma.

In fact, Nick's picture was of a guy. With a beard.

"Nick wins," Lisha said blithely.

"I have a feeling this was not one of my brighter ideas." Karma sighed. And then, out of curiosity, she read the letter from the girl from Mary, Kansas.

Dear Jazz,

I know I don't look like the Asian girl whose picture you put on TV, but if you ever need a replacement who looks like you, I'm available.

People really are desperate, Karma thought. *People will do anything to be on television. This girl doesn't look anything like Jazz at all. And did she really think that Jazz herself was going to read her letter?*

Karma methodically and quickly started opening envelopes, barely noticing the sounds of her friends doing the same. For each one, she didn't even bother with the letter, just taking a quick glance at the photo.

A quick look was usually plenty.

An hour later the group had made four huge piles of photographs.

Blondes, redheads, brunettes, and guys. Not more than six of the photos were of females with Asian features, and one of those was old enough to be Karma's grandmother. The other five looked absolutely nothing like her.

Karma eyed the unopened envelopes. There were only a dozen or so left. "Okay, this was the loser idea of all loser ideas," she decided. "If anyone tells me 'I told you so' I will personally bury them in all these photos."

She reached for one of the last ones without much enthusiasm.

"Karma?"

It was Lisha's voice.

"Yeah," Karma replied, still struggling to open her letter, which had been taped shut. "What's up? Did Coolio send his photo in, too? Or how about Chelsea Clinton?"

"Noooo," Lisha said, trying to control the excitement in her voice. "I think you'd better look at this one."

Everyone looked over at Lisha, who handed an eight-by-ten photo to Karma.

Karma looked at it.

I can't believe it, she thought, feeling both elated and scared to death. *That's me!* Wordlessly, she held it up to her friends.

"Whoa," Nick breathed. "Freaky."

"It looks just like you!" Chelsea exclaimed.

"Who sent this?" Karma demanded.

Lisha handed her the letter. "Her name's Tran," Lisha said. "She lives in Galveston, Texas. And you gotta admit, Karma, she looks just *like* you."

Karma looked again at the picture, her heart pounding in her chest.

No doubt about it.

It's me.

Karma hung up the phone in her bedroom and walked back into the living room. It was that evening, one of Karma's few nights off from Jimi's, and all the interns were sprawled on the living-room rug, eating Chinese takeout directly from the small white cartons. Karma had told them that this was a New York City tradition.

"Belch," Nick commanded his dog. Belch belched.

"Good person," Nick said, giving Belch a piece of five-flavored chicken from his container.

"Good *person*?" Lisha echoed.

"I told you, he's offended by the D-word," Nick explained, patting Belch's head. "Now, double belch," Nick instructed the dog.

Belch belched once, and then again.

"Yeah!" Nick exulted, giving Belch more chicken. "What a person!" His friends gave him dubious looks. "Okay, what a canine," he relented.

"Do you feed him beer beforehand, or what?" Lisha asked, swirling some cold noodles with sesame sauce around on her fork.

"No beer," Nick said. "It's a trade secret."

Chelsea looked up at Karma. "So, what happened?"

"She's coming tomorrow," Karma announced, taking a seat in the easy chair that seemed to dwarf her tiny body. "That was Sumtimes, calling from the office. Tran's coming tomorrow morning."

"Sumtimes is still at the office?" Alan marveled.

"She's married to her job, I guess," Nick said, scratching Belch lovingly under his chin.

"They're flying her first class from Houston," Karma reported. "She'll be at the office at two in the afternoon."

Nick looked at his watch. "You guys want to watch the tape of the first Ali-Frazier fight?" he asked. "ESPN's putting it on in five minutes."

"I'd rather watch today's Trash-cam video," Lisha said, licking some sesame sauce off her finger. "Who picked up the camera?"

"Sky," Nick said.

"Not me, man," Sky said. "I thought you were getting it after Jazz left."

"She was still in the office when I left," Nick explained. "I thought you said you'd get it when you dropped off those files she wanted."

The two guys stared at each other.

"So neither one of you got the Trash-cam," Alan said.

"So we don't get to watch what Jazz does in the secrecy of her office until tomorrow night," Lisha said with a shrug. "It's no biggie that the camera's still there."

"Oh, yes, it is," Alan said slowly.

Everyone looked at him.

"It's Wednesday night," he explained. "Jazz's office gets cleaned on Wednesday nights. I mean *really* cleaned, every inch. Which means the cleaning person could find the camera. Correction. *Will* find the camera."

That thought was so horrible that no one spoke for a long moment.

"Our lives are over," Sky finally said.

"We don't know that the cleaning guy is gonna find it," Nick said. "We might luck out."

"And we might not," Chelsea added. She turned to Nick and Sky. "How could you guys do something so stupid?"

"A misunderstanding," Sky explained. "I guess we got our signals crossed."

"Great," Lisha snorted. "Just great. We could all six go down because the two of you got your signals crossed."

They were all silent again.

"Okay, here's what we'll do," Sky decided. "The steady-cam guy gave me keys. I'll go in way early tomorrow. If we luck out, and her office door isn't locked, I'll get the camera out. If it's still there, that is."

"Tomorrow *morning*?" Chelsea screeched. "That's too late!"

"Yeah, maybe you should go tonight," Karma suggested nervously.

Sky shook his head. "I'm not cleared for night access security. None of us are. None of us can get past the guard downstairs."

"So, in other words, we could be totally screwed," Lisha concluded.

"We could be," Sky agreed. "But let's hope we're not." He looked down at his food. "I seem to have lost my appetite."

"I'm feeling kind of nauseous myself," Alan agreed.

"We can't just sit here!" Lisha said. "We have to do something!"

"You got any brilliant ideas?" Nick asked her.

"We should go give the guard some story and see if we can get into the office," Lisha insisted.

"Forget it," Sky snapped. "No way will that work. The security is super-tight. We are out of luck until tomorrow."

The room grew quiet again.

"Look, we always knew there was a possiblity of our getting caught," Alan finally said. "That's a chance we all agreed we were willing to take."

"If that camera is missing, Jazz'll fire all of us, you know," Sky said.

"Not only that," Karma chimed in, "she'll ruin us. Bye-bye major network for me."

"She won't know it's our camera," Nick pointed out, fiddling with his earring.

"She'll find out, somehow," Sky said. "You know she will." He got up. "Look, I'm gonna go watch the fight and try not to think about my career in TV being over before it even got started."

"I'm outta here, too," Nick said, getting up. He leaned down and kissed Chelsea quickly. "You taste like sweet-and-sour shrimp," he said, nuzzling her neck.

"Aren't you worried about the camera?" Chelsea asked him.

Nick scratched his chin. "Kinda. But I kinda think worrying about it is a waste of time, too. I mean, whatever is gonna happen is gonna happen, right?"

"Well, I'll worry enough for both of us," Chelsea said, her voice high and strained.

"I guess I'll go do that guy-bonding-over-sports thing," Alan said dryly, dumping his empty Chinese-food container into the garbage in the kitchen. He reached for Chelsea's hand and gave it a squeeze. "Try not to make yourself crazy over this, okay? Whatever happens, we're in it together."

Chelsea nodded at him gratefully, and the three guys left, Belch at their heels.

The three girls looked at each other.

"I can't believe Sky and Nick messed this up so badly," Chelsea said.

"Okay, we're not gonna freak out here," Karma decided. "We're gonna put this totally out of our minds until tomorrow."

"When the police pick us up," Lisha said darkly.

"Don't think like that," Karma said. "Anyway, what we're doing isn't actually illegal. I don't think."

"If we get caught, my mother will just kill me," Chelsea lamented.

"You guys," Karma whined. "I am changing the subject. As of now. Someone say something." She picked up the rest of the Chinese-food trash and dumped it into the wastepaper basket.

"I don't think any of us would look very good in one of those orange jumpsuits Sela Flynn was wearing," Lisha said.

"That is not changing the subject!" Karma cried. "And we're not going to jail!"

"We could, you don't know!" Chelsea said. "How are we—" she began as the phone rang again.

"It's probably Sumtimes again," Karma said, reaching for the portable phone. "Hello?"

"Lemme talk to Lisha," a deep male voice said.

"Who's calling?" Karma asked.

"Just put her on," the voice snapped.

Karma put her hand over the phone. "It's some guy," she told Lisha. "He won't tell me his name, he just said to put you on."

Lisha's face paled.

Harley, Karma thought. *The guy who called before, the one who's wanted by the FBI.*

She took her hand off the receiver. "Uh, listen, whoever you are," she said. "Lisha moved. No forwarding address."

"That's bull and you know it," the voice rasped in her ear. "Tell her to get her ass on this phone. Now."

"Aren't you a lovely human being," Karma said. "Have a swell life. Bye." She hung up.

"Harley," Lisha said, staring at Karma.

"What a charmer," Karma said. "Were you really involved with this guy?"

"I—" Lisha began.

The phone rang again.

Karma snatched it up. "Listen, you—"

"No, you listen." The same voice, low and sinister, came into Karma's ear. "Tell Lisha her Harley is on his way to New York. I know where she lives. I know where she works. Tell her I'll call her when I get there. And if she knows what's good for her, she'll see me."

The phone went dead in Karma's hand.

"I'm living in a really, really bad soap opera here," Karma said, hanging up the phone. She told Lisha everything Harley had said.

"Oh, God," Lisha moaned, dropping her head into her hands.

"What is with him?" Chelsea asked.

"I can't tell you," Lisha said, her voice muffled by her hands.

"But you're really scared, I can tell!" Chelsea exclaimed. "We want to help you!"

"No one can help me." Lisha raised her head and looked at her friends, her face a mask of misery and fear. "No one."

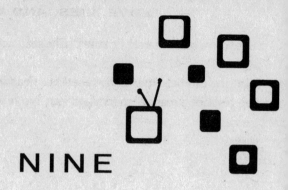

NINE

"Jazz! Jazz! Over here!"

"Just one more shot, Jazz! Look this way!"

Jazz Stewart, nineteen-year-old megastar, selected by *People* magazine as one of the most beautiful people in the world, obliged the photographer and turned toward him. She was wearing faded jeans with a leopard-print bra top under a distressed-leather motorcycle jacket, which fell artfully off her shoulders. Her eyes were hidden behind large black-framed sunglasses; her trademark long, white-blond hair flowed across her shoulders.

"She's so perfect looking," Chelsea said, watching Jazz pose.

"You would be, too, if you'd had as much plastic surgery as she has," Lisha commented.

"I am so nervous," Karma said, twisting some of her hair around her finger. She looked at her watch. "The plane is about to land. And someone who looks just like me is about to walk in here."

It was the next afternoon, and the three girls, along with Jazz and her entourage, were at La Guardia Airport to pick up Tran, Karma's look-alike. Jazz had decided to make it into a media event, and she'd had her public-relations people put the word out to the press. The press had, per usual, shown up in droves. Private security circled the group, keeping the curious crowd back.

"You think she's a long-lost sister from Korea, or something?" Chelsea asked Karma.

"According to my mother, I didn't have any sisters," Karma said.

"Maybe she's a brother who *used* to be a sister," Lisha quipped. "That would be *so* much more up *Trash*'s alley!"

"I am in such a great mood," Chelsea said happily. "I mean, this is so exciting! Jazz actually got a limo for us! And best of all, the Trash-cam was still in its hiding place this morning. Is life great, or what?"

"That Trash-cam thing was a really close call." Karma shook her head. "We are so lucky we didn't get busted."

When Sky had arrived at Jazz's office early that morning, they'd all been sweating bullets. But much to their relief, the camera was right where he had hidden it, behind some books and files on a shelf across from Jazz's huge, dalmatian-print desk. Just as Sky was about to remove the camera, however, he'd heard voices in the hallway, so he'd pushed the camera back into its hiding place before he snuck out of the office.

They learned all this via a hurried phone call from Sky, shortly before seven o'clock that morning.

"Hey, Jazz, how come you're looking for your intern's look-alike?" a reporter yelled out.

"We heard your intern needs a kidney transplant and you're searching for a donor, is that true?" another called.

"*Kidney transplant?*" Karma hissed to her friends.

"Hey, I never divulge to you guys why I do anything," Jazz told the reporters. She cocked her head to one side. "But maybe after this I'll have a contest to find *my* look-alike. And then this intern look-alike can work her butt off for my look-alike." She smiled coolly. "That's what interns do, you know."

"The plane just hit the gate, Jazz," an assistant reported breathlessly, running over to the superstar.

A crowd of people hurriedly deplaned, swarming around the press, the onlookers, Jazz, and her entourage.

"I don't see anyone who looks like me," Karma said nervously.

"She's on this flight, for sure," Chelsea insisted, peering into the crowd. "Sumtimes arranged it, and Sumtimes never messes anything up."

A pretty, young African-American woman in a white Rice University sweatshirt and jeans tapped Karma on the shoulder.

"Yeah?" Karma asked, still searching for a face that looked like hers.

"I'm Tran," the girl said, grinning.

Jazz, who was standing only a few feet from Karma and her friends, overheard the girl. She turned and stared at her.

"You're *who*?" Lisha asked.

"Tran," the girl repeated easily. "Tran Johnson. Tran is short for Tranquille." She spelled her name for Karma. "My mother gave us all kinds of odd names."

"But . . . you're black," Karma said ridiculously.

"Acute powers of observation," Tran said. She turned to Jazz. "Hey, I loved flying first class. They really treat you great up there, you know? Thanks, Jazz!"

Jazz folded her arms as cameras snapped away at Tran and Karma. "This is a scam, right?" she asked.

"Kinda," Tran grinned at Jazz. "Wow, you are even more incredible looking in person than you are on the tube. I'm a major *Trash* fan. I watch it at college. All my friends do. We even plan our class schedules around it!"

"But . . . but the photo," Karma sputtered. "Where did you get a photo that looked just like me?"

"Well, it's like this," Tran said. "I'm a computer-science grad student at Rice. I was taping the show when the spot came on. So I froze the photo of you, made a copy, put it into my computer, and enhanced it to change it a little. You know, so I'd look like you, but not dressed like you."

Jazz slowly walked over to Tran and stood in her face, just staring at the girl.

For a brief moment everyone was quiet, waiting to see what she would do. "Why'd you do it?" Jazz asked Tran.

Tran shrugged. "To see if it would work—and it did! And hey, I got a great first-class plane ride out of it. And I'm getting to meet you. Not bad!" A camera flashed, and Tran posed, a broad smile on her face. "Not to mention getting my picture in the paper," she added.

Jazz is going to kill her, Karma thought to herself. *Of course she'll have to stand in line, because I'm going to kill this girl first, myself.*

But much to Karma's surprise, Jazz laughed. "I like the way your mind works," she told Tran. "Very *Trashy.*"

"I was hoping you'd appreciate it," Tran said. "So, are you just going to put me back on a plane to Texas? I was really digging first class, so don't downgrade me now."

Jazz laughed again. "Hey, I think you should come on my show before you go back to Texas. What do you think?"

"Do I still get to stay at The Plaza Hotel?" Tran asked.

"Sure," Jazz agreed. She put her arm around Tran. "Okay, paparazzi," she called to the photographers, "get some good shots of me and my new bud, Tranquille. I love a woman with a truly diabolical mind!"

The photographers snapped away, and one reporter hurried over to Karma. "Are you disappointed?"

"I don't know," she said honestly. "I'm . . . stunned, that's what I am."

The reporter turned to Chelsea, pen poised over a spiral notebook. "What do you think, Chutney? And how's your life been going since you became a hero?"

"What do you think of Sela Flynn judging that fashion show? Did you hear that she just signed a six-figure book deal? And sold the movie rights?" another reporter called out to them.

"Let's get out of here," Chelsea told Karma, pulling on her arm.

The three girls hurried away, and got into the back of the black limo Jazz had rented for them. Jazz's personal limo with the black-and-white dalmatian-spotted doors was in front of theirs.

"Now, that was truly bizarre," Lisha said as the driver pulled away from the curb.

"I'm still reeling, here." Karma let her head fall back against the cool, black leather. "I really thought I'd found my double."

"I suppose we should have wondered how a girl who lives in Texas ended up in a New York City crosstown bus a few days ago, anyway," Chelsea pointed out.

"I just figured she was visiting here, or something," Karma said lamely. She shook her head. "I can't believe all this."

"So . . . we still don't know who your double is," Lisha said. She leaned forward and opened the small refrigerator in the back of the limo.

"Back to square one," Karma agreed. She watched Lisha rummage through the fridge. "What's in there?"

"Champagne!" Lisha exclaimed happily, pulling out a small bottle. "I say we drink it."

"We can't do that," Chelsea said quickly. "For one thing, we're underage. And for another thing, it'll get charged to Jazz."

"For one thing, Jazz couldn't care less if we're underage, since *she's* underage," Lisha shot back. "And for another thing, Jazz does not go over the bills. Some accountant wonk does."

She deftly opened the champagne bottle with a satisfying *pop*. Then she poured some into three plastic champagne flutes she found next to the refrigerator.

"I could get used to this," Karma said, sipping her champagne. She watched the world go by through the window of the limo. "Can you believe Jazz's reaction to Tran?"

"Yeah, actually, I can," Lisha said. "Her *Trashiness* appreciates a good scam, even when it's a scam on her." She looked over at Chelsea, who was staring at the champagne in the glass she was holding. "Are you going to look at it or drink it?"

"I know y'all are going to get a real kick out of this," Chelsea said, "but I've never had champagne before."

"You're kidding," Karma said.

"No champagne, no sex—what have you been doing for eighteen years?" Lisha teased.

"Being a good girl," Chelsea said with a sigh. "A very, *very* good girl."

"Highly overrated," Lisha said, sipping her champagne. "Drink up."

Chelsea hesitated. "It still doesn't seem right to drink this."

"Look at it this way," Karma said. "We're in a limo that *Trash* is paying for. We dodged a huge bullet this morning with the Trash-cam, and you're young, cute, smart, single, and living in New York City."

"And another thing," Lisha added. "When this glamorous ride ends, you're gonna have to go walk Jazz's dogs and scoop their poop. So I say live for the moment."

"You've both got a point." Chelsea took a small sip of the champagne. "It's good! Fizzy!"

Karma stared out the window. "Who was the girl I saw in that bus?" she mused out loud.

"It wasn't Tran, that's for sure," Lisha said dryly.

"Well, I'm back to the reflection theory," Chelsea said. "And because Demetrius said he saw someone he thought was you, it was already in your mind."

"I guess," Karma agreed halfheartedly. But even as she said it, in her heart, she didn't believe it was true.

Someone is out there, she thought to herself. *Someone who looks just like me. I saw her. I know I did. And I won't be at peace until I find her.*

Whoever she is. However long it takes.

☆

"Yo, Kushner, Jennings, in my office," Roxanne bellowed at them.

It was six o'clock that evening, and Karma and Chelsea had just passed the open door to Bigfoot's office on their way home.

"Damn, we were almost out of here," Karma whispered to Chelsea.

"On the double!" Roxanne yelled.

The girls walked into her office. Her cast was, as per usual, propped up on her desk. Today it was clad in pink leather, which matched her pink leather miniskirt.

"Hi, Roxanne," Karma said pleasantly. "What's up?"

"Cut the chitchat," Roxanne snapped. "Where's my info on Kettering's kid?"

"Uh . . . it's really . . . coming along," Karma said brightly. She turned to Chelsea. "Right, Chelsea?"

"Oh, right!" Chelsea agreed.

"Be specific," Roxanne demanded. She inhaled sharply through her teeth. "My foot is killing me today again."

"Maybe you should go back to the doctor," Karma suggested, eager to change the subject. "You can't mess around with a gunshot wound. I mean, you could have, like, gangrene under there, or something!"

"I don't have gangrene," Bigfoot said in a withering voice. "And I don't need an intern to give me medical advice, do I?"

"Intern, medical advice—that was a joke, right?" Karma suggested hopefully.

"Are you under the impression that I find you amusing in any way?" Roxanne asked.

"Not really," Karma admitted.

"So, back to the subject at hand," Roxanne said. "The Kettering girl in Australia? You've talked to her?"

"Right!" Karma agreed. "We've talked to her!" She could feel Chelsea's eyes shooting daggers at her.

"That is, Chelsea talked to her," she continued.

"And?" Roxanne asked irritably. "Am I supposed to coax it out of you?"

"Tell her what Chelsea said, Chelsea," Karma said.

"The girl's name is Chelsea?" Bigfoot questioned.

"Isn't that a funny coincidence?" Karma asked. "Chelsea and Chelsea! Ha-ha!"

"So, is she coming on the show?" Roxanne demanded.

"She . . . isn't interested," Chelsea invented.

"That's not the answer I want to hear," Roxanne said. "I thought I agreed to put you on this because you were going to have so much rapport with this girl."

"Well, you can't make someone do what they don't want to do," Karma said quickly. "But it was a good try! Hey, I say we get that guy whose mom and dad shot down—"

"Listen, you two." Roxanne pitched her voice low. "I did not get where I am by giving up. I never give up. I want *this girl* for my show."

"But—" Karma began.

"Forget 'but,' " Bigfoot said. "Clearly the two of you can't handle this. I want Kettering's phone number on my desk first thing tomorrow morning."

"But—" Karma began again.

"Do the words *shut up* ring a bell with you?" Roxanne yelled. "*I want the phone number.* I'll call her myself. Now get out of here."

Karma and Chelsea scurried out of Bigfoot's office. They took the elevator down to the lobby, not speaking until they were actually out on the street.

Chelsea turned to Karma, her eyes blazing. "You realize I'm going to kill you, don't you?"

"Come on, Chels, we can figure a way out of this—"

"Roxanne wants Chelsea Kettering's phone number!" Chelsea screeched, panic rising in her voice. "*I'm* Chelsea Kettering!"

"Not so loud!" Karma hissed.

"Why not? My life is ruined, anyway!"

"Just . . . calm down," Karma instructed her. "Don't panic. Take deep breaths."

"Deep breaths? *Deep breaths?*"

"You're hyperventilating, Chels—"

"O-mi-god, o-mi-god, my life is wrecked, it's over, it's—"

Karma took Chelsea by the shoulders. "I'm telling you, there is a way out of this," she insisted. "Bigfoot is not—I repeat, *not*—going to find out who you are. Now breathe in and out slowly so I know you're not going to faint in the middle of West End Avenue."

Chelsea obliged, taking deep, slow breaths even as she gave Karma the evil eye.

"Better," Karma assured her, trying to smile at her friend. "Okay, I have a plan."

"This whole thing started with one of your plans!"

"Look, all we have to do is to tell her that . . . we lost the phone number!" Karma suggested.

Chelsea gave her a withering look.

"Okay, stupid idea," Karma agreed. "I'll come up with something better. Let's walk. I think better when I walk."

They headed toward their apartment, dodging between the people scurrying home from work.

"Okay, how about this," Karma said, stepping around a white-uniformed nanny wheeling a baby carriage. "We tell Bigfoot that Chelsea Kettering is on a trip to America. We give her a phone number. There's a recording. Bigfoot leaves a message. Chelsea Kettering never returns the call."

"Are you on drugs?" Chelsea cried. "What phone number? What recording?"

"We'll get a friend involved," Karma said, thinking fast. "I'll get one of my friends from Long Island. We get her to make a recording, and blah-blah-blah. This'll work!"

"I doubt it," Chelsea muttered.

"It will," Karma insisted. "I promise you on my word of honor as one of your two best friends in this world that Bigfoot will not find out the truth about you. Okay?"

"No," Chelsea said bluntly. "I'm so scared I feel like barfing."

The girls turned the corner and headed into their building, waving to Antoine the doorman as they hurried past him.

Karma kept up a steady stream of reassuring patter as they took the elevator up to their apartment and undid the three locks on the front door.

"I'm gonna call my friend Alice right now," Karma was saying as they walked into the living room. Then she stopped.

Because Lisha, Nick, Sky, and Alan were all sitting there in horrible, scary silence.

"Someone died," Karma guessed, grabbing for Chelsea's hand for support.

"Yeah, us," Sky said bluntly.

"What are you talking about?" Chelsea asked fearfully.

Sky cocked his head toward the coffee table. The Trash-cam sat in the center of it. "I got the camera out of Jazz's office while you guys were at the airport," he explained.

"But that's good!" Karma cried.

"It would be if there had been any film in it," Sky said. "I didn't check until just now. We were gonna put the video on and see what we'd caught in Jazz's office."

"Only someone beat us to it," Lisha added.

"You mean—" Karma began.

"Exactly," Nick said. "Someone did find the Trash-cam. They just didn't move it.

"Instead, they stole our film."

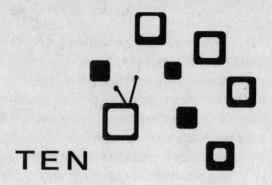

TEN

"If we all get arrested and there's a trial, I'm throwing myself on the mercy of the court," Alan said as the six interns got on the elevator in their office building the next morning.

They had been up almost all night the night before, going over their crisis again and again. Who could have stolen their film? Why would someone take the film and leave the camera? Nick suggested that maybe Jazz would do it, just to psych them out. But no one else believed this. They did, however, all believe that they were in deep, deep trouble.

"Look, like I said last night," Karma began as she pushed the button for their floor, "no one knows the camera belongs to us."

"It wouldn't be very hard to trace the camera to me," Sky said, his lips thin with tension. "I'm the one who borrowed it."

"Let's just not jump to conclusions," Lisha said firmly. "We'll take it as it comes."

"I could confess," Sky said. "I mean, they're gonna get me, anyway. And maybe that would save you guys from—"

The elevator stopped on the third floor, and Jazz's secretary, Winston, got on.

"Yeah," Winston said, pushing the button for the tenth floor, where the largest conference room was located. "How's life?"

"Just keen," Lisha replied sarcastically.

Winston looked at Karma. "Roxanne said to remind you that she expects the phone number on her desk ASAP this morning. She said you'd know what she was talking about. And she wants you and Chutney in her office at noon, sharp."

"Right," Karma agreed.

The elevator stopped at their floor, and the interns all got out. They looked to the right and to the left.

"No cops," Sky announced.

"'Morning," Demetrius called cheerfully as he walked by, sipping a cup of coffee. "Hi," he added with a grin, gazing down at Karma. "How are you?"

"I've been better," Karma confessed.

Demetrius looked at the ashen-faced group. "You guys look like you just got indicted for murder."

"Have you seen Jazz this morning?" Karma asked him.

"Yeah, I was just in a meeting with her," he said. "What's up?"

"What kind of mood was she in?" Lisha asked anxiously.

"Bad," Demetrius said. "But that's just because she's up so early to get into makeup for a photo shoot for *Spin* magazine."

"She didn't happen to...mention any of us by name, did she?" Karma asked brightly.

"I don't think she mentioned anyone but herself by name," Demetrius said with a chuckle. "She is her favorite topic of conversation." His brow furrowed as he looked at Karma. "Is something wrong?"

"We...I can't really talk about it," Karma said evasively.

"Okay." Demetrius leaned down and touched Karma's arm. "Hey, can I talk to you a minute?"

"Sure," Karma said. "I'll meet you in the employees' lounge." As soon as Demetrius walked away, she turned to her friends and spoke in a low voice. "We look totally suspicious standing here. Let's separate and act normal."

The group said their good-byes and headed in different directions, except for Chelsea and Karma.

Chelsea grabbed her friend's arm. "What about the phone number for you-know-who?" she hissed.

"I'm on top of it," Karma assured her, trying to sound more confident than she actually felt.

"You are not!" Chelsea accused. "You tried calling your bud Alice last night and she wasn't home! I was there! And now Bigfoot wants—"

"I'll take care of it," Karma promised.

"How?" Chelsea demanded.

"'Morning," Sumtimes said, stepping out of the elevator. She was wearing black jeans, a man's T-shirt, and a tuxedo jacket. Her bald head shone under the fluorescent lights, and black bowling-ball earrings danced in her ears. "Hey, what do you guys think of the name Felicia?"

"Uh, great name," Chelsea said.

"Good, because this week I'm Felicia Sumtimes," Sumtimes said. "You're on dog-poop detail this morning, Chutney, so follow me."

Chelsea gave Karma a pleading look and headed off with Sumtimes.

Karma hurried toward the lounge, her thoughts flying. *I've got to protect Chelsea, no matter what,* she thought. *But between the missing film and Roxanne's search for Chelsea Kettering, I feel like I'm coming unraveled.*

"My life is a shambles," she announced to Demetrius when she hit the lounge. She immediately headed for the Mr. Coffee and poured herself a cup.

"How's that?" Demetrius asked.

"Just take my word for it," Karma advised. "If I live through this day, it'll be a miracle." She sipped her coffee. "What's up?"

"I was going to ask you the same thing," Demetrius said. "The six of you looked really weird standing by the elevator just now."

"We did?" Karma asked. "Like, you mean we looked suspicious?"

Demetrius made a face. "What are you talking about?"

Karma sighed and sat down next to him on the shabby couch. "Nothing. Forget it. I'm just losing my mind." She took a sip of her hot coffee and made a face. "Ugh. Cheap swill again."

"I've been thinking about you," Demetrius said softly.

"Yeah, the same," she admitted.

He put his arm around her shoulders. "Are you upset about what that girl Tran did yesterday?"

"I'm over it," Karma decided.

"Maybe I was wrong about that girl I saw on Broadway that I thought was you," Demetrius said. "The more I think about it, the more I think I must have just had you on my mind, and so—"

"So you thought some other cute little Asian babe was me," Karma finished for him. "And I guess it really must have been my own reflection I saw in the bus window. The mind can play bizarre tricks on you." She nudged her shoulder into Demetrius. "But I've decided to take your mistaking someone else for me as a compliment. Like you were just so preoccupied with images of the beauty that is me, or something."

"Yeah?" he asked, smiling.

"Yeah. Besides, frankly I've got much bigger traumas in my life to worry about right now."

"Can I help?"

"I wish," Karma said. She took another sip of her coffee. "I guess I'd

better get to the cubicle that laughingly passes itself off as my office."
She started to get up.

"Wait." Demetrius stopped her. "I was hoping we could do something together tonight."

"If I'm not in prison," Karma muttered.

"Pardon me?"

"Nothing," Karma said. "I'd love to, but I have to work at Jimi's."

"How about if I drop by Jimi's? Or does the club frown upon having your boyfriend hang out while you're working?"

Boyfriend? Karma thought. *Did he just refer to himself as my boyfriend?*

"It's fine for you to show up," she told him. "Believe me, they love it when someone who looks like he just stepped off the cover of a romance novel hangs out. It adds cachet. Gorgeous women will tear off your clothes."

"There's only one gorgeous woman I'm interested in having tear off my clothes," Demetrius said, his voice low. He quickly leaned over and gave her a soft kiss on her lips.

"Interesting offer," Karma admitted contemplatively.

"We should discuss it further," Demetrius said, a smile twitching at his mouth. He kissed her again.

"That almost makes up for the crisis that is currently my life." Karma sighed.

"Listen, I wish you would tell me what's worrying you," Demetrius said. "Maybe I can help."

Karma stood up. "I know you have, like, the world's broadest shoulders to cry on, but right now I am sworn to secrecy."

Demetrius stood up, too. "Okay. But if you change your mind—"

"You'll be the first to know, I promise," she told him. Then she stood on tiptoe and tried to reach his lips with hers. When that didn't work he simply lifted her up, his strong hands spanning her tiny waist, and he brought her lips to his.

"We can't go on meeting like this," she said as he held her in the air.

"Oh yeah, we can," Demetrius insisted, gazing into her eyes.

"But...we're at work," she said feebly. "Someone could come in."

"Yeah," he agreed.

But when he kissed her again, she forgot to care.

Chelsea met Karma in front of Bigfoot's office. Her secretary's desk was empty. It was exactly five minutes before twelve.

"When I wasn't walking Jazz's monster dogs, I spent the morning with my head draped over the porcelain throne," Chelsea hissed. "Did you reach your friend Alice? Did you give Roxanne her phone number?"

"No," Karma admitted.

"Oh, God, my life is over," Chelsea moaned.

"It was a dumb idea," Karma confessed. "Bigfoot would never believe that Chelsea Kettering was in Australia one day and in America the next."

"So what do we do, then?" Chelsea asked, her voice rising with hysteria.

"Something better. We—"

"Kushner, Jennings, you're late," Roxanne snapped, sticking her head out of her office.

"It's four minutes before twe—"

"Just get in here." Roxanne disappeared into her office.

Chelsea gave Karma a panicked look, then they headed into Roxanne's office.

"Sit," Roxanne barked.

They sat. Bigfoot hobbled around the desk and sat in her oversized leather chair, propping her foot up on a well-positioned swivel chair instead of on her desk.

"How's the foot?" Karma asked.

"It sucks," Roxanne said, her face pinched. "I've got a doctor's appointment right after this. He says it shouldn't be hurting so much."

"Gee, maybe you'd better head over there," Karma said. "The traffic can be murder—"

"Look at the top of my desk, both of you," she commanded.

Karma and Chelsea obediently stared at her desk.

"What do you see there, Chutney?"

"Two magazines, a file folder," Chelsea recited dutifully.

"Do you see a phone number?"

"No," Chelsea said.

"Gee, neither do I," Roxanne said. "Do you two want to know what utter incompetence is? Great, I'll tell you. Utter incompetence is two interns who botch an assignment and then after they botch it can't even manage to remember to get a simple thing like a phone number on my desk!"

"There's a very reasonable explanation for that," Karma said.

"Oh, really?" Bigfoot asked coolly. "How ducky." She turned to Chelsea. "Why don't you enlighten me."

"Me?" Chelsea managed. "I . . . I . . ." she stammered.

At that moment Roxanne's intercom buzzed. She pressed the black button on the intercom. "What?" she snapped into it.

"Roxanne, there's a phone call for you from Australia," came Winston's lilting voice. "It's someone named Chelsea Kettering. Shall I take a message?"

"I'll take it," Roxanne said quickly. She looked up at Karma.

"She's right on time," Karma said smoothly.

"You arranged this?" Roxanne asked.

"Chelsea did it." Karma caught sight of Chelsea out of the corner of her eye.

She looks like she's going to melt into a puddle of fear, she thought. *Hang in there, Chels.*

"I'll put this on the speakerphone," Roxanne told them. She pressed a button, then picked up her phone. "Roxanne Renault," she said into the phone. Her voice, in utter contrast to the way she spoke to them, was smooth and sweet.

"This is Chelsea Kettering. I understand you wanted to speak with me." The voice coming out of the speakerphone sounded young and American.

"I'm so glad you called me," Roxanne said warmly. "I really do appreciate it. You sound so . . . American."

"I lived in America until I was twelve," the voice said.

"Really?" Bigfoot replied. "Where?"

"Are you kidding? I can't say," the voice went on. "Say, *Trash* is very popular over here," the voice said.

"Really?" Roxanne exclaimed. "How terrific! Are you a fan?"

"I watch when I can," the voice said. "I'm pretty busy with college and all."

"I understand completely," said Roxanne, her voice dripping sincerity. "So, let me explain why I wanted to speak with you, Chelsea."

"I already spoke with someone from your show," the voice said. "Someone named Chelsea Jennings, I think she said?"

"Right," Roxanne agreed.

"She explained the show you have planned. I want to tell you how nice she was, by the way. You're really lucky to have her working for you."

"We all love her here at *Trash*," Bigfoot assured the voice on the phone. "I want you to understand that if you agree to appear on *Trash*, you could help millions of kids out there who feel like they have a shameful family secret. You'd be a hero."

"I'm just not interested," the voice said. "I wanted to tell you myself. There's nothing you can say that will change my mind."

"What if we gave money to your favorite charity?" Roxanne suggested.

"No—"

"I'd hate to see you get trashed on TV when you're not going to be there to defend yourself," Roxanne said, trying a different tack.

"And I'd hate to have to sue you for invasion of my privacy or character defamation." the voice countered.

"Well, I'm disappointed," Roxanne said. "But I certainly respect your feelings. Why don't you give me your phone number, and perhaps we can chat about this again after you've had a chance to think about it some more."

"Chelsea Jennings already has my phone number," the voice responded.

"Just for my own records," Roxanne coaxed sweetly, picking up a pencil.

The voice on the phone quickly gave her a phone number with a country code and a prefix for Australia.

"Thanks," Roxanne said. "And listen, Chelsea, I know you've been through a lot. But let's just keep the lines of communication open, okay? I'm on your side."

"Thanks," the voice replied. "And tell Chelsea thanks for me, too. Frankly, she's the only one I'd even consider talking with again." She hung up.

Bigfoot turned to Chelsea. "That was Chelsea Kettering," she said.

"Yup," Chelsea squeaked. She looked over at Karma, who smiled at her with encouragement.

"I told you the two Chelseas would bond," Karma asserted.

"Uh-huh," Roxanne said. "You expect me to believe that Chelsea Kettering just called me from Australia."

"She did," Karma confirmed.

"It couldn't be that the two of you cooked this up because you never really got ahold of this Chelsea Kettering babe at all, could it?" Roxanne asked.

Karma could actually *hear* Chelsea's stomach churning.

"Look, Roxanne—" Chelsea began.

"How about if I just dial this phony little phone number, huh?" Bigfoot sneered. "How much you want to bet there is no such number and no such person? And how much you want to bet I get the two of you fired for this little stunt?" She quickly dialed the number the voice on the phone had given her.

Chelsea actually buried her face in her hands.

Ring. Ring. Ring.

"It's ringing," Karma pointed out. "I guess that means it's an actual phone number."

"Probably dumb luck," Roxanne snapped.

Ring. Ring.

"Mum?" a female Australian-accented voice said into the phone. "I'm just running out—"

"This isn't 'Mum,' " Roxanne said. "May I speak to Chelsea Kettering?"

"There's no such person here," the voice said.

Roxanne gave the interns a look of smug triumph. "Sorry to have bothered you—"

"My roommate's name is Chelsea Gardner," the voice continued, "if that's who you wanted. Eighteen? American?"

"Ri-right," Roxanne stammered, taken aback.

"Sorry I thought you were my mum—she always calls when I'm running out. Did you want to leave a message for Chels? She was on the phone with someone just a minute ago, and then she left."

"No, no message," Roxanne said. She hung up the phone.

"I told you Chelsea Kettering changed her last name," Karma reminded her.

Roxanne narrowed her eyes. "Okay. So you weren't lying. So you really did find her and Chelsea really did talk to her. I was wrong."

"We accept your apology," Karma said sweetly.

"I'm still going to find a way to get that girl on *Trash*," Roxanne said. "You heard it here first."

"Was there anything else you wanted?" Karma asked.

"No, get out," she told them.

Karma and Chelsea scurried out of her office and ran down the hall and around the corner.

"What just happened in there?" Chelsea asked, her hand to her forehead.

"You heard her. We talked to Chelsea Gardner—a.k.a. Chelsea Kettering. In Australia."

"Karma, I think I'm losing my mind," Chelsea said.

Karma pulled her close and checked to make sure the coast was clear. "It's like this," she whispered. "I called my stockbroker this morning, who called a friend in Australia, who called her daughter, who agreed to pretend to be you. I gave her all the pertinent poop, she pulled it off. I told them all it was part of an elaborate practical joke, and no one asked me any questions. Simple!"

"Simple? Only you would call that simple. And who was the other girl, the Australian one?"

"Same person!" Karma said. "According to my broker, she's this ace actress. She did a great American accent, didn't you think?"

"And you even thought to have her answer as the roommate in case Roxanne called back?" Chelsea asked.

"I tried to cover all the bases," Karma said. "I thought Roxanne might smell a rat. She's a bitch, but she's not stupid."

"God, you're a genius!" Chelsea was exultant. "But why didn't you tell me? I thought I was going to have a stroke in there!"

"I never got a chance to!" Karma explained. "I was going to tell you before we went into Bigfoot's office, but there was no time!"

Chelsea grabbed Karma's hands. "She bought it! Bigfoot really bought it!" She threw her arms around Karma. "You are so brilliant!"

"Hey, how come you two look so happy?" Lisha said, rounding the corner with a pile of files in her arms.

"Karma just completely threw Bigfoot off the trail of Chelsea Kettering, daughter of the mass murderer," Chelsea whispered. "I feel like this huge weight has been lifted from my shoulders!"

"I'm happy for you." Lisha's voice was flat. "So now you won't get fired before the rest of us are."

"You don't look so terrific," Karma noted. "I guess you're worried about the missing film, huh."

"Yeah, there's that," Lisha agreed. "But I also just got another phone call from Harley."

"He called you at work?" Chelsea asked.

"Home, work, he doesn't care," Lisha said. Her fingers were white, she was gripping the files in her hands so hard.

"Maybe we could get Sky to call him and threaten him, or something," Chelsea suggested.

"First of all, I don't know where he's calling me from, so I can't call him back. Second of all, threats would only make it worse."

"But . . . there must be something we can do," Chelsea said.

"Yeah," Lisha replied. "Pray. Because he is one scary guy. I mean really scary. And he won't be satisfied until he's ruined my life."

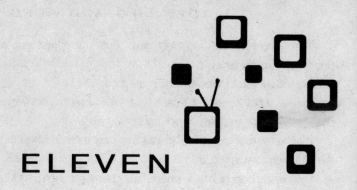

ELEVEN

"It sure is crowded in here," Sky observed as he looked around Jimi's, sipping an organic special shake made with fruit juice and ginseng.

It was that evening, and Sky and Alan had stopped into Jimi's to hang out. Karma, clad in her Jimi's T-shirt, was behind the juice bar, as usual, cranking out exotic juice cocktails for the teen clientele. Since Alan was both notoriously shy and in love with Chelsea, Karma had been surprised when he had immediately asked the girl sitting next to him at the juice bar to dance. That was fifteen minutes earlier. Sky just sat there, staring morosely into his shake.

"It's always crowded in here," Karma replied, refilling a near-empty dish of goldfish-shaped pretzels on the bar. She peered into the crowd, hoping that at any moment she'd see Demetrius walking toward her.

Sky sighed and picked up one of the goldfish. "What is the meaning of life, Karma?"

"Too deep for me," she replied.

"For me, too," he agreed. "My life used to be real simple, you know? Then I started at *Trash*—"

"You're bummed about the missing tape," Karma guessed.

"Aren't you?" Sky asked.

"Yeah," she conceded. "I feel like I'm waiting for the other shoe to fall. But I've been trying to just put it out of my mind, because, like, it's totally out of our control."

"Out of control is not my favorite way to be," Sky admitted.

"Nothing happened today, Sky," Karma observed. "Maybe we all dodged a bullet."

"Maybe we're all gonna die tomorrow," he replied darkly.

The music changed from a Tori Amos ballad to a classic dance groove by the B-52s, and fake snow began to fall on the wildly gyrating bodies on the dance floor. Up above on the balcony level that circled the second floor of Jimi's, a bunch of kids were dancing with the giant mechanical robot, who was clad in a Jimi's T-shirt.

"Why don't you go dance?" Karma suggested as she wiped the bar with a wet cloth. "Alan's out there, somewhere."

"Easy for him. He knows that the girl he loves really loves someone else," Sky said, picking up another goldfish pretzel.

"Meaning Chelsea," Karma filled in.

Sky nodded. "But the girl I love is free, totally free, and she still treats me like I'm her brother."

"Lisha," Karma stated.

"The beauteous, infuriating Luscious Lisha, right on the first guess." Sky ran his fingers through his dark hair. "She's your roommate, Karma, maybe you can enlighten me. What does she want?"

"Lisha's kind of . . . secretive," Karma explained. "I mean, I love her to death, but there's all kinds of things about her I don't know."

"Join the club." He sighed, then looked over at the dance floor morosely. "Anyway, for the time being, I'm a fool for love. She's the only girl I can think about."

"Hey, bartender, where's my carrot juice?" a skinny guy in a torn Metallica T-shirt, standing down at the end of the bar, demanded imperiously.

"Coming," Karma called back. She turned back to Sky. "Look, just because you love Lisha doesn't mean you can't have fun."

"Wanna bet?" Sky replied.

"Yeah!" Karma exclaimed. "Look at me, for example. I'm crazed for Demetrius, but that doesn't mean I can't live without him."

"Speak of the devil," Sky said, cocking his head toward the front door of Jimi's. Demetrius had just gotten past the bouncer, who, unlike bouncers at regular clubs, checked everyone's ID to make sure they were *under* a certain age.

"Is the man poetry in motion, or what?" Karma sighed, watching Demetrius walk across the club toward her.

"Yo, sweetheart, my carrot juice?" the guy down the bar called to Karma.

"Yeah, it's coming," she called, still watching Demetrius. "Chill out. Stress is very bad for you."

And then there he was, standing in front of her, smiling at her. "Hi," Demetrius said.

"Hi," Karma replied, grinning back.

"I'm getting depressed just looking at the two of you," Sky commented.

"Yeah, unrequited love is a bitch," Karma agreed, not taking her eyes off Demetrius.

"Look, if I don't have my carrot juice in the next thirty seconds, you're in big trouble, babe," the guy down the juice bar yelled.

"Her name isn't 'babe,'" Demetrius replied.

"Do I care?" the guy jeered. "Man, you people ought to go back to your own country and quit taking jobs away from Americans."

Karma, Demetrius, and Sky all turned to the guy at the same moment. Demetrius began to walk over to him, but Karma reached across the bar to stop him. "I'll handle it," she said. She walked over to the rude guy and stared at him. "You need to apologize to me," she said evenly.

"Go read about it in a fortune cookie." The guy sneered. Then he held up the corners of his eyes to make them slant, and he made a face at her.

"That does it," Demetrius said. He took three long strides down the bar and then lifted the guy up by the front of his T-shirt. Sky was standing next to him, his arms folded menacingly. "You were saying?" Demetrius asked.

"It was just a joke, man," the guy mumbled, dangling in the air.

"It wasn't funny," Demetrius said. "It was stupid. *You're* stupid. What's your name?"

"Paul," the guy mumbled.

"Well, Paul," Demetrius said, "how about if you apologize to my friend?"

"Yeah, yeah," the guy said.

"That's not an apology, Paul," Sky pointed out. "You'll have to do better."

"I apologize," Paul said gruffly. "I was out of line."

"Right," Demetrius agreed. "And now you're also out of here." He put the guy down.

"You can't kick me out!" Paul blustered.

"Let's just say we're strongly suggesting you leave," Sky explained. "Or we will make your life very unpleasant."

The guy fixed his T-shirt and sneered at them. "This club sucks, anyway." He headed for the door.

"What a lovely human being," Karma said.

"He's been drinking," Demetrius said. "I smelled it on his breath."

"He must have snuck the stuff in," Karma said. "Alcohol is a major no-no in here."

"Does that kind of stuff happen to you very often?" Sky asked Karma.

"No, to tell you the truth," she said. "Once in a blue moon." She glanced down the bar and saw people were waiting three deep for service.

"I gotta hustle," she told them. "I'll be back." She hurried to take care of her station.

"How great is she?" Demetrius asked, watching Karma.

"Real great," Sky agreed. "You're a lucky guy."

"No kidding," Demetrius agreed. "You hang out here a lot?"

"Nah," Sky said. "I came by with Alan. I'm nursing a broken heart, man."

"That's rough."

"Tell me about it," Sky agreed. "And then there's the fact that I'm about to get the *Trash* ax—"

"No way," Demetrius interrupted.

"Not just fired," Sky continued, his voice stressed. "Ruined. I'll never get another job in TV. My rep will be wrecked—"

"What are you talking about?" Demetrius asked, confused.

Sky hesitated. "I can't tell you."

"Then why did you bring it up?"

"I shouldn't have," Sky said. "Forget it."

"Hey, I'm a pretty good listener," Demetrius said. "So if you want to talk—"

"Nah, but thanks, man," Sky said. "I'm just so stressed that I'm—"

"Hey, your friend isn't very funny," Paul said, lurching back over to them.

Demetrius and Sky could both smell the alcohol on his breath, even stronger than before.

"I could have sworn I told you to leave," Demetrius reminded him mildly.

"I ran into your Chinese girlfriend by the door," Paul jeered, stumbling drunkenly. "I tried to apologize to her again, right? She pretended she didn't even know me!"

"You're wrecked," Sky said with disgust. "You were talking to the wall."

"I know who I was talkin' to, man," Paul mumbled. "What a snooty bi—"

Demetrius reached for Paul's T-shirt again. "Don't make me do something you will regret," he said, his voice low.

"And don't make me help him," Sky added.

"Just turn around and head for the door," Demetrius told Paul, taking him by the shoulders and spinning him around. "And this time go out it. And don't come back."

Paul mumbled something under his breath and stumbled toward the door.

"I think I'll make sure he actually gets outside this time," Sky decided, following Paul.

Karma finished serving her customers, and right after Sky took off after Paul, she looked over at Demetrius, who was watching the couples on the dance floor. A tall gorgeous blonde in a red miniskirt and thigh-high stockings came over to him and said something Karma couldn't hear. Whatever she said made him laugh, then he said something back to her. Now she laughed.

They look so cute together, Karma thought morosely. *Anyone would expect him to be with a girl who looks like her, instead of with a girl who looks like me.*

Now the blonde was speaking to Demetrius again, and pulling on his arm, as if to lead him to the dance floor. He shook his head no. The blonde seemed to be pleading with him in a teasing way, pulling on his arm. Finally he laughed again, relented, and headed to the dance floor with the girl.

Okay, it doesn't necessarily mean anything, Karma told herself even as her fingers tightened so much around a bottle of carob powder that her knuckles turned white. *It's just a dance. This is a dance club. Anybody can dance with anybody, and—*

"Excuse me, please, could I order a drink?"

Karma reluctantly tore her eyes away from Demetrius and the blonde, and turned around to face her customer.

And then she gasped.

Because she was staring face to face with herself.

Karma hurried toward the diner on the corner, her heart pounding in her chest. The events of the past half hour played themselves over in her mind. She had tried to talk to the girl at the bar, but the girl had been ready to run away. Karma had begged her to meet for coffee, then she'd begged her manager to let her out early. And then, with a quick lie to Demetrius about a stomachache, she had cut out of Jimi's to meet the girl.

I don't know why I didn't tell Demetrius the truth, she thought, *but I just couldn't. I have to know who this girl is first, before I can share it with anyone else.*

At least now I know I was right. Someone does look just like me. I'm not losing my mind.

But who is she? I don't even know her name.

Karma raced into the diner and saw the girl sitting in a back booth, a cup of coffee in front of her.

It could be me, she realized wildly. *It's like I'm looking at myself. Except that she's dressed in pressed chinos and a pink polo shirt, conservative preppie clothes I wouldn't be caught dead in.*

"Hi," Karma said, sliding into the booth across from the girl.

"I can't stay very long," the girl mumbled. She even had a New York accent, like Karma, though not quite as thick.

Karma just stared at her. "Who are you?"

"Menu?" the Greek waiter asked briskly, appearing at the table.

"Just coffee," Karma said.

"Hey, you two are twins," the waiter said. "Cute." He walked away.

"Are we?" Karma asked, her eyes searching the girl's.

"I don't know," the girl said, her voice low.

"You have to admit we look just like each other," Karma said. "What's your name?"

"Janelle Cho," the girl said.

"Mine's Karma Kushner. I was adopted from Korea, by a Jewish-American couple who live on Long Island. That's where I grew up." She waited for Janelle to offer her own background, but was greeted by silence. "What about you?" she finally asked.

"I was adopted, too," Janelle reluctantly said, staring into her coffee. "From Korea. By Korean-Americans. I grew up on Staten Island. I'm in the city this summer for early classes at Columbia."

"How old are you?" Karma asked.

"Eighteen," Janelle said.

Karma felt as if her heart was pounding so loud that surely Janelle could hear it. "What's your birthday?" she asked.

"I don't know," Janelle said. "My family celebrates the day they adopted me as my birthday."

"Were you that young when they adopted you?" Karma asked.

"I was only a few days old."

"So, what's the day you celebrate?" Karma pressed.

"April eighteenth," Janelle said.

Karma sucked in her breath. "My birthday is April second." She stared hard at the other girl. "We're . . . we're twins. I think."

Tears of happiness came to her eyes. *This is so incredible,* she thought. *I have a twin sister. We've been living a few miles from each other all our lives. I want to know everything about her. It's so fantastic and wonderful and—*

"I don't have a twin," Janelle said stubbornly.

"Look, I didn't believe you existed, either!" Karma exclaimed. "My mother swore to me I didn't have any siblings at all. But I guess she got told the wrong information. You must have already been adopted, because they didn't get me until I was two."

They were silent as the waiter set Karma's coffee down.

Janelle looked at her. "Listen—Karma, is it?"

Karma nodded.

"The truth is, I know about that thing on *Trash,* where you were looking for your double—"

"You saw it?"

Janelle shook her head no. "My friend Amy did. She told me about it. I told her she was mistaken, that she just thought it looked like me because all Asians look alike to non-Asians—"

"I think that sometimes, too!" Karma exclaimed.

"But deep down inside, I didn't believe that," Janelle continued. "I had this terrible feeling that Amy was right."

"But why is that terrible?" Karma asked, confused.

"Because I'm very happy with my life just the way it is," Janelle said tersely. "I don't need it complicated."

Karma shook her head in confusion. "Look, am I missing something here? We're twins. And we didn't know each other even existed before. I'm not here to wreck your world or anything!"

"I don't mean to offend you," Janelle said. "But I'd rather...I'd rather just pretend we don't know about each other."

"But...but why?" Karma asked, a sinking feeling in her heart.

"My parents are very conservative people," Janelle explained. "We're also very, very American, even though their parents came here from Korea. We've really broken all our ties with that country, and you'd just be a reminder of—"

"Of what?" Karma exploded. "We were both innocent babies! We didn't do anything wrong! No one did, unless you count the fact that someone lied about each of us having a twin—"

"Look, no one knows I'm adopted, okay?" Janelle said sharply. "That's how my parents want it. That's how *I* want it."

"So...so you don't even want to get to know me?" Karma faltered. "You want to pretend you never met me?"

Janelle stood up. "Can't you understand? I don't want anyone to know I'm adopted. Your life was fine before, and so was mine." She threw some money on the table. "Good luck, Karma. I think it's better if we just go on like this never happened." She turned around to leave.

"Wait!" Karma said quickly. She reached for a napkin and took a pen out of her backpack. "At least let's swap phone numbers."

"I won't use it," Janelle said.

"You might change your mind," Karma said, holding the napkin out.

Reluctantly, Janelle took the napkin and stuffed it into the pocket of her chinos. She jotted hers down and pushed it at Karma. Then, with one last look at Karma, she turned and headed out the door.

Karma felt as if someone had punched her in the stomach. And she also felt as if her heart was breaking.

But how can my heart break for someone I didn't even know existed an hour ago? she thought.

Because she's my sister, her own voice answered in her head. *My twin sister.*

And she doesn't want to have anything to do with me.

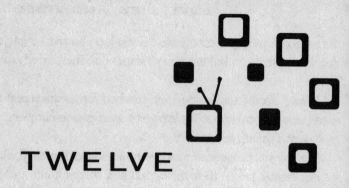

TWELVE

"Demetrius?"

It was fifteen minutes later. Karma had sat in the booth at the diner, staring into space, not knowing what to do or how to feel, totally confused. Finally she'd paid for her coffee and walked back down the block to Jimi's to see if Demetrius was still there.

And he was.

Sitting with the gorgeous blonde.

"Hi!" he said, his eyes lighting up when he saw her. "I thought you went home sick!"

"Evidently," she replied, giving the blonde a cool look.

"Oh, this is Candi," Demetrius said. "Candi, this is Karma."

"I bet you dot the *i* in Candi with a little heart," Karma said coolly.

I'd like to pull her bleached hair out by its black roots, she thought nastily. *This is definitely not my night.*

"I did when I was ten," Candi said. "Demetrius was just telling me all about you."

"I'm so sure," Karma said flatly.

"Really," the blonde insisted. "And I was telling him about my fiancé, who's in the navy—he's coming home next weekend and I can't wait. And he was telling me all about you."

"Well, I'm just as wonderful as he said I was," Karma said, rising to the occasion.

Candi laughed. "Well, then, you must be really fantastic!"

"Do you have to go back to work?" Demetrius asked.

"Not unless my manager sees me," Karma said. "Let's duck out instead."

"Great idea." Demetrius got up. He looked at Candi. "You don't mind?"

"Not at all," she assured him. "It was really nice to meet you, Demetrius. You, too, Karma."

They headed for the door. "I was so sure she was going to be a bitch," Karma admitted.

"Prejudging people can be dangerous," he pointed out.

"Oh, yeah, Mr. Perfect?" she asked archly. "Like you've never done such a thing in your life?"

"Who, me?" Demetrius asked, his voice teasing. He put his arm around her shoulders. "I'm so glad to see you. I thought you were gone for the night."

"So did I," Karma said. "Hey, where's Sky and Alan?"

"Left," Demetrius said. "We're on our own. Are you hungry?"

"No," she said. "I'm confused."

They hit the cool outside air and Demetrius turned to face her. "About us?"

"About my life," Karma said.

"Well, that's pretty enigmatic," he said.

"Yeah, that's me, Miss Mysterious," Karma cracked. "Wanna walk some? To the little park by Cooper Union? Maybe?"

"Fine." Demetrius took her hand and they walked slowly down the block in companionable silence.

"The weirdest thing in the world just happened to me," she finally said.

"You were abducted by aliens," he guessed.

"I'm serious," Karma said. And then she proceeded to tell him about meeting Janelle Cho.

"Wow," Demetrius uttered as they reached the park. "That is incredible!"

"She has to be my twin sister," Karma said. "She must be the one you saw on Broadway that time, and it was her I saw on the bus."

"It's amazing you two never ran into each other before," he mused.

"Not really," she said, sitting down on one of the swings and rocking slowly. "I mean, she grew up on Staten Island, I grew up on Long Island. They might as well be opposite sides of the country. But now she's here for college and I'm here for work, and ... well, you know the rest."

"So, you're happy, aren't you?" Demetrius asked. He got behind her and pushed her lightly in the swing.

"I would be if she was," Karma said. "But she's not."

"That's hard to believe," he commented.

"Believe it," she said. "She said her family is conservative, and no one knows she's adopted. And that's how she wants to keep it. It's like she's ... she's ashamed that I exist!" Karma felt hot tears threaten her eyes.

Demetrius came around to the front of the swing, grabbing the chains that held it up between his hands. "Maybe she just needs some time," he suggested, looking into Karma's eyes.

"I don't think so," Karma said sadly. "She didn't like me. She didn't want to know me."

"It's her loss," he said softly.

"You think?"

"I know," he insisted. Then he leaned over and kissed her softly on her lips.

"It's hard to understand, you know?" Karma said, her eyes searching his. "How can she just . . . just *discard* me like that?"

"I don't know," Demetrius admitted.

"I gave her my phone number," Karma said.

"Maybe she'll call you."

"I'm not holding my breath." She kicked the heels of her boots into the dirt. "But I'm not going to just drop this, either."

"No?"

"It's not my style," Karma said firmly. "I'm gonna get as much information from my parents about my adoption as I can, and . . . hey! I just thought of something!"

"What?" Demetrius asked, rocking her in the swing by slowly moving the chains in his fingers.

"I could have other sisters or brothers, right? If my parents didn't know about Janelle, there could be others they don't know about, right?"

"Makes sense," he agreed.

"I've never thought that much about where I'm from, or how it happened that I got put up for adoption," Karma admitted. "But now—"

"Now you want to know," Demetrius concluded.

"Yeah," she said. "I'll do the research. I'll come up with a plan—"

Demetrius laughed. "I love this about you!"

"What?"

"Your enthusiasm," he said. "Your ambition."

"You don't think it's a pain in the butt?" Karma asked.

He stopped swinging her and stared into her eyes, the moonlight glinting off her raven hair. "Oh, Karma, don't you know how I feel about you?"

"You . . . like me a lot?" she ventured, her voice low.

Demetrius gently lifted her up until she was standing on the swing, which put her face just about level with his. His large hands held her fast, and she wrapped her arms around his shoulders. Then he kissed her, slowly, softly.

"Demetrius," she murmured, her face buried in his neck.

"Karma," he whispered back. "There's no one else like you. No one." He kissed her neck, one hand holding her waist, the other holding her hair back off her face. Finally his lips came to hers again, their bodies pressed together, until time and space and everything in the world but the feel and taste and scent of each other was swept away.

"Yo, find a bedroom!" a drunken young male voice yelled. Someone else laughed. There was the sound of a bottle breaking.

"Maybe we'd better take this show on the road," Karma whispered.

"Good idea," he agreed.

"Come home with me," she said.

"You mean—?" There was a question in his eyes.

"I don't know," Karma said. "But I do know I want to be alone with you. In private."

"Me, too," Demetrius agreed.

Karma jumped down from the swing, and they walked to the street to hail a taxi.

When the cab pulled up in front of Karma's apartment building, she got out while Demetrius paid the fare.

"Nice night, huh?" he said, taking a sniff of the cool evening air. He stared up at the clear sky.

"It actually cooled off," Karma noted, looking up, too. She saw a light streak across the sky. "Hey! A shooting star! Did you see it?"

"Yeah," Demetrius said. "You never see those in Manhattan." He looked down at Karma. "You know what that means, don't you?"

"What?"

He put his arms around her. "This is a very special night. A magical night. And now you need to make a wish."

Karma closed her eyes. *What do I want to wish for?* she wondered. *That Janelle will want to know me? That we'll find whoever took the Trash-cam videotape without all of us getting caught and fired? That*

Chelsea's identity is protected? That Lisha works out whatever her mysterious problems are? That I become a millionaire sometime soon?

She opened her eyes again. "I think I'm suffering some wish-option overdose," she said.

He laughed. "Too many things you want?"

"Yeah," she confessed. "I'm greedy." She smiled into his eyes. "So maybe I should wish for something that seems to be coming true already." Then she stood on tiptoe and managed to reach his mouth with hers.

"Hey, you two."

They turned around. Lisha was striding toward them.

"Making out on the street?" she teased.

"We were just going in," Karma told her. "What are you doing up?"

"I got hungry," Lisha said as the three of them walked into the building. "There's nothing in our fridge, per usual. Chelsea is across the hall with Nick, so I decided to go to the Greek place for a burger."

A young guy none of them knew was sitting behind Antoine's desk in the lobby.

"Where's Antoine?" Karma asked.

"Quick trip to the trotters," the guy said with a wink. "I'm his cousin Manny."

"You'd better not let the building manager catch you here instead of Antoine," Lisha said. "He'll fire Antoine real fast."

"Hey, the manager of your building drinks like a fish, man," Manny said. "He's always passed out this time of night. Don't you know nothin' about where you live?"

"Evidently not," Karma said wryly as they headed for the elevator. She gazed into Demetrius's eyes.

"Please, just hold off on the love sports until you get to Karma's room, okay?" Lisha said. "I'm a single woman these days."

"Your choice," Demetrius said. "Sky is crazy about you, you know."

"I like Sky," Lisha said.

"But . . ." Karma began.

"But I'm flying solo right now," Lisha explained.

The elevator stopped and they got off and walked down the hall to their apartment. When they reached the door, they all stopped and stared.

Because it wasn't locked.

In fact, it was open just a crack.

"Did you leave this door open?" Karma asked Lisha sharply.

"No way," Lisha said. "I locked all the locks when I left."

"Then how did it get open?" Karma asked.

"I don't know," Lisha replied. "Chelsea, maybe."

"Let me go in first," Demetrius said, moving in front of the girls.

"Thanks, macho man," Karma said, stopping him, "but you can get killed by a crazed junkie with a gun just as easily as we can. We should go call the police."

But before they could move, the front door swung open.

A tall, handsome guy with shaggy black hair and intense blue eyes was staring at them.

"Come on in," the guy said, his eyes glinting with menace.

"How did you—" Lisha began.

"It was real easy," the guy said. "Your locks wouldn't keep out an armless crackhead, baby."

"Let's go." Demetrius reached out to pull Karma and Lisha away from the door.

"Not so fast," the guy said.

That's when he pulled out the pistol and pointed it at them. "I'm inviting you in, in the nicest way I know how."

Karma, Demetrius, and Lisha stepped into their apartment, their hearts pounding in their chests, while the guy kept his gun trained on them. He closed the door behind them, his eyes locked on Lisha.

"Long time no see, baby," he said.

"You know him?" Demetrius asked Lisha incredulously.

"Yeah," Lisha said. "Demetrius, Karma . . . this is Harley."

Coming January 2005 from Berkley Jam

It's the hottest summer job ever...

TRASH TALK

Cherie Bennett & Jeff Gottesfeld

Six girls and boys are about to have one hot summer. They've been chosen to move to New York City to be interns on the new reality talk show *Trash*.

But what goes on while the cameras are rolling is nothing compared to the happenings behind the lights.

Includes the two books in the popular series: *Good Girls, Bad Boys* and *Dirty Big Secrets*

0-425-20121-X
www.penguin.com

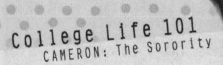

Now a Berkley Jam paperback

Maybe joining a
sorority wasn't the
best idea, after all...

College Life 101
CAMERON: The Sorority

National Bestselling Author
Wendy Corsi Staub

0-425-19727-1